THE MAKING OF A DRAGON

She is so terrified that she can hardly breathe. Her arms feel stiff as ice, her forehead is hot. There are sounds in her ears that have nothing to do with Alfreida's spell. Her feet ache and itch in ways she has never felt before. Enormous tears roll from her eyes and she bids farewell in her mind to home and family.

Fingers lengthen, turning into talons, growing long, glistening claws. Golden hair lifts and twines, turning into two twisted arching horns, forming a perfect valentine over the long, green, scaled snout. Skin hardens and shines, segmenting into scales.

Alfreida howls with delight. "I did it! *I did it!*" she crows.

In the pentacle the huge, brown eyes of the dragon continue to shed perfect tears.

"Chelsea Quinn Yarbro's A BAROQUE FABLE is not only a wry and charming novel, it's also the first book I know of that manages to be half fairy tale and half musical comedy. Watch out for singing trolls!"

—Craig Shaw Gardner
author of *A Malady of Magicks*

Berkley Books by Chelsea Quinn Yarbro

MESSAGES FROM MICHAEL
MORE MESSAGES FROM MICHAEL
A BAROQUE FABLE

A BAROQUE FABLE

CHELSEA QUINN YARBRO

BERKLEY BOOKS, NEW YORK

This is a fairy tale. Characters, institutions,
circumstances, outcomes, *consequences*, locations, and
all the rest are taken from other fairy tales and from my
imagination. Actual persons, places, institutions,
circumstances, outcomes, *consequences*, locations, and
all the rest are not found in fairy tales, and that includes
this one.

A BAROQUE FABLE

A Berkley Book/published by arrangement with
the author

PRINTING HISTORY
Berkley edition/July 1986

All rights reserved.
Copyright © 1986 by Chelsea Quinn Yarbro.
This book may not be reproduced in whole or in part,
by mimeograph or any other means, without permission.
For information address: The Berkley Publishing Group,
200 Madison Avenue, New York, NY 10016.

ISBN: 0-425-09081-7

A BERKLEY BOOK ® TM 757,375
Berkley Books are published by The Berkley Publishing Group
200 Madison Avenue, New York, NY 10016.
The name "BERKLEY" and the stylized "B" with design are
trademarks belonging to Berkley Publishing Corporation.

PRINTED IN THE UNITED STATES OF AMERICA

ACKNOWLEDGMENTS

Those who have been
associated with
A Baroque Fable in previous
theatrical
forms have my heartfelt
thanks
for all their help and hard
work,
as well as their many
insights.

For
Cedric and Jan Clute
and all the rest of the gang
from the late, lamented
Magic Cellar

A BAROQUE FABLE

The Beginning

THIS STORY TAKES place once-upon-a-time; not a real time that has come and gone, or a time that has yet to happen, or even quite a high-and-far-off (-out) time where so many stories take place; this is a time that never happened but ought to have, in one of those places that are called fabulous since, of course, they exist only in fables.

Because this is one of those tales, it must begin with a proper little verse, something pompous and frivolous, to set the tone of the thing and to bow to tradition.

> *That special once-upon-a-time is here*
> *When wonders and nostalgic dreams abound*
> *When aggravations of this world all leave*
> *And for a while care knits up its sleeve.*
> *Here you may gather cherished memories around*
> *And merrily indulge, your conscience clear,*
> *The special whimsy and delight you found*
> *When younger, in the realms of make-believe.*

So much for tradition.

Now that you are in the mood, think of towering powdered wigs and cascades of lace, of adorable heroines and staunch heroes, of mighty wizards and malefic sorcerers, of perspicacious kings and odious tyrants, of soothsayers and enchantments, and all the other stuff of faery, for this is that once-upon-a-time, where even witches had a sense of fashion.

1

• • •

We begin in the darkest part of the Woebegone Wood, a place known as the Wailing Gorge. Trees unlucky enough to grow here are festooned with so much moss that it is difficult to know what they are like underneath. There is very little light here, and what small amount of it reaches down through the overgrowth is a murky color, as if it had run out of breath. A river rushes down from the craggy heights in a hurry to get away, and it has very little manners about how it goes. Everything here is dank and the smell is miasmic.

There are two sets of inhabitants here. One is a large family of Trolls who roister much of the time. They live in the caves behind the falls and it is rare that anyone sees them, which is probably just as well. The other is an elderly witch (who nonetheless has some pretentions to beauty of a particular sort), her abominable familiar who is an obnoxious floofy cat, and her servant (more about her in a moment).

Alfreida Broomtail, the witch, lives in a hut, one of those low-slung hovels with a thatched roof that has things growing out of it. There are very few windows, all of them tiny and hard to see through, and generally one of them is full of Liripoop who spends most of the time polishing his claws with his tongue. There are excellent reasons not to disturb him. Beneath one of the windows is a large, rickety table that takes up most of the wall and about a quarter of the floor. It is covered with jars and bottles and vials and sachets and boxes and small cooking pots that send off various dreadful odors. This is where Alfreida spends most of her time when she is not too busy with her personal toilette. Occasionally she sweeps everything off the roughhewn surface, and so there are heaps and piles of unidentified debris on the floor—the rats and spiders are very territorial about them. Naturally there is a fireplace, with the traditional cauldron hanging on a blackened iron hook over the glowing coals. The hearth is very neat, and the smells coming from the cauldron are delicious; Alfreida is much too busy to cook, and the task is left to her servant.

For illumination there are candles in tilting sconces tacked to the walls wherever there is room for them, and so haphazard are they that their flames appear to lurch around the room, from hearth to door to table to bed and back to the hearth again. Little wax stalagmites rise under the candles, their relative heights revealing how long the sconce above has been there.

Alfreida herself is busy at the table sorting out cobwebs. She is a fine, scrawny ruin of a woman, with bones poking at her skin like unfriendly tenants. This afternoon she is wearing a splendid, ancient dress of a rusty, muddy shade that might once have been dark blue. The brocade taffeta is shapeless and without shine, and the scraps of lace at the corsage and the cuffs only serve to make the whole ensemble appear more bedraggled. Over the years she has lived alone, she has got into the habit of talking to herself. It is quite useless to talk to Liripoop, who rarely pays attention to anything except his own vanity.

"Bats' toes, bats' toes, where are they? What sly things they are, oh, yes." With a cry she seizes a lump of a jar and pulls the stopper out. "There. Theretherethere!" Delightedly she drops some small, anonymous bits into the pot sitting by her right elbow. "Now for the kernels of gallowsbane fruit!" Her twiggy fingers hover over the confusion and she clicks them with impatience.

On the windowsill, Liripoop regards her contemptuously. He stretches out his front paws, crosses them just so, and lets his claws out to their full, glorious, scimitar length.

"And now, wartflower. Where's the wartflower. No good reason for it to be missing, that's what I say." She reaches down, pushing several containers aside, but finally stands back in vexation. "There are some things that don't know when funny is funny."

From the distance, the Trolls can be heard singing. They usually start about this time every afternoon and have sometimes kept at it all night.

> *"Gruesomely churns the water down*
> *Bringing us victims, hey-ho!*
> *Horses and riders washed down*
> *Who simply forgot to say woah!*
> *Murky and damp our houses are*
> *Deep in the slime and mud caves—"*

Alfreida grits her teeth and makes a face in the direction of the horrible song. "Some people!" she mutters.

> *"While to the tune of frightened screams*
> *Our mummy whimpers and—"*

"Liripoop, can't you—" Alfreida complains, as she always does.

> "—raves . . .
> Chorus:
> Lollopping, slobbering—"

"—do something to—"

> "—monstrous Trolls!
> We hide under bridges, we hide in deep holes!
> We gibber and scribble—"

Alfreida takes up the largest bottle she can easily reach and heaves it in the general direction of the sounds. The bottle smashes satisfyingly and sends a thin, noxious odor through the room to blend with the others.

> "—our names in the ooze!
> We feast on whomever, whenever we choose!"

"They'll be at it all night at this rate!" Alfreida shouts to the ceiling. She claps her hands on her hips and glares at Liripoop. "You could *do* something; you know you could. But there you sit! Some people don't know what lucky is."

Ever so delicately, Liripoop yawns, taking great care to show all of his long, pointed teeth. The tip of his plume of a tail gives one ominous twitch.

"It's all very well for you," Alfreida rails at him. "All you ever have to do is sit there and wait for the mice to come. You're not so put upon as others I could name." She reaches for a featherduster made with nettles, but does little more than wave it threateningly in the air. (Above her, one or two bats are changed into snails; one of them drops onto the table and lands in a box of ground ginger.) She knows better than to get into a row with Liripoop; he knows it, too.

> "Morbidly through the gloom we slosh,
> Our thick, icky limbs distorted!
> Quaking our prey that—"

As much to save face as anything, Alfreida stomps over to the door and pulls it open. "You! Trolls! Much more noise out of you and I'll set the cacodemons on you!" She sounds more irritated than she is. If the truth were known, she actually looks forward to these afternoon tussles with the Trolls.

> *"—ichor we plaster our reeking walls—"*

Alfreida slams the door and braces it with her back, the very picture of the chatelaine defending the castle. She glares at the nearest candle and is satisfied only when the little flame quivers and goes out. It would be too much to say that she smiles, but she changes enough to be pleased. "A body can't get an indecent spell done without them caterwauling about how special they are and breaking into one's concentration. It's a shame they're not so modest as some of us."

Liripoop blinks very thoroughly.

Beyond the door, the song of the Trolls grows rowdier and a bit louder. Alfreida gives up her post and goes back to the table. "Where did I leave off?"

If this question is directed at Liripoop, he ignores it superbly.

She busies herself with sorting out bottles and at last finds a badly blown bottle with a wax seal across the top. With an eager cry, she grabs it and breaks the wax off at once. "Oh, yes, what a fine vintage it is!" she cackles as she pours out the gooey substance into the pot. "This is just what's needed."

Delicately Liripoop gets down from the sill and stalks away toward the hearth where he begins a most fastidious grooming of his tail.

"Just listen to them. Those Trolls!" Alfreida says sotto voce. She is trying to find just the right wooden spoon to stir her concoction. "No shame at all, the way they carry on." There is no spoon to be found, and at last she relents, screeching, "Esmeralda!" (Remember, she has a servant.) She potters over to the far end of the table, hoping that perhaps she will find what she needs there. "Those Trolls have no sense of the order of things. What if I should go around trying to be so impressive? Not that I haven't got things to recommend me."

Liripoop yowls and makes a face that on a human would be a smirk.

"I won't have you entertaining those notions," Alfreida warns him, but with little force. "In my youth, I will have you know, I was thought to be most remarkable for my appearance. Even Osgood said—that wretch!—I was very, very unusual." She lifts a spoon and considers it, but apparently it is not what she needs, for she puts it down once more. "But I'm not like those Trolls, not at all. *Esmeralda!* I know a bit more about conduct and courtesy, you may be sure of that."

Liripoop abandons his washing and finds a perfect spot; he gathers all his paws together, drops his chin on them and drapes his tail over his nose. His mad orange eyes do not quite close.

In her zeal to find the spoon, Alfreida oversets three little boxes. They fall to the floor and spill out three dissimilar dusts. "Exterpation!" Her hands raise up, gathered as tightly as her twig-fingers will permit. She is on the verge of a fine tantrum. "Es-mer-al-da!"

Timidly the door is opened and Alfreida's unfortunate servant comes into the hut. In spite of the torn clothes and smudge of dirt on her cheek, it is clear to anyone with decent vision and half a brain that this is one of the loveliest females ever to grace a once-upon-a-time. She is fair and glowing; her complexion is softer and more delicate than a rose petal; her hair falls in ridiculously perfect flaxen waves; her eyes, fringed with long, sweeping lashes, are the same deep shade as the best Dutch chocolate. At the moment she looks on Alfreida with pretty dismay. "Yes?"

"About time!" Alfreida shrieks.

"You told me to give your spiders"—here she shudders, a blossom in the wind—"pedicures."

"What an abominable creature you are. You made a perfect mull of drowning kittens yesterday and now this!" Her temper flares more brightly. "A spoon! My spell requires a spoon! What have you done with the spoons?"

"I . . . washed them," Esmeralda ventures, not daring to raise her voice above a breathless whisper.

"Washed them? *Washed* them? What is the matter with you? Don't you know enough not to *wash* things? Some people take too much on their judgment!" She stamps closer to Esmeralda, who shrinks back. "Not content with everything else, you're washing things!"

"But—"

"If I want a thing washed, I will tell you to wash it, do you understand me? Some people don't know when to listen. Some people don't know when to let others do the thinking! Some people assume they're able to . . . to . . ." Alfreida has turned an alarming shade of puce, and she gasps for air. In the sudden silence, the Trolls are heard once again, more off-key than ever.

"—and scribble our names in the ooze!—"

"A-A-A-a-a-a-gh-h-h!" goes Alfreida, shoving the door closed.

"Mercy," Esmeralda breathes.

"Not from me, you little blither-head," Alfreida crows, having found a victim on whom to vent her wrath. "You've done one thing too many, and you'll have to take the brunt of my punishment for your mistakes. Yes, yesyesyes. You think I'm an old soft-hearted creature, don't you? like some others I could mention, but I'll have a chance to learn otherwise."

Esmeralda stares in horror at the witch. "But I've tried to obey you. I've done as you wished, and I haven't attempted to escape or do you any disservice, just as I promised."

"And you think I paid any notice of that?" Alfreida scoffs. "What a moron you must think I am. Just a silly old woman, who only needs a little cajoling before she changes her mind about everything." Alfreida looks down at Liripoop and coos, "You could tell her a thing or two, couldn't you?" The cat does not respond, which is wise of it. "You sly wench! I'll turn you over to the Trolls if you go too far. You'll discover how well-off you've been with me, if you end up with the Trolls. Some people think that reasonableness and lenience is weakness, but that's poppycock. You're in the Woebegone Wood now, you pretty nit, and you'd better think twice about what you do and say." Her pebble-gray eyes reveal no trace of emotion, but her face is stretched out in a grotesque smile.

"But honestly, Mistress Broomtail, I have never wanted to turn against you. You've warned me that all my family's crops would be blighted if I did, and I cannot be the instrument of their distress." Esmeralda lifts her hands (the nails, miraculously, are clean and unbroken) to her cheeks and starts to weep.

"It is strange that you would try to trick me. I can see through every word, you dizzard. There are some who might be taken in by you, but not me." She raises her hands ominously. "There are some who might take vengeance on you in other ways."

"Oh, gracious," Esmeralda whispers.

"You're not going to get away with that twaddle about your poor papa's acres, no, you're not." Her expression changes to one of the most spurious good will. "Still missing your family, are you? After all this time? How sweet."

Liripoop gives a loud cat-snort but shows no other sign of paying attention.

With an enchanting little sniff, Esmeralda tries to stop her tears. "Oh, you cannot know how much I miss my home and family. It was so wonderful to be there, with my father and my mother and brothers and sisters and—"

"It sounds too crowded to stand," Alfreida mutters with an impatient and ominous twitch to the ragged wisps of black lace at her elbows.

"—and our little dog Slurpy. We were so happy, helping each other and singing nice songs in the evening while we scrubbed the little cottage clean again." Her sigh is a faint, adorable loss of air through her partly opened lips.

"Oh, for the use of a genie, just for a minute," Alfreida beseeches the air, her eyes turned up toward the smoke-blacked beams of her hovel. "There are some people who could learn a trick or two from a genie."

"But don't you see?" Esmeralda asks. "It was so wonderful because we all loved each other and helped each other and we were all happy to do this, and we were all the better for it." She clasps her hands together as she remembers.

"All the better for it? All the better for it, she says," Alfreida warns the pots and vials in front of her. "All the better for what, you great gawk?" She picks up the stopper from a jar and wags it at Esmeralda. "You listen to me, you horrible creature. You were none of you happy. You were none of you improving yourselves and helping each other, you were making sure you got what you want, and that's all there is to it. The rest is a lot of goopy talk. You believe something like that, you'll believe that sweeping up after the Trolls could be fun!" She flings the stopper into the air. "I don't know. I bring you here, I try to show you what's what, and all you can do is talk about drudgery as if it were some kind of picnic, a treat!"

Here Esmeralda touches her throat with her beautiful fingers. "Don't you know that so long as we are kind, others will be kind in return?"

"Listen to the nonsense," Alfreida admonishes Liripoop, who pays no attention at all. She shakes her head as she looks at Esmeralda. "What kind of fairy tale were *you* living in? Bah! Bahbahbah! Some people don't have the first notion of the world." She flounces away from the table making an angry show of herself. "Some people don't know why they're liked, what they are worth to the world. No they don't. Some people think that they need only look wistful and the world will do what they want. Well, we don't all have soft hair and melting eyes and rosy skin like a certain dummy I could name. We don't all bat our lashes and whisper pretty little things to get our way."

Esmeralda cannot bring herself to rebuke Alfreida for her behavior, though she knows it is rude. Instead, she does as her mother taught her. "I'm sure your friends must be good and kind, and treasure you. They know and appreciate all your good qualities and think you quite becoming—"

"Me?" This is almost more than Alfreida can stomach.

"Striking, anyway," Esmeralda amends. She looks away from Alfreida, uncertain how to go on, and not wishing to give offense to her abductress. "It is very sad, you know. Since you've brought me to this dark forest, I've not been able to discover anything that pleases you. I've tried to do as you wish, and I respect your abilities, and I . . . I want to assure you that I would not do anything to give you reason to . . . take the action you said you might." She turns her pleading eyes to Alfreida. "Why will you not tell me what I am to do to please you?"

Alfreida snorts. "Haven't you paid attention to anything I've said? Are you really as dense as all that? If you think to fool me with a deep game, you had better change your mind. You do not know what I am capable of doing, especially when I'm bored."

"Bored?" Esmeralda repeats, seizing on what she hopes is a clue to Alfreida's unpredictable behavior. "Is that it? You are alone here, but for your cat and the Trolls. Oh, I should have realized." Her eyes shine with inspiration. "You miss your friends, don't you? I should never have reminded you of how lonely you've become. Forgive me, please."

"Forgive something so ridiculous! What an odd idea she has of forgiveness," Alfreida remarks to Liripoop, her scraggled brows moving up and down to indicate something of significance. When Alfreida's brows waggle, it is a very bad sign.

"I do realize that I'm not the best companion for you, but I will try to improve. Tell me what you wish me to study—not anything too awful—and I will do my best to learn it, so that I can offer you some intelligent conversation when we are finished with the work of the day." Her eyes are growing pensive now, and she droops where she stands. Her pretty, amazingly clean frock shows off her posture to the best advantage and her half-closed lips would appear pouting on anyone less patently innocent.

"So you wish to please me? Will you listen to it, Liripoop, the moron wants to please me. How delightful." Her tone is filled with something that Esmeralda does not recognize; it is malice. "There must be some little thing I could think of, if I put my mind to it. What do you say, Liripoop? Isn't there something that would be simply perfect?"

Liripoop gives a slow, studied stretch, then drops his chin back on his feet.

For once, Esmeralda has the good sense to be apprehensive. "I didn't mean . . . I don't want to be a bother to you, but if there is something . . . you might not want to . . ." Even dithering, she is lovely, which Alfreida notices with a cultivated sneer.

"You want to please me, and the way you are, no matter what you did, you would please someone, I'm sure." She reaches out, tapping her long, hooked fingernails on one of the metal pots. The noise is like pebbles or teeth rolled down a metal washboard. "I'm sure," she muses, her eyes half closing, taking on an expression very like Liripoop's. "Yes. But what if you were changed? What then?" The sly eyes do not open, but they whisk from Esmeralda's face to the cat's and back again. "What if you were plain? What if you were ugly? What if you were hideous? What if you were frightful? Do you think anyone would be glad to have you help them, and make you feel so happy? Not a chance, not a chance. No one would want you near them, no one! That idiot dog of yours would bite you if he didn't run howling out of the room." Alfreida cackles with glee at the thought, exactly as all wicked witches are supposed to do. "We'd see what's what then, wouldn't we?"

Esmeralda had turned divinely pale. "What are you saying? Why should such things make a difference? I am certain that you have let your disappointments sour you, and I am sorry for it. It isn't possible that you could be right." Her indignation is almost as splendid to behold as her dismay was. "It is just that you are an unfortunate, neglected, unhappy old witch!"

Both Alfreida and Esmeralda are stupefied by her outburst, as much because it is a pretty good summary of the problem than anything else. Liripoop licks his nose in a thorough and studious manner.

"What was that?" Alfreida demands ominously.

"Oh, dear," Esmeralda cries, shrinking back. "What a dreadful thing for me to say to you. What can I have been thinking of, to speak of you in that way?"

"It wasn't your family's crops," Alfreida declares with a slow nod. "They'll be eating weeds before the summer is over, you spiteful little worm."

Esmeralda looks around the hut, overcome by distress. "I never meant that, never. I was . . . foolish! stupid!"

"That you were," Alfreida agrees with spurious good will.

"I'd do anything to make amends. I beg your pardon." She curtsies, as graceful as a willow bending in the wind. This does nothing to appease Alfreida, who rolls up her eyes in exasperation.

"What a ninny it is. What an aggravating ninny." Her chuckle is low and nasty. "And it expects me to forgive and forget the insult. Well, I'm not so blind as some I could name. And I'm not so namby-pamby."

"No, certainly you're not. You have great perspicacity," Esmeralda assures her, eager to placate her captress. "You are more learned and erudite than anyone I've ever met."

"Fine words for someone who should be scratching out bequests," Alfreida warns her, then pauses. "You do want to get back into my good graces, don't you. You're not just saying that to convince me you're harmless."

Esmeralda is not wise enough to be nervous at this sudden change of humor on Alfreida's part, so she nods earnestly, the color coming back into her cheeks. "Oh, yes. Yes, it would mean so much to me. And then my family would not have to starve and I would be able to tend to the chores you have set me in a manner you will like." She smiles mistily. Or perhaps she is merely nearsighted.

"Indeed," Alfreida says with a permissive wave of her hand. "Well, then I will have to think about it, won't I?"

"Oh, please; yes, please," Esmeralda breathes.

Alfreida shakes her head and looks down once more at her pots. "Some people are remarkably dense." She smiles, a jagged, crocodile sort of smile. "I'll have to give you that chance, won't I? It wouldn't do for me to prohibit you. No, not at all."

"Thank you, thank you," Esmeralda whispers, all but dropping to her knees in gratitude. "I knew you could not be so cold-hearted to forbid me to have the opportunity to redeem myself in your good opinion."

"What mouthfuls you say," Alfreida remarks sweetly. "If you'll just go to the cave and get my grimoire, I'll see what I can come up with for you to do." She indicates the door. "Be sure you close it firmly. I need time to think, and the Trolls are making too much noise for that."

"The grimoire. Yes, I will fetch it. Right away." She rushes to the door and with some effort tugs it open.

> "—in the mold-green moonlight
> Where horror unknown waits and—"

"SHUT IT!" Alfreida bellows, and glares in secret satisfaction at the door. "That will keep her busy while I make a few preparations. Something like this requires planning and concentration, and no one can manage that with an abominably sweet wretch prattling along about goodness and happiness."

Liripoop gives a low purr; he knows what's coming.

"And when she comes back, I'll show her." Alfreida begins to hum, her tone-deaf meanderings painful to everyone including Liripoop, who turns his back on Alfreida and ignores the whole thing. "What a pretty little cotton-head she is, no doubt about it. High time she learned it's a rougher world than she knows. Yes. Yesyesyes. When she comes back, I'll turn her into a toad." This gives Alfreida such amusement that she has to jig about the room in order to accommodate her mirth. As she goes, she kicks the occasional bit of furniture out of her way. "Must have a good open space, mustn't we? Large enough to do the work. Toad magic, now that takes a smallish pentacle." She begins to pace out the lines on the floor, then stops abruptly. "Not a toad. No, that's far too easy. An obnoxious thing like her, she'd find someone who likes toads. It must be worse than that."

Liripoop is no help at all.

"What about a sickly bat? One of those weak ones, that are always falling into people's hair? What would that cream-puff do when a flighty old lady fainted at the sight of her?" She looks toward her cat, as if expecting approval, but Liripoop pays no attention. "If not a bat, what about something large and terrible, something really unpleasant?" The notion appeals to Alfreida as she says this, and her grin is unnerving to see. "I think that I might come up with a spell or two that would do the trick." She hops experimentally. "A slip of a thing like Esmeralda is going to take more than a jot of magic to get up to size, but there are some who are thought to be the best around who are not equal to my abilities, not that I would think to boast of it." Her voice has turned sweetly modest, not a very pleasant thing at all.

Liripoop rolls onto his back and looks up at her in an expectant way, then utters a few strange cat sounds which Alfreida listens to attentively. When he has finished this, he rolls back into a ball and claps his paws over his eyes.

"Why, I never thought about that at all," Alfreida says to him, as if in conversation. "It didn't occur to me. I must not be completely myself today, to have overlooked such an obvious thing." A speculative gleam comes into her eyes. "And there would be real advantages to your plan, Liripoop. You're always showing me the way, I must admit it." She looks about among the pots. "What might work best? Tigers and lions are out—I haven't got the space for them. But there are other things . . ." She reaches out for some white powder. "The pentacle first, I think, while I work out what I am going to do with her." Alfreida kicks a few more bits of furniture into the corners of the room. Other bits of legs and arms of chairs already broken there attest to how regular a habit this is with her. When she has cleared a good portion of the center of the room, she wets her fingers and holds them up. "No draft except for the chimney, and that's to be expected."

Liripoop rolls closer to the hearth, as if to aid her, or it may be that he is only exercising good judgment.

"The floor will do as it is," Alfreida announces to the air. She begins to pace and measure as she goes, still holding the box of white powder. "I won't need the candles; I won't want to keep anything *in.*" Her laughter has degenerated to a cackle. "And then, it's only a matter of choosing the right form and putting her in it." The cackle grows worse. Alfreida is beginning to enjoy herself, something that bodes very little good for anyone other than Alfreida. "The pentacle, the pentacle. And that disgusting creature!" It would be too much to say that she actually skips, but she comes dangerously close to it. "She'll be quite hideous, quite, *quite* hideous. How delightful it will be."

As if in protest, Liripoop gets up, stretches, and then leaps up to the narrow stone projection that serves as a mantle above the hearth. He recommences washing his tail.

"What would make her feel most awful?" This occupies her thoughts briefly. "And what would cause the greatest uproar? What would bring all the neighbors running to stare and curse?" Her eyes widen suddenly. "I have it! I have it! Extirpation, I have it!" This time her hop is more emphatic. "A dragon, that's it. A dragon. I'll turn that syrupy blossom into a horrible, repulsive, ghastly, horrendous dragon, with scales and flames. That will cause tongues to wag, even among the Trolls." The more she contemplates this, the happier it makes her. She opens her box of white powder and begins the task of marking out the pentacle on the floor. She croons to herself as she goes. "A dragon, Esmeralda a dragon. Why, there hasn't been a dragon in the Woebegone Wood for centuries, and almost everyone's forgotten what they're like. And to have them know that I did it, well, it would be about time for some of them to realize the talents I possess are not to be trifled with." She has finished about half the pentacle and she pauses to look over her work. "Coming along very nicely. What do you say, Liripoop?"

The cat could not be bothered.

Nothing daunted, Alfreida continues with her chores. "Think of it. All the nobility from Addlepate and Alabaster-on-Gelasta will come riding out here, and I'll have them! What a plate of understanding charity and help they'll serve Esmeralda! And what *I* will do to *them.*" She finds this so amusing that she almost drops the box of white powder. "What fun it's going to be! Ah! And what a lasting lesson it's going to give to a remarkably stupid fuzzy-brain." She is growing more and more enthusiastic for her dire project; the ramifications are becoming apparent to her, and the more of them she recognizes, the better she feels. "Those know-it-alls in Addlepate. Well! Humgudgeon thinks he's the master enchanter in these parts. Fat lot of boasting, that's all he's good for. Why, I could out-enchant the whole lot of them, including Humgudgeon. I've got more imagination than any of them, I've shown that over and over. My skills keep getting better." She stops congratulating herself to put the finishing touches on her pentacle. "There's more evil in my little—"

> ". . . hide in deep holes!
> We —"

Alfreida screams as Esmeralda hastens to close the door behind her, once again shutting out the rowdy carolling of the Trolls.

"Will you warn a body when you're coming, you inexcusable dottard? All this skulking about makes me nervy." Alfreida glowers at Esmeralda, pouting as she does.

Esmeralda is chagrinned, and she blushes rosily. "I'm sorry, Mistress Broomtail. I never intended to frighten you."

As if it were not bad enough to have been startled, this revelation is almost more than Alfreida can bear. "Frighten? You, frighten me? Will you listen to this loathsome abomination?" Suddenly Alfreida laughs, anticipating the revenge she is about to achieve.

"Mistress Broomtail, I—" Esmeralda says apprehensively, her mouth turning down, but not enough to mar the shape and curve of it.

"Don't interrupt me," Alfreida orders. "I'm thinking." So saying, she takes the time to walk around the pentacle once more, as much to congratulate herself for her cleverness as to be certain she has performed her magic correctly. "Quite satisfactory, I should think. There are those who would say that it takes more than the spells and a pentacle to do things right, but they haven't the experience that some of us can claim."

This is more promising than Esmeralda had feared it might be, and so she tremblingly proffers the tome she has brought. "I have . . . your book, Mistress Broomtail."

"Book?" Alfreida turns and abruptly snatches the volume from Esmeralda. "It had better be the right one," she warns as she starts to open it. In fact, she owns no more than three books, and the other two are nothing like her grimoire, one being a small volume on herbs, and the other a dissertation on manners and fashion now more than thirty years out of date.

"Ah. Well, you can get things right on occasion, can't you, especially when you're told just what to do."

Esmeralda can think of nothing to say in response, and so for a change she remains silent. Her hands lie against the folds of her sprigged muslin skirt, joined delicately. Somehow or other she has managed to keep her shoes clean and they still have a trace of polish to them. She looks wistfully toward Liripoop, wanting to pet him, but afraid of what he might do, since he has shown himself to be disinclined to attention from her in the past.

"I'm almost ready," Alfreida announces after she peers at the various containers on her table. "I have everything I need, I think."

"Do you want me to leave?" Always before when Alfreida has been about to do magic, she has ordered Esmeralda out of the hovel, no matter what the time or the weather. It being a dank afternoon with promise of a gelid night, Esmeralda cannot help but look longingly at the hearth where the fire still has a little life in it and the cauldron bubbles.

"Oh, no. Nonono. Wouldn't think of it. You ought to see what I can do when I'm in fine form. This is as good a time as any. But"—she points to the center of the room— "I want you to stand there. For your . . . protection." Her giggle is like shards of ice sliding over metal.

Liripoop opens his eyes indignantly, then assumes his usual inscrutable pose.

"Is there any place in particular I should stand? I don't want to interfere," Esmeralda says. She is concerned about this sudden change of demeanour on Alfreida's part. She knows that she ought to trust others, but for once she has trouble convincing herself of this.

"You see the star? Well, you go and stand in the middle of it, so you'll be safe."

"This five-pointed one?" Esmeralda asks, still uneasy.

"Perfect. Now don't move, and don't speak, and don't do anything unless I tell you to, all right?" Once again she giggles and, if anything, it is worse than before.

"I scuffed one of the points. Should I fix it?" Esmeralda looks at the pentagram, not wanting to disobey Alfreida, but worried that there might be some hazard if the pentagram is not correct. Alfreida has often railed at her when magical things were not just so.

"Um?" Alfreida murmurs, looking up from the book. "Oh,

I see. Well, yes. You can fix it. Make sure it comes to a nice, sharp point. You do that." She goes back to struggling with the book, which is very large and unwieldy, which is traditional for important grimoires.

Esmeralda sets the corner of the pentacle to rights, then moves back again, standing quietly and adorably at the center. She lowers her eyes demurely.

"Where would they put *dragon* in a book like this?" Alfreida wonders aloud as she turns the pages.

"Under *D*," Esmeralda says, grateful now that she has the protection of the pentacle. She is very much afraid of things like dragons and wyverns and gryphons. She is also afraid of witches and Trolls, but that is another matter.

"What a helpful little wretch it is," Alfreida grumbles as she fingers the pages. "Ah, yes, here it is. Under *D*." She peers at the page. *"Whilst hopping on the ryte foote thou dost repeat: Latchetail ryscr* . . . Aha! That's got it. Here we go." She puts the book on the one clear space on the table, canting it out precariously, then reaches for various bits of powders and dried oddments, strewing them about. All the while she chants, turning first this direction then that, describing strange shapes in the air with her skinny fingers. Her voice, never soothing, becomes increasingly strident. There is a light in her eyes that more hardened souls than Esmeralda would find disturbing.

"Prigin kardapest dinguremer apenlau!" The words of the spell are strange to both Esmeralda and Alfreida, and neither of them knows if they are pronounced correctly. They sound sinister because they are so very unfamiliar, which causes more apprehension to fill Esmeralda. Alfreida is inspired by what she is saying, and goes into the second part of the spell with considerable verve.

The air in the hovel, never very clear, becomes first dingy and then sunk into gloom. Strange flickers of acidic green and orange move along the beams like St. Elmo's Fire. There are sounds that cannot be identified coming from the walls, and rustlings move along the floor as if the place were being invaded by hoards of invisible mice.

> *"Cebalpontigerdig yepwig.*
> *Lesegho hapdoff kopasil yepwig.*
> *Shybid esterkring tillclet pantu!"*

The chant goes on, growing so loud that it almost competes with the carousing Trolls (to give the Trolls their due, they fell silent when the spell began. They may be Trolls, but they are not total boors).

And what is happening to Esmeralda? She is so terrified that she can hardly bring herself to breathe. Her arms feel stiff as old ice, her forehead is so hot that she would not touch it if she could, for fear of raising blisters on her fingers. There are sounds in her ears that have nothing to do with what Alfreida is yodeling outside the pentacle. Her feet ache and itch in ways she has never felt before. Enormous tears roll from her perfect eyes and she bids farewell in her mind to home, family, hearth, and Slurpy.

Alfreida is prancing and leaping now, throwing herself into the ritual so frantically that she realizes that tomorrow she will be one mass of sore joints and sour disposition. Yet for the moment she is caught up in the spell as much as the object of her corybantic frenzy. She bounds into the air, tossing the last of the herbs in the general direction of the pentacle. Then she spins giddily around the entire pentacle (widdershins, of course) and ends up before her fire, panting and triumphant.

The air in the hut crackles and fizzes. Four new, distinct and incompatible stenches are released from the pentacle. Strange, obscuring clouds roil up, turning various noxious colors as they go. Jars and boxes skitter on the table and a strange stretching groan fills the room.

Pop! Whirrr! and fingers lengthen, turning into talons, growing long, glistening claws. Toes thrust through the ends of shiny shoes, more claws appear. Golden hair lifts and twines, stiffening as it goes, turning into two twisted, arching horns forming a perfect valentine over the long, green, scaled snout. Hummmm! Zip! Ping! Joints shorten, reach, change, shift. Esmeralda gasps and a tiny puff of smoke clouds out of her mouth. Skin hardens and shines, segmenting into scales.

Alfreida howls with delight as the last of the colored mists fades away and the hovel is once again quiet. "I did it! *I did it!*" she crows.

Liripoop blinks slowly, keeping his thoughts to himself.

"I'll have to make sure that those idiots in Alabaster-on-Gelasta find out about this. They'll want to know there's a dragon about. And Humgudgeon will want to know that

Alabaster-on-Gelasta knows." She actually rubs her hands together in malefic anticipation.

In the pentacle, the huge brown eyes of the dragon continue to shed perfect tears.

Interlude

A SHAPE GOES out from the Woebegone Wood, a Shape that is many things, a bit of soot blown against the sky, perhaps a bird no one has been before. Sometimes it drifts, sometimes it lurches, sometimes it tumbles with the wind, but always, always, it goes toward Addlepate, carrying something with it, and beneath it, where its shadow passes, the Woebegone Wood falls silent.

Complication Number One

IF HUMGUDGEON IX, Protector Extraordinary of Addlepate is known for anything, aside from malice, it is caprice. He likes nothing so much as exercising his right to have an absolute whim, one that every minion of his court will have to leap to indulge or face *the consequences*. Humgudgeon is a short, pudgy man who is inevitably called handsome, since to say anything else is to woo disaster (see *the consequences*, above). He has been known to order his whole court to pack up and move in the middle of the night, and take them all, without warning, to visit a noble who is currently enjoying the dubious advantage of his favor. These Protectoral Progresses always cause chaos, which is precisely what pleases Humgudgeon the most. He prides himself on the amount of upset he can bring about, which can be a dangerous thing in a ruler, no matter how much fun it might seem to be.

At the moment, he has ordered the court to go away on a picnic, never mind the rain, and has the afternoon free to contemplate new mischief. For that purpose, he has gone to his study where he can recline on the cushion and sip from various cups while he turns various schemes over in his mind, consulting his raven from time to time, for like Alfreida, he has a familiar. He prides himself on his decadence, and at the moment is doing it in the effete style.

The Shape has almost reached the castle where Humgudgeon is plotting. It has made good time and has farther to go. It circles around the towers and finally begins its descent.

"Yes, we'll think of something for them," Humgudgeon muses, taking more of whatever-it-is in the gold cup. "A tasty little plague, perhaps. There's much to be said for plague. It is such a complete disaster, brings everything to a halt. You may prefer calamities a bit more solid and theatrical," he goes on to the raven. "Fires and floods and the rest of them, but you're wrong, my dear. It devastates me to say that you are wrong, but there it is. There is no poetry in your notion. Ruins should be poetic." He touches his dark, greasy hair and smooths it back from his brow. "Those poor dears, still thinking that my attention is elsewhere, occupied with other matters. But Alabaster-on-Gelasta will meet its doom, and all in good time. I will relish it. Oh, yes, it is a wonderful thought." He becomes positively jovial as he goes on. "Think of it, my dear. People dying, the nation bankrupt, commerce halted, agriculture nonexistent, the King in chains—imagine Rupert in chains, won't you?—the entire court turned to corpses or paupers over night. Pretty, very pretty." He fills another cup with a greenish substance kept in a jar of chalcedony. "And that wizard of his . . . something will have to be done about

him. There's a temptation to do the obvious and chop off his
head, but that lacks finesse. You must appreciate how necessary finesse can be to enterprises like this. Truly, you must."

The raven is not particularly impressed, but unlike Liripoop, who always permits himself to express his disdain, the
raven remains silent and vaguely preoccupied. Then something outside the narrow window attracts its attention, and it
points its beak toward the opening, not daring to make a
sound as the Shape passes quite near. The raven remains very
still, as if listening.

Humgudgeon is drinking from a different goblet, and his
loquacity continues. "I've considered the possibility that he
has protected himself. Rupert is a bit of an ass, but you cannot
be too careful with kings who keep wizards. You see, I don't
underestimate the brilliance of Sigmund Snafflebrain. I realize
he's talented. Some would say he has genius, but that may be
taking it a bit too far. It's always hard to imagine genius without malice, isn't it?" He turns toward the raven, who has been
looking out the window. "There is something bothering you?"
An edge has come into his voice, just a hint of condemnation
for the lack of attention the raven has given him, and ordinarily it would be enough to cause the bird to become attentive
again (otherwise, there are *consequences*). However, this
time, the raven takes a moment before he looks again in the
general direction of the master of the castle.

"Am I boring you?" Humgudgeon asks, in obvious and
dreadful sarcasm.

The raven makes a low sound. Nervously it preens the
long quills on its wings.

"Is there something you'd rather do? Would you prefer
that I work these problems out on my own, so that you need
not be interrupted in whatever it is you do?" He waits, filling
the silence with more of the liquid in the cup.

Outside the Shape hovers and then departs, speeding away
in the direction of Alabaster-on-Gelasta.

It takes a little time for Humgudgeon to finish what is in
the goblet, and when he raises his beady, piggish eyes they are
decidedly muzzy. "I've given it a lot of thought," he says, not
getting all the syllables quite right. "I know that it is Sigmund
we must defeat before anything can be done about Rupert.
Always get the wizard first, that's my motto. Doubtless it is
Sigmund who is the true power in Alabaster-on-Gelasta. I'll

find out how he does whatever he's done, and then Rupert's rule will be ended, and I can begin my occupation. You want to know how I am going to do this, now that you're giving me your notice, my dear? I'm not going to give them away to someone as unreliable as you. That would be foolish, and I am never foolish. He toasts himself with yet another goblet and drinks. The lace at his wrist becomes stained, and some of the threads are eaten away, as if what is in the goblet is faintly corrosive.

Before Humgudgeon can quite finish the goblet, there is a knock at the door. It is urgent, almost desperate, and a voice is heard calling out through the planking: "Your Maleficence! Your Maleficence!"

"I gave orders I was not to be disturbed," Humgudgeon calls out, showing his teeth in an expression that is anything but a smile. "You're disturbing me."

"A thousand pardons, Your Maleficence. If it were not a mater of life and death..." The pounding is renewed and Humgudgeon glares at it.

"Whose life and death?" he demands, casting an irate glance at the raven. "All right. Enter. But this had better be worth the disturbance or you will suffer for it."

The enormous door groans inward on ancient hinges and a man in the wreck of a military uniform with his wig askew stumbles in to fall at Humgudgeon's feet. "Your Maleficence, we have tried to follow your orders, but... Tottering-in-the-Wold has fallen to vandal hoards. The Umbrous Stronghold is besieged! We tried!"

"How very distressing," Humgudgeon says, carefully drawing his feet back so that the poor fellow before him cannot touch any part of him.

"The city was sacked, the ships were sunk, the castle was razed and they gave the marshal a bloody nose." With each new element of disaster, the man in the shredded uniform tries to get his head lower than it was. By the end of his recitation, his forehead is on the floor.

"Dear me." Humgudgeon reached for a fan and snaps it open. "Downwind, vartlet."

Obediently the man drags himself along the floor to a different vantage point. "The food is gone, the water is poisoned, the fires are spreading and it is the flea season," he informs Humgudgeon in a quaking tone.

"You're most alarming," Humgudgeon says, fanning himself with vigor and raising an eyebrow in the direction of the raven.

Finally the poor fellow raises his head. "Well?" he beseeches.

"Well?" Humgudgeon echoes, astonished that the man should still be there.

"You're the Protector Extraordinary. Do something!" This time when he lowers his head to the stones, it is because he has almost fainted.

"What?" Humgudgeon demands. "Surely you don't expect me to go there, actually put myself in danger, do you? Do you?" He finds the man's audacity quite invigorating if completely ridiculous.

The messenger sighs. "But—"

"Gracious, it's sounds dreadful there. Why would I deliberately go someplace where all those mishaps are occurring? I wouldn't dream of it." He gives an indignant snap to his fan.

"But Your Maleficence, think!" He clasps his hands together and extends them toward Humgudgeon, who slaps them away with his closed fan.

"I have thought. I know that it would be a great mistake to go anyplace where the vandals are wrecking castles. This is where I prefer to be." He reaches out for another goblet and takes a deep drink. Of course he would not consider offering a taste of anything to the prostrate messenger.

"Then a spell or two, Your Maleficence. You must do something. You cannot let them perish without lifting a finger."

Humgudgeon's lower lip thrusts out farther than it had been. "That's all you can think of isn't it? I spend all my time being Protector Extraordinary, and then when the going gets difficult, you want me to take care of you, of everyone in Addlepate. You none of you think of me, do you?" He takes another sip from the goblet, looking away from the figure lying at his feet. "It isn't the least bit fair of you."

"But we're your subjects, Your Maleficence," the wretched messenger protests.

"And precious little good you've done me," Humgudgeon reminds him. "Getting killed and burnt and sacked like that."

"Save them, I implore you, I beg you," the messenger cries out, once again reaching to touch Humgudgeon's foot.

"Don't *do* that," Humgudgeon orders, getting out of range again. He looks toward the raven. "Well, my dear, what do you think? The problem is that if I do this once, make an exception for you, they will all expect it later, and then I will be stuck with having to save them all the time. You see that, don't you?" Slowly he reaches out his hand and makes an arcane gesture. There is a small manifestation like a little whirlwind that fades quickly. Humgudgeon sighs. "There. One spell, as you wished. But that's all I'm going to do. Don't ask me for another thing." Humgudgeon is often sulky and this is one of those oftens.

With a relieved whimper, the messenger loses consciousness, but not before he chokes out his thanks to the Protector Extraordinary.

Now that the messenger is out cold, Humgudgeon takes a chance and nudges him with his toe. "Goodness me," he says to himself when the messenger does little more than twitch. He slides sideways and leans toward a concealed door not far from his mound of cushions that has been serving for a throne. "Chumley," he beckons.

The concealed door bulges, then swings open, and Chumley shambles into the room. He is large and lumpish and may be distantly related to the Trolls. He is a creature of simple pleasures and simpler mind. He makes a sound that is a grunting kind of laugh that no word exists for, but for the sake of having an indication of it, will be called "hurm." As he lumbers toward Humgudgeon, he goes "Hurm. Hurm. Hurm." in a kind of anticipation. "Master want Chumley? Master call Chumley. Chumley play now? Chumley want play." This is a fairly complex conversation for Chumley and he tires of it quickly.

"Of course, dear boy. You must be allowed to play. Growing boys need plenty of recreation." He drinks from yet another goblet before indicating the messenger in the tattered uniform. "See this? You may have this to play with."

"Hurm. Hurm. Chumley want play with him. Hurm. Him play toy." He lurches toward the unconscious man, then bends over to prod him with one spade-like hand. "Hurm. Want more play." He pokes harder, then leans down, and grabbing the unfortunate messenger by an arm and a leg, proceeds to half-carry, half-drag him toward the door he came from.

"You may do just as you wish, dear boy. But take him

away. He is dreadful clutter where he is."

Chumley is happy to oblige. "Chumley—hurm—take. Chumley play." And with these ominous words, he vanishes and the concealed door is once again closed.

"A-a-a-ahhh yes." Humgudgeon shakes his head slowly. "You see how it is, my dear," he protests to the raven. "Not a moment passes but they make the most incredible demands on me. There's nothing I can do to stop them. Thank goodness for Chumley. I don't know what I would do without him. I have other *consequences* I might employ, but most of them are exhausting. Chumley is simplicity itself." He tastes something in one of the smaller goblets, spits out what he has in his mouth and empties the rest on the floor. "One cannot help but wonder where they dream these things up. Whoever sent that to me will have something to answer for, I promise you."

From behind the concealed door there comes a single, ghastly breaking sound, and then a heavy thud.

Humgudgeon chooses to pay no notice to this. He selects another goblet and continues. "There's nothing I can do to stop these silly demands, though I've certainly tried. You favor drastic means, I know," he remarks to the raven, "but that's messy and not neat. You must perceive the need to be neat. There's no point in dealing with them if it only serves to make matters worse. If I am to decimate my country, it ought to be tidy, so the rest will not become too upset. Still, I can't let them bother me all the time, so it might become necessary to find other means. It isn't the least practical to spend all my time worrying about finding a way to keep them from taking up all my time. No advantage in an arrangement like that. I require some time for myself, don't I? Of course I do, my dear." He refills his current goblet and drinks from it with real satisfaction. "This is more like it. Whoever sent this one will have some sort of favor from me, perhaps I will take my court to visit him. That would be an honor."

The raven flaps around the room once, croaking a few times, and then returns to its perch where it waggles its head several times as ravens often do, then busies itself with setting its feathers in order.

"I *do* wish you would learn to speak," Humgudgeon complains. "It's so inconvenient having to decipher those sounds of yours. I'll attend to it shortly. But a creature like you, truly, you should be able to speak."

Just then there is another knock at the door and a terrified voice calls out, "Your Maleficence! Your Maleficence!"

"Go away," Humgudgeon answers.

"It's important, Your Maleficence!" the voice protests in desperation. "You could be in danger!"

"Goodness!" For Humgudgeon, this is a curse word. "In danger?"

"Yes, Your Maleficence!"

"Oh, all right. You may come in. But this had better be real danger, or you will answer for it." He sets his current goblet aside and taps the tips of his pudgy fingers together. "You may enter."

The door yawns open and a man staggers in. He is disheveled, one of his eyes has been impressively blackened, his right arm is in a makeshift sling and he is breathing heavily. "Your Maleficence," he pants, trying to bow properly.

"This had better be as important as you say," Humgudgeon informs him with a smile. Tap-tap-tap go his fingers.

"Your Maleficence, the townspeople are revolting!"

Tap-tap-tap. His smile becomes a grin. "Of course."

"It's going on right now!" the man insists. "The magistrates sent me. They're afraid they'll be lynched."

"They always are," Humgudgeon remarks, adding, "lynched, I mean."

"Even now there is still a chance to save some of them. The poor have run riot, and are tearing their way through all the shops and are calling for blood. They say they are starving and that you are a tyrant."

"How perceptive," Humgudgeon murmurs.

"They have sworn to bring you down," the man goes on, less certainly than before.

"Must they do this? Every spring, it's the same complaints, the same riots." He looks at this second messenger. "New magistrates, of course, but that's to be expected." He sighs. "I have to let them have a little fun, haven't I? Still, a few magistrates are a small price to pay." He leans back on his cushions.

"You don't understand. They say they will hang us all. They say they will pull down the castle walls. They say they will blow up the city. They say they will fill the rivers with blood—"

"Yes, yes," Humgudgeon interrupts this recitation. "It's

the same old thing. I've heard it hundreds of time. How far out of hand has it got?"

"They're in all the streets and——"

This time Humgudgeon is not about to indulge the messenger. "How close are they to the castle, that's what I want to know."

The messenger blanches. "Not far. Near the fish market, when I broke away from them."

"That's south," Humgudgeon muses.

"Hurry. If you don't do something, they'll all be hung!" the messenger exclaims rather wildly.

"That's hanged," Humgudgeon corrects him gently. "How fast would you guess they were moving, considering there are so many shops to wreck there in the fish market?"

"I . . . I don't know. I . . . I didn't stop to——" His voice is getting higher and higher.

"Would you say they had reached the taxing booth?" Humgudgeon inquires.

"Probably," the messenger allows. His eyes move uncertainly about the room, as if he expects it to be invaded at any moment.

"Then I suppose I will have to do something." Humgudgeon yawns at the notion. "If they are so rambunctious, I'll have to teach them a lesson, again." He pushes himself up on his elbow and begins to mutter strange and clashing syllables under his breath while making disturbing passes in the air with his hand. The room grows oddly dark and there are strange spots of brightness that hang in the air after his hand has moved.

"Your Maleficence ——" the messenger begins uncertainly.

"Hush!" Humgudgeon orders. "I'm concentrating."

A few more passes, a few more bits of light, and then something strange zips out the window.

"There," Humgudgeon declares with satisfaction as he leans back on the cushions.

Outside a sudden noise like an underground explosion or a collapsing, crowded sports arena fills the air. Screams and howls and shrieks erupt, and then suddenly fall silent.

"There," Humgudgeon says, regarding the messenger with a bemused expression. "That's better."

The messenger stares back in horror. "But you killed——"

"They breed like rabbits, dear fellow, like veritable minks.

They won't miss a few." As he speaks, a single brick hurtles through the window. "How annoying," Humgudgeon snaps. "I thought I'd got them all. That's easily remedied." He makes a few more passes, and once again something forms and leaves the room.

"Don't—" the messenger protests, trying to stop the thing Humgudgeon is sending out. As he tries to grasp the thing, a shudder goes through him, and he drops, twitching, to the floor. Beyond the window there is a yelp and the rumble of falling masonry.

Humgudgeon watches the messenger. "Mercy. I don't know my own strength." He reaches for a goblet. "Well, perhaps it's better this way." He takes a deep drink, then calls out, "Chumley."

The concealed door creaks open and Chumley lurches into the room. "Hurm. Hurm. 'Nother play toy for Chumley?" He looks down with schoolboy chagrin at his enormous, splayed feet. "Other play toy broke. Chumley broke other. Hurm."

"You really must learn to be more careful, Chumley," Humgudgeon tells him, not too severely. "It is very difficult for me to get you new play toys all the time. Truly, dear boy, you ought to try to be more gentle with your toys." In spite of the reprimand, Humgudgeon cannot help smiling as he admonishes Chumley.

"Chumley sorry," he says contritely.

"You'd better be, or I won't give you this one." He indicates the quivering messenger.

Poor Chumley is about to burst into tears, being basically soft-hearted under his crudeness, and he is often seized with fits of sentimentality, and never more so than when offered new toys. "Chumley promise. Chumley not break play toy."

"See that you don't. Or not too quickly, in any case," Humgudgeon instructs him. "Very well, dear boy. Take him away."

Chumley's face is wreathed in delighted smiles, which is a most unnerving sight. "Got new play toy! Chumley got play toy!" He grabs the ankles of the second messenger and begins to drag him toward the concealed door. "Chumley play. Hurm. Hurm. Hurm." And with the last "hurm" he is gone, and the door closes behind him.

"You see?" Humgudgeon asks his raven as he selects a goblet at random. "Never a moment's rest. I tell you, my dear, there's just too much to do. This Protector Extraordinary position is not at all the marvelous station so many think it is." He slides back against the cushions, making himself very comfortable. "Now, if I were Good, like Rupert, that would be different. Any fool can be Good. It requires no ability at all, no esthetic, no gifts. But Bad . . . my dear, it takes real planning and purpose to be Bad." With this revelation, he begins to sing:

> *"And the thing of it is that I'm evil*
> *I am vile and slimy and bad;*
> *I am given to tortures Medieval*
> *With results most lamentably sad, so sad.*
> *It is hard to imagine more malice*
> *Than's contained in the muck of my mind;*
> *It would soon overflow the whole palace*
> *If I hadn't an outlet outlined.*

> *"Let me tell you it takes dedication*
> *And a talent sent up from below*
> *With years of true edification*
> *For evil to flower and grow, and grow.*
> *It's an honor, it's proud and it's lonely*
> *To champion all that is ill:*
> *I'll hold out to the last, yes, if only*
> *To make myself eviler still!*

"And when you consider the sacrifices I've made, my dear. So many, many sacrifices," Humgudgeon observes to his raven. "The poor things. It's enough to make you lose faith my dear, when you see what it is that gets ahead in the world." He finishes off the goblet and is annoyed to find that all but two of them are empty. He is about to ring for a servant, when the door opens and a sinister figure insinuates itself into the room.

"Your Maleficence," whispers the Spy. That is all the name he has. Once he might have had another, and for a while he had a number, but all that has faded from his mind. Now he is simply the Spy.

"What? Who said that?" Humgudgeon demands. He grabs hold of one of the goblets so he will have something to throw, should it be necessary.

The Spy slides out of the shadows and reveals himself in a shabby travesty of court dress. His bow is shabby, too. "It is I,

Your Maleficence. I have returned." He is able to make this simple announcement seem fraught with significance.

"Well, why don't you speak up? What do you want?" He stares as the Spy comes closer. "Oh. It's you." He turns to his raven. "I told you we'd see him again, my dear. You doubted, I know, but my threats are effective, you see." He sets the empty goblet aside and chooses one that is full as he leans back. "Well?"

"Terrible news, Your Maleficence," the Spy begins. "I shudder to tell you."

Humgudgeon grins. "Terrible, you say?"

"You'll be furious," the Spy says uncertainly.

"Furious?" Humgudgeon is postively delighted.

"I'm afraid so, Your Maleficence. It is quite, quite dreadful." This admission shames him and he averts his eyes.

"Gracious, how bad is it?" He settles himself back for a good denunciation.

The Spy, however, hedges. "I followed your instruction to the letter, Your Maleficence. You must believe that I did. I would not attempt to fool you. I watched the Crown Prince, the Duke of Wappor, the Count of Murmoor, the eldest daughter of the Baron Onguent, the one-eyed verger, and the second stable boy." He starts to pace nervously. He is often nervous.

"Well?"

"I intercepted their messages, I opened their letters, I crept through their parties, I hid in their closets, I waited beneath their beds, I perched in the trees, I—"

"Marvelous," Humgudgeon breathes.

"—bribed the Chamberlain, the Chatelaine, the Seneschel, the Pursuivant—"

"Yes," Humgudgeon interrupts gleefully. "Yes, of course you did. All as I instructed you. The question is, Spy, what did you discover?"

The miserable Spy averts his eyes again. "Nothing," he says when he had got up enough courage to speak.

The good humor which had filled Humgudgeon evaporates almost at once. His complexion turns a distressing shade of plum, very ripe plum. "What?!" he thunders.

"I tried, Your Maleficence," the Spy protests quickly, all but going down on his hands and knees. His manner is abject. "I tried everything I knew, and still I couldn't find anything. I'm sorry, so *sorry*, Your Maleficence. It won't happen again,

I promise you, Your Maleficence—"

Humgudgeon interrupts his babbling. "Chum-ley!" he bellows at the top of his lungs.

The Spy turns an even more sickly shade as the concealed door begins to swing open on groaning hinges. "No. Wait. Wait, Your Maleficence. Don't do this. Don't. Please. I know I can still be of use to you. Give me a chance." He reached out and grabs the skirt of Humgudgeon's brocaded coat, kissing it fervently.

Chumley looms in the door. "More play toy? Want more play toy. Hurm. Hurm. Play."

"I'll go to Alabaster-on-Gelasta," the Spy vows, speaking even faster than before. "I'll spy on Rupert. I'll find out what the wizard's secrets are. I will. Really I will. I'm subtle, Your Maleficence. I'll get the truth out of Sigmund Snafflebrain. You wait, I'll do it." He looks desperately toward Chumley, who is licking his lips. "And I'll alarm them. I'll dream up some story about enemies and invasions and treachery. I'll get them worked up and frightened and ready to jump. I'll bring in real chaos." He cringes as Humgudgeon reaches out to touch him.

"Chumley want play now. Like new play toy. Hurm." He comes a few steps closer.

The Spy has tried to take refuge behind Humgudgeon, and he speaks in a wail. "I'll plant the seeds of anarchy. I'll corrupt the army. I'll suborn the palace staff—"

Humgudgeon sighs with boredom. "Never mind, Chumley. Not this one. At least, not yet. Maybe next time, if he fails again." This last threat is brazenly directed at the Spy, who drops to his knees, weak with apprehension and relief.

"No play toy?" Chumley asks, despondent at the news.

"No." Humgudgeon makes a wave of his hand, which Chumley sadly obeys, leaving the Protector Extraordinary alone with the Spy.

"Ah . . . thank you, thank you, Your Maleficence."

Humgudgeon allows the Spy to kiss his hand, then leans back once more. "It was nothing. And remember, if you do not deliver all that you have promised, and soon, Chumley will be waiting for you. Think of this as a delay, a stay of execution, as it were. And strive to do as you've said you will." He empties one of the goblets and stares hard at the Spy. "If you do not succeed, Chumley will be waiting for his new toy. And you know how hard boys his size can be on their toys. Don't you. Keep that in mind, dear fellow. It really is most important."

The Spy bows almost double. "Yes. I will. I certainly will. You have my word on that, Your Maleficence." He has not yet summoned the nerve to get to his feet, but he does make a kind of crablike movement toward the door.

"You will leave for Alabaster-on-Gelasta at once. Today, in fact. I want you gone by sundown." Humgudgeon is taking some measure of satisfaction on the Spy's acute discomfort.

"As you say, Your Maleficence. Your word is my command. I hurry to obey you. I certainly do." He inches his way toward the door.

"You will mastermind the downfall of King Rupert and that wizard of his. I expect you to do this quickly." He takes the last of the goblets and starts to drink from it. "And on the way out, you might tell them to send up some more drinks for me. All this magic and planning makes me thirsty. See to it, won't you, Spy?"

"An honor, Your Maleficence. An undeserved honor." He has made it halfway across the room now and some of his panic is leaving him. "Is there anything else?"

Humgudgeon yawns. "You will also do your best to get rid of Queen Hortensia. She is more than even I can bear."

"My pleasure, Your Maleficence," the Spy assures him, now at the door.

"Go, Spy," Humgudgeon says sweetly.

The Spy gets to his feet and bows deeply. "I am gone, Your Maleficence."

As the door closes, Humgudgeon leans back, looking in the general direction of the raven. "If he succeeds, Rupert will at last be in my power. If the Spy does his work well, I will reward him. That's the least I can do. Service should always be rewarded." He chuckles with the innocent pleasure of a boy pulling wings off of flies. "What shall we give him? The rack?" He waits for the raven's response, but there is none. "A little severe, don't you think? No doubt you prefer the strappado, but I must disagree. It lacks subtlety and it's far too quick. This sort of thing must be done carefully, with loving artistry." He sighs again, thinking of the fun he will have. "If he gets past the peasants' revolt, he'll be in Alabaster-on-Gelasta by Wednesday week. That gives me time to think and to prepare something new, especially for him. I *know* he'll appreciate it. An invention all my own." Humgudgeon all but bounces with excitement. "A wonderful, varied, impossibly slow torture." He studies the raven. "You may be right, my dear. Such a treat might be too good for him. I would hardly want to waste it." His attention is caught by a new sound as three liveried servants arrive, bearing enormous trays, each laden with a variety of goblets and bottles.

"Now which do you think," Humgudgeon asks angelically, "has the most poison?"

Another Interlude

THE SHAPE RIDES on the breezes, now looking a bit like a hawk, now more like a beautiful and deadly orchid plucked by the wind from it arboreal moorings. Sometimes it spins, other times it coils lazily on fingers of the wind. It passes over Addlepate and across the Dubious Marches to the pleasant and fertile plains of Alabaster-on-Gelasta. Although there appears to be no actual course to its wafting, it inevitably ends up circling the castle of King Rupert, coming to rest for a little while on the sill of the largest window of the Wizard's Tower, where it crouches, leeching some of the brightness from the early afternoon sunlight.

A Series Of Developments

EVERYONE AGREES THAT Sigmund Snafflebrain is brilliant, although they have an assortment of reasons for thinking so. His perspicacity is reputed throughout the world; there is some debate about his methods. Undoubtedly Sigmund knows everything and eventually he may reveal it all. However, he is possessed of an attention span rather less than a sentence in length, which makes worming things out of him next to impossible.

The Wizard's Tower in the castle of King Rupert of Alabaster-on-Gelasta is a marvel to behold, not only for the amazing variety of things it contains, but the total randomicity of their arrangement. Sigmund potters around in the room quite blissfully, comfortable and content with the disorder. His wizard's robes are velvet, of a benefic green color. Mismatched cuffs and jabots of lace are his usual ornaments and he wears a truly ridiculous periwig which most often is askew. He stares out the window after the Shape in an absent-minded way (this is not significant: he does everything in an absent-minded way), and after a while, starts to talk to himself, which he usually does when he is trying to concentrate.

"In the notable suggestion of my worthy colleague concerning the . . . the . . . concerning the . . ." He glances toward the window in a vaguely expectant way, then starts again. "In the notable suggestion of my worthy colleague I have . . . in hand? . . . I have . . . uh . . . have received . . . hum . . . have rewound?" He clears his throat and has another go at it. "In the notable suggestion of my worthy col . . . In the notab . . . In . . . the . . . the . . . Hum!" He claps once, as if the air might contain his lost thought. "I know there was something I have to . . . to . . . remember. Confound it! Gone again! There was something . . . some . . . thing . . . I had to . . . whatever." He shakes himself as if he were just coming awake. "Where was I? Oh, yes? . . . Oh, no. . . . Oh, well." He is philosophical about these lapses, which is sensible, considering how frequently they occur. He wanders over to his astrolabe and stares at it with delight and an almost total lack of recognition. As he folds his hands under his chin the better to gaze at it, the door to his study opens and a very handsome and upright young man comes into the room. (Do not think it odd that he does not knock—no one knocks on Sigmund's door because often as not he will forget to answer it.)

"Good day, Sigmund," the young man says briskly, being an energetic sort of fellow. His clothes are elegant and rich and arranged with great perfection. Everything about him bespeaks resolution and purpose. "What have you discovered today?"

"Who's that?" Sigmund asks as he looks around. "Oh. Now I see you . . . and I'll have your name in a minute ahem." He peers sternly at the young man. "See you every day . . . don't I? . . . don't I? . . . see you?"

The young man puts one foot on the only safe three-legged stool in the room and braces one arm on his knee. He tucks his lace-trimmed tricorn under his arm. "Prince Andre, Sigmund."

Sigmund wags a finger at him in admonishment. "You didn't have to tell me. I knew you at once . . . at . . . once. . . . I remember you well . . . see you . . . every . . . day." Finally a thought he has been searching for quite some time surfaces and he beams as he cries out merrily. "I have it! I enchanted it! I enchanted it!"

This causes Prince Andre to raise his brows; he has rarely heard Sigmund speak so emphatically. "What?" he inquires politely.

"What, what?" Sigmund asks, an expression of pleasant anticipation on his features.

"What did you enchant?"

Sigmund blinks. "Did I enchant something?"

Prince Andre knows it is useless to protest. "You said you did."

"Ah. And when did I say that?" He is clearly intrigued.

"Just now," Prince Andre says patiently.

"Did I? . . . I wonder what I meant by it?"

Now Prince Andre cannot help but be a wee bit exasperated. "I don't know."

"Do *I* know?" Sigmund asks with genuine interest.

"You didn't say," Prince Andre tells him with a little less cordiality than before.

"Oh . . . then perhaps I have a . . . a . . . you know . . . a . . . secret. That's it." He gives his attention (such as it is) to Prince Andre. "By the way, what are you doing here? Have you . . . been here long?"

"No, not long," Prince Andre admits. "I am here to find out about the Woebegone Wood."

Sigmund is taken aback. "Whatever for?"

"There's a dragon loose in the Wood, or so I've heard. There was a merchant who called at the castle only this morning," Prince Andre goes on with growing enthusiasm, "who said he had had it from two men-at-arms, who swore it was true. Can you imagine? A dragon!"

"Yes." Sigmund nods after a thoughtful moment. "I can imagine a dragon." He stares off into space. "A dragon? With scales and flames and . . . things? . . . that sort of dragon? . . . hum?"

"That is what I have come to ask you," Prince Andre informs him.

Sigmund folds his hands under his chin. "And what have I said?"

At this, Prince Andrew permits himself to sigh. "You've said nothing so far."

"That's odd," Sigmund declares, turning away. "I thought we'd been saying . . . some . . . thing . . ." This is a dangerous sign, for there is no telling how long it might take to get Sigmund back on the subject again once he wanders off it.

"About the dragon . . ." Prince Andre begins, trying to catch Sigmund's attention. "You were going to tell me something, weren't you?"

"No doubt," Sigmund says in a puzzled tone. "No doubt I was . . . I often do . . . but it escapes me . . . just now . . . Don't trouble your head about it; I don't."

"Yes," Prince Andre says to himself with a hint of disappointment. "I realize that."

Sigmund brightens again. "It will come back to me . . . always does, you know . . . not all at once, but it does come back to me."

Another person comes into the study in the Wizard's Tower: Prince Andre's sister, the Princess Felicia. She is just as pretty as a Princess should be, all rigged out in rose and silver. Her sack-back dress glistens, her petticoats are a froth of silver lace, her cuffs are edged in rose and silver, and the corsage of her dress has the most delicate and tantalizing little ruff of silver set with peridot. Her shoes are silver brocade with rose-colored buckles. Her very fair locks are gathered up into an artless knot, threaded with long rose ribbands. At her throat is a small choker of diamonds and more peridots. Only the discontented downward turn of her rosebud mouth indicates she is not pleased with her state.

"There's another one!" Sigmund exclaims. "Don't bother to tell me . . . I know who you are . . . and I'll have it . . . in a . . . a—"

"Why, Felicia," Prince Andre says in some surprise. "What are you doing here?"

She looks at her brother in languid dissatisfaction. "I have just been told about the dragon in the Woebegone Wood. My, but it sounds dull."

"What sounds dull?" Sigmund asks with a show of interest.

"'It' sounds dull," Prince Andre responds without thinking of what he is saying.

"Oh . . . well . . . then there's no hope for . . . it." Sigmund shakes his head sadly.

Prince Andre finds this a bit more difficult to follow than most of Sigmund's conversational meanderings. "For what?"

"For it. No hope at all." His eye is caught by a stuffed blowfish and he examines it in rapt silence.

Princess Felicia sinks down on the single bench in the room. Her skirts and petticoats frame her charmingly. "I wish I knew what the dragon was really like. I suppose all dragons are just like everything else, each the same as the other." She opens her silver lace fan. "How boring. Poor dragon." With a wistful sadness, she addresses Sigmund. "Is the dragon so very uninteresting? Royal Mama said you would know."

Sigmund is distracted from the enthralling blowfish. "If she said so . . . I'm sure I must . . . know. But I can't seem to . . . remember . . . just now . . . to remember . . . to remember . . . about the . . . about the . . . the . . ."

"About the dragon," Prince Andre interjects.

"The dragon?" Sigmund turns to Prince Andre in astonishment. "What about it?"

"Is there one? Is there really a dragon in the Woebegone Wood?" Prince Andre asks, doing his best to contain his temper.

"Of course there is," Sigmund says, turning slightly huffy. "What have I just . . . been . . . you know . . . telling you?"

"I must confess, I wasn't quite sure," Prince Andre remarks.

"What did you . . . think I meant?" Sigmund asks in confusion.

Luckily, Princess Felicia takes to musing aloud, or an even more frustrating argument might have got started between Prince Andre and Sigmund. "I thought that perhaps for once things would be different. That things would be exciting and thrilling. I should have realized that things are never different." Her downcast eyes are free from tears, but they have that aged and hollow look that only the young can achieve.

"Not . . . not different things . . . I thought it was dragons. Dragons . . . not dif . . . ferent things." Sigmund looks to Prince Andre for an explanation.

"It is dragons, Sigmund," Prince Andre agrees in a resigned voice.

"Oh. Well. Then that settles 'it.'" He beams at the Prince and Princess as if they had all accomplished something remarkable.

But Princess Felicia is unaware of this. "I thought that it would be like this. Dragons are dull. What do you want one for, anyway? What good is a dragon?"

Prince Andre stands even straighter. "Well, it *is* a Prince's duty to catch dragons. It's expected of us."

"But why? What would you do with it if you caught it?" She folds her fan again, petulantly gazing down at the toe of her shoe.

"I'd keep it, I suppose," he answers, with less certainty than usual. It is clear that he has not considered this before she inquired.

"After all . . . duty," Sigmund reminds them. Since neither Prince Andre nor Princess Felicia are aware he is paying attention, they are both disconcerted by his remark. "You know . . . a Prince and all that . . . must go after dragons . . . his duty."

"All right," Princess Felicia sulks. "But even if you got one, what would you do with it once you had it? You can't keep it here at the palace. There's no space for it. Dragons must take up acres of space. Royal Papa never caught one, and we haven't the room."

"We could *make* room," Prince Andre says mulishly.

"But where? You know as well as I do, Andre, that—"

"I don't know," Prince Andre says shortly. "I guess we could keep it in the mews. There's plenty of room back of the wyvern's cage."

"Yes," Sigmund says, grinning impishly. "Keep it in the mews . . . in the mews . . . to, you know . . . *a-mews* him." This, luckily, is Sigmund's only pun, and he alone appreciates it. He shakes with laughter while the Prince and Princess remain obstinately silent.

In this juncture, another figure sallies into the room: Queen Hortensia. She is an impressive woman, not so much dressed as upholstered. Her panniers would provide comfortable seating for a party of three, her towering wig is festooned with jewels and ornaments in such profusion that it is astonishing that she can walk upright. Her tall cane has a very large champagne-colored topaz at its crown. She is a woman whose life is a series of avalanches; avalanches of sensibility, of sentiment and temperament that often make for awkwardness in her family. She catches sight of her two offspring and flings out her arms. The cascades of golden lace that fall from her elbows sweep out in an alarming manner, almost snagging some of the unidentified goodies that Sigmund has collected. "My precious little petunias! I thought I might find you here."

Sigmund looks up while the Prince and Princess look at anything but their mother. "Ah. Your Majesty . . . it *is* Your Majesty, isn't it?"

"Yes, Sigmund," Queen Hortensia says in the most purple tones. "It is I. You may rise. Indeed," she adds critically, "you may bow." Even Sigmund is not so absent-minded that he would dare to ignore such an order. He claps one hand to his periwig to keep it on while he bends double to honor her. "Now you may rise," Queen Hortensia says when she is satisfied. "Now, my precious Royal Darlings," she coos to her children. "What have you been doing? It's been over an hour since I've seen you."

Prince Andre assumes his briskest manner. "Royal

Mama," he says, coming to attention before her. "There is a dragon in the Woebegone Wood. I should very much like to go and catch it. I feel it is my duty as a Prince to do so."

Queen Hortensia directs her question to the wizard. "Sigmund, is the creature truly a dragon?"

"What creature, Your Majesty? There are all sorts of creatures . . . all sorts . . . not all dragons . . . not—"

She cuts him short. "The creature in the Woebegone Wood: is it a dragon or is it not?"

"Now?" Sigmund inquires tentatively.

"Yes. Now." For emphasis, she taps the floor with the point of her tall cane.

"Of course it is; now." Sigmund smiles at Queen Hortensia in the mildest way.

Prince Andre leaps at his chance. "There, Royal Mama, do you see? There *is* a dragon. I shall go and catch it, as any Prince would want to do. It will be wonderful. I will be a hero. You will be proud of me." His expression is more hopeful than confident.

"Do nothing rash, my dearest child," Queen Hortensia tells him as she puts her hand to his cheek (this attention brings him the most acute embarrassment). "First we must request leave of your Royal Papa. It is fitting that you should be granted his mandate before undertaking such a venture. Surely Royal Papa will decide what's best to be done. He is the King, remember."

This is not promising, but Prince Andre bows, doing his best to conceal his misgivings.

Princess Felicia plucks at one of the folds of Queen Hortensia's voluminous skirt. "Royal Mama . . ." she falters.

Queen Hortensia turns and beams at her. "What is it, my azure-eyed azalea?"

The Princess does not even bother to look disgusted. "I think I might like to go with Andre when he hunts the dragon. Life here is so very, very dull. I am sure that the dragon is dull, too, but it will be a different sort of dull, at least."

"But my own sweet little lilac," Queen Hortensia exclaims, "why do you want to do such a thing? You are not bred to such trials, and there is no earthly reason for you to expose yourself to the unpleasantness of such a venture. The Woebegone Wood is a terrible place, without any comforts at all. Here you are surrounded by caring servants and a devoted family. Nothing is denied you. What possible attraction could a dark, filthy forest hold for you, when you can have the delights of this court to fill your days?"

"I don't know," she sighs. "No attraction, probably, but for a little while it might be different." Once again she opens her fan.

"Your Royal Papa shall consider it," Queen Hortensia informs her, which most usually means "no." "Far be it from me to rule on such an important matter. I am your mother, and for that reason, I know my judgment might fail me through the dictates of my heart. Your Royal Papa's stern good sense will prevail. He will tell you what is to be done, and you shall abide by his edict. Now then, Sigmund." She rounds on him with authority.

"Oh, yes, indeed, yes, there is a dragon in the Woebegone Wood," he says at once. "Certainly . . . to be sure . . . there is a . . . a . . ."

Queen Hortensia is not willing to tolerate much of this. "What is the dragon like, can you tell me that?"

"The dragon?" Sigmund peers into the middle-distance. "The dragon is . . . dragon-like. You know . . . like a dragon. Scales, flames . . . dragon things . . . seen one dragon and you've seen them all . . . dragons, that is." He shrugs. "This one can't be much different."

"Well enough," Queen Hortensia says at her most decisive. "I want you all to come along with me to the Throne Room. We shall ask Toby to decide. This is a very grave matter, and the King must be the one to rule upon it." She herds the other three toward the door, then stands imperiously as they begin their descent of the winding stairs. As they pass Sigmund's private quarters, he almost gets away, for he starts to wander off toward his sitting room, his manner even more abstracted than usual.

"Sigmund!" Queen Hortensia says in stern rebuke.

"Oh." He gives her a bemused stare. "You're still here. I thought . . . you know . . . you had . . . left." He makes a peculiar gesture. "It's my familiar. . . ."

Prince Andre laughs. "You've never had a familiar, Sigmund."

"No . . ." he agrees vaguely. "But perhaps . . . I *ought* to have . . . a familiar. . . ." He allows himself to be directed down the stairs, the Prince and Princess ahead of him, Queen Hortensia behind him.

This is a palace of mirrors and windows, so that it is

always very bright and pleasant. There are almost no dark corners and even the dungeons—unused for several decades except to store wine—have good-sized windows and fluffy comforters on the snug little cots in the cells.

To run ahead of the little group and get to the Throne Room before the Queen and her party do, take a short cut across the terrace and slip in past the King's Page Francis (or Frances, no one seems really certain about this), who is drousing on a highbacked chair.

There are two thrones in the Throne Room: one is quite imposing and covered with gilt where it is not damask and brocade. The other is almost an easy chair, and it is here that King Rupert, looking something like a cross between the King of Hearts and Santa Claus, is seated. His wig is about the only imposing thing about him, and it is topped with a small, tasteful crown. In his hands he holds knitting needles; on the left side of the throne there is an enormous ball of yarn, and on the right, a heap of whatever-it-is he is knitting this time.

Near the throne is a middle-aged man, portly and good-humored, dressed in a conservative coat (narrow skirts, no elaborate lacing) and unpowdered wig. This is Eustace, who is the fifteenth Official Torturer of Alabaster-on-Gelasta, the officing having passed from father to son in a distinguished line. Since Alabaster-on-Gelasta gave up on torturing in his grandfather's time, Eustace has little to occupy himself but the invention of newer and better instruments of torture, and it is one of these that he is trying to explain from the plans.

"See the improvements, Your Majesty. It is a much more efficient design, a marked improvement over my last effort. These levers here make the pincers open and that pulley there does the stretching. Do let me construct one and try it out, if only to see that it works properly. I promise I won't hurt anyone. Much." He has to add this last, because he has great faith in his inventions.

King Rupert does not respond, but he does say, "Knit one, purl one," to indicate he is listening, after a fashion.

Eustace is used to this, and he goes on with determination. "Oh, please, Your Majesty. I've never had a chance to experiment with any of my designs. Never. And I would so like to have the chance. How do you know your confidence in me is justified if you do not put me to the test. It quite fills me with worry, the notion that you will need me to torture someone someday and I will not really know how to go about it."

"Knit two, purl one, knit one . . ." King Rupert looks up at last. "Let me think about it, Eustace."

"All right," he says carefully. King Rupert has said this before and so far he has not had opportunity to practice his craft. "Torturing has been the family business for fifteen generations. If I never torture anyone, how will I uphold the family honor?"

"Knit one. Well, your father never had the chance, either," King Rupert says reasonably. "He became philosophical in time. You might try philosophy, Eustace." He resumes his knitting with more determination.

"Very well, Your Majesty," says Eustace, who knows when he's beaten. He gives half a bow and withdraws from the Throne Room.

"Purl two, knit one, purl one, knit two and repeat to the end of the row. Busy hands are happy hands, eh? Francis?" He does not wait for an answer, but sings a little ditty about his own approach to being a monarch.

> "If ever I a monarch see who happily is reigning
> Without a hobby to his name, I'll say that he is feigning;
> For ev'ry monarch surely is entrapped in his position
> And without a hobby it can be a serious condition.
> Oh, happy is the monarch who
> Knows very much as all of you
> That he needs something more to do—
> A harmless little hobby.

> "Some English Kings I've read about are worthy of
>   attention:
> One had a knack of having wives, another, of
>   demention.
> And every French King has his own peculiar excesses:
> Some care for fishing in dry lakes and some for wearing
>   dresses.
> Oh, happy is the monarch who
> Finds good escape and entre nous
> That little something extra, too:
> A harmless little hobby.

> "So every single afternoon while on the throne I'm
>   sitting

*I'm not precisely all alone—you see, I have my
   knitting.
Affairs of state can jog along with none of my devising
While sweaters, mufflers and the like come from my
   improvising.
Oh, happy is the monarch who
Though not exactly destined to
Discovers that his derring-do
Is less fun than his hobby.*

"Knit one, purl one, knit two. And a very good idea that is.
The world would get on very much better if more monarchs
followed it." He settles back on the throne, prepared to spend
the rest of the day working on his latest creation.

But it is not to be. Queen Hortensia, the Prince and Princess, and Sigmund have reached the Throne Room at last, and
Queen Hortensia nudges Francis (or Frances) awake with the
end of her cane.

Francis (or Frances) stumbles to his (or her) feet and proceeds to announce: "Her Majesty, Queen Hortensia Winnifred
Penelope—"

"Never mind that. Toby—" Queen Hortensia surges forward, arms outstretched, a lace handkerchief clutched in the
hand that does not hold her cane.

"His Highness, Prince Andre Victor Halli—"

"Don't bother," Prince Andre says, following his mother
toward the man on the throne.

"Her Highness," continues Francis (or Frances), determined. "Princess Felicia Augusta Laetic—"

Princess Felicia sighs. "Please."

One figure remains at the door, and Francis (or Frances)
approaches him cautiously. "Sigmund Snafflebrain?"

"Oh, yes, yes . . . yes, it is I. Yes, indeed. Or at least . . ."
he continues less certainly, "I think it is."

King Rupert calls out, "You needn't, Francis. Don't let us
bother you."

With this for permission, Francis (or Frances) retires once
again to the chair and slumps down in it, half-asleep already.

Before Queen Hortensia can launch into what is tradition-
ally a long harangue, King Rupert says to her, "Now, my
love, what do you want of me? Knit one, purl one, knit two,
purl one, knit three, purl—you've made me drop a stitch."

"We have just now come from a conference with Sigmund," Queen Hortensia announces, calling out, "Sigmund!"

"Hello, Sigmund," King Rupert says as he attempts to pick up the stitch again. "You can't help me with this, can you?"

"I . . . don't think . . . magic for knitting . . . no," Sigmund says, although he comes much nearer and begins to inspect what King Rupert has done thus far. "Interesting," he muses.

"Your dear children were with him as they are with me now," she goes on ominously. "Children!"

The Prince bows, the Princess curtsies, and they say in almost the same voice, "Hello, Royal Papa."

"Toby!" Queen Hortensia goes on in portentous accents, "you will never guess what they were discussing."

"The dragon in the Woebegone Wood," King Rupert says, keeping up his knitting.

"How did you guess that?" Queen Hortensia demands, irritated to have the wind taken out of her sails. "Well, you shall never be able to imagine in a thousand years what your darling son and Heir to the Throne wants to do."

"He wants to catch it," King Rupert says quietly.

This is more annoying to Queen Hortensia, who had planned to spend a fair amount of time dragging out the suspense of this revelation. "You're very clever this morning, Toby. What have you been doing with yourself?"

"Knitting," he says patiently and obviously. "But I was told about the dragon earlier, my love. What else would happen but that Andre would want to catch it? That is what Princes do, after all. Right wrongs, rescue maidens, catch dragons, you've said so yourself. Any Prince is bound to think of this as a golden opportunity. You'd scarcely think him a credit to us if he didn't want to catch the dragon, would you? Knit one, purl one, knit two, purl two and repeat to the end of the row. Would you?" Over the years, he has developed his own way of dealing with Queen Hortensia.

"Yes, yes, of course you're right, dear Toby," she agrees in some irritation. "But this is not the question. We are not talking about Princes in general, but of Andre. You must realize that the venture is dangerous. He might be attacked by that savage beast. Or by other monsters living in the Wood."

"Oh, is it savage?" King Rupert asks Sigmund.

Sigmund looks up. "Savage? Oh . . . yes . . . I think so . . .

savage . . . usually are, you know . . . savage . . . dragons are."
He gives a beatific smile.

"There, you see?" Queen Hortensia pounces. "How can
you let your only son, your precious child, the hope of your
whole kingdom, go into the Woebegone Wood where there are
who knows how many dangerous and vile and disgusting
creatures. He will meet with certain disaster. It is not to be
borne, Toby; it is not." She brings her lace handkerchief up to
her eyes.

"Knit two, purl two, yarn over, knit one, purl two and so
on to the end of the row." This is King Rupert's way of refusing to get involved in Queen Hortensia's emotional avalanches.

"You aren't listening to me, Toby," Queen Hortensia
chides him. "You are deliberately ignoring me and the peril
we all face. How I must suffer because of you." There are few
things she enjoys more than suffering.

"Now, now, Hortensia." Unlike his spouse, King Rupert
has never come up with a nickname for Queen Hortensia. "It
is very affecting, of course. Your sensibilities must positively
rev—rebel at the thought of the anguish and worry you would
feel while Prince Andre is away, but you have known since his
birth that he has a Prince's duties and obligations. Indeed,
you, my love, have been the one who has constantly reminded
him of this when he desired to undertake diversions that were
not consistent with his place and role in life." Having stopped
Queen Hortensia for the moment, he signals his son. "Andre,
come here."

"Royal Papa?" He rarely bows, but he likes his father, and
so he inclines his head.

"What your mother says is quite true. Dragons are fierce
things and the Woebegone Wood is an unfriendly place. If you
are looking for a romp, it is not the place for you. However,
you are a Prince and you should get in some Princely deeds
before you try being King. So if you want to go, it is up to
you." King Rupert beams at Prince Andre. "If I'd had the
chance when I was a Prince, I would have gone in a shot, but
don't let that influence you. Dear me, no." He chuckles
quietly to himself.

"Sire, you overwhelm me," Prince Andre says, pressing
his tricorn to his heart.

"I do?" King Rupert is startled and pleased. "Well,

remember that. Yes, yes, do remember it, if you will."

While the King is so well-disposed, Princess Felicia steps forward. "Royal Papa," she ventures prettily, "if it is quite all right with you, I would like to go with Andre. Nothing exciting has ever happened to me. I think hunting dragons might be a bit exciting, at least it will not be the same dull things I've done every day of my life. I could carry a spear, or make sketches for a tapestry, or something." It would be too much to say that color mounts in her cheeks, but there is a touch more animation to her than usual.

"Could you? Why, that would give you a splendid hobby, wouldn't it? Tapestries, that's the thing! By all means, you should go. If Andre says you can, you should go." He is fairly bouncing with enthusiasm now, and he looks from his daughter to his son.

Princess Felicia turns to her brother and looks pleadingly at him. "Oh, dear Andre, will you take me with you?"

Prince Andre is not eager to be wheedled by his sister, and so he makes none of the objections that spring to his mind. Instead, he replies, "Why, certainly. It might be very dull with only a cook and a squire for company, though. I wouldn't want you to be bored."

"I can be bored anywhere," Princess Felicia reminds him with a trace of pride. "Everything bores me."

All this is too much for Queen Hortensia. Her bosom swells and she turns her eyes tragically upward, clasping her hands together on her tall cane. "Is no one going to listen to me? Are my precious little blossoms to be torn from me, still tender and untried, to be flung into the hazards of the world without a mother to protect them? Must I endure this? Does no one care for a mother's torment?"

King Rupert reaches out, half rising from his throne, to pat her joined hands. "Very commendable, Hortensia. I'm sure your torment does you great credit."

This overwhelms Queen Hortensia. "How cruel! Oh!"

"Remember how it was the first time Andre's hair was cut, my dear. You must not let these things distress you so. You will make yourself miserable and cause our children unneeded worry if you succumb to all your fears and doubts this way. Try knitting. It makes a wonderful difference," King Rupert promises her, then he regards the Prince and Princess. "Well, I leave it to you children to work it out with Sigmund. You'll want to plan carefully and to anticipate problems. That's what hunting dragons is all about. You'd best plan to take Leander with you. He's a superb crumpet maker and you can't trek off to the Woebegone Wood without a good supply of crumpets, dear me, no. Not the sort of thing you can expect to find there, from all I hear." He picks up his knitting needles again. "Crumpets are just the things. Leander will look after you very well." With this last announcement, he resumes his hobby. "Knit one, purl two, knot two, purl one, knit one, purl two and so on to the end of the row."

"Royal Papa," Princess Felicia inquires, "what are you knitting this time?"

King Rupert holds the mass of knitwear out for them to admire. "I haven't the slightest idea. Fascinating, isn't it?"

Sigmund concurs in his own way. "Strange . . . significant. Very . . . significant."

"Oh!" cries King Rupert, delighted at having done something significant at last. "Of what?"

"I don't . . . quite know . . . but significant . . . oh yes, . . . very . . . sig . . . nif . . . i . . . cant . . ." It is clear that something has distracted him, and while he is attempting to recover himself, the door to the Throne Room opens and Professor Ambicopernicus strides into the room.

Professor Ambicopernicus is an Exotic. In the midst of all this Baroque and Rococo, he is Byzantine. His clothes are seven hundred years out of date and he wears them with considerable dash. His dalmatic is a deep blue velvet, embroidered with all sorts of mystical symbols (the Professor actually made up a few, so as to look impressive). His surcote is of bright red brocaded silk. His turban (of course he has a turban) is of scarlet and gold cloth, fastened with an enormous pin of emeralds and tourmalines. Under his arm, he carries a huge tome on his special subject; he is the Court Astrologer.

Francis (or Frances) manages to make the announcement. "Professor O. Ambicopernicus!" That done, he (or she) goes back to sleep.

"Your Majesty! Your Majesty! A word with you. This is very important."

"Really? So many important things in one day," King Rupert says, taking his seat once more.

"I have just discovered that today Mars and Mercury form a trine with Jupiter. And do you know what that means?" He raises up his book as if prepared to use it as a weapon in an argument.

"No. What does it mean?" King Rupert asks, leaning forward with interest.

"I don't know either. I haven't the slightest idea. I was hoping you might have a notion. I know it is significant of something."

"Significant!" King Rupert says enthusiastically. "Like my knitting!"

"No . . . not the . . same thing . . . not at all . . . the same thing . . . no." Sigmund has not got anyone's attention.

With an effort, Professor Ambicopernicus opens his enormous volume and reads quickly. "Here! I believe I have found it. I may reveal what the stars tell me. 'It is a day for great ventures!' "—here, the Prince and Princess exchange glances —" 'A day for great deeds. A day for wonderful discoveries. A time of surprises. An opportunity for growth. A climate of change. A time to pay taxes.' " This not only brings the Professor up short, everyone else in the Throne Room (and awake) is taken aback.

"Taxes," exclaims Sigmund. "I knew . . . there was something . . . I hadn't . . . done . . . taxes. That's it . . . taxes."

Professor Ambicopernicus (whose first initial, do not forget, is O) angrily tears off the bottom of the page. "Nonsense. There are no good days for paying taxes. How did that get in there." He closes his book with as much of a snap as a volume so big will produce. "But Your Majesty should be advised that today is the best day of all days for great ventures, for changes, for enterprises, for adventure, for—"

"Hunting dragons?" King Rupert interjects.

"Why," Professor Ambicopernicus muses, "I suppose so. There is adventure and enterprise in dragon hunting. There is nothing in the stars that would forbid the hunting of dragons."

"Then we must set out this very day!" Prince Andre declares. "There are a thousand things to attend to. I must make my plans."

Queen Hortensia brings one trembling hand (and lace handkerchief) to her bosom. "Oh! Oh! So soon!"

Princess Felicia, warming to the excitement, drops a curtsy to her parents. "I shall go and find a shawl. Perhaps I shall gather lilies. Perhaps I will take my lute, to while away the tedium of the journey. I will certainly be bored." She follows her brother out of the Throne Room.

King Rupert gazes after them. "That's it. Run along, Felicia. Yes, that's simply splendid. Good to see young people like that, full of vigor and romance; ready to forge ahead into life, meeting challenge and adversity with shining eyes. What joy! Ah, youth! Ready to grasp the world by the horns. Oh, yes!"

From the door of the Throne Room, Prince Andre calls back, "I shall send Francis to the kitchen. I must speak with Leander."

Francis (or Frances) rouses at once and stumbles for the door, almost knocking over the person approaching. As he (or she) leaves the room, he (or she) announces: "It is the Official Torturer again, Your Majesty."

"Eustace! Just a moment. We are sorting out so many things." King Rupert motions the man forward.

Prince Andre continues from the door, "Leander will be my squire, for Armand can't be trusted in a fight. You remember what happened at the Tournament last spring, and if he will quail at a joust, who knows what he might do in real combat. No, Leander is the better choice, and he will be able to tend to us and make our crumpets, as well."

"Your Majesty . . ." Eustace begins, trying to get a word in edgewise. He is holding a model in his hands, a terrible thing with saw teeth and winches and spikes. "It *is* urgent."

King Rupert does not pay him any mind. "That's splendid, Andre, simply splendid. Wonderful. Off you go, children." He sighs with contentment as he watches Prince Andre and Princess Felicia depart to do their packing. "Did you see that, my love? They're both of them brimming over with excitement. It does my heart good to see it."

Queen Hortensia has just one word for so callous a reaction. "Beast!"

"Well, no . . ." Sigmund corrects her after considering the accusation. "Not . . . just at present."

"You'll want a little time to yourself, my dear," King Rupert suggests to Queen Hortensia. "You have had a series of shocks today and your sensibilities are no doubt riven with anguish. I wouldn't want to impose on you while you quiet your apprehensions. Much better if you have a good cry, don't you think?" He is hopeful that she will accept his advice, and he hurriedly says to the others, "After all these developments,

I feel the need of a little refreshment. Let us all go and have strawberries and candied violets on the terrace. We will have an opportunity to bid the Prince and Princess farewell when they depart, and we will be able to enjoy the splendor of the afternoon. That's the idea." He looks from Professor Ambicopernicus to Sigmund to Eustace. "Do join me, won't you?"

Eustace holds up his model more emphatically. "But, Your Majesty, I wanted you to see—"

"Yes, yes. I'll look it over once we've had our snack. Come along. No doubt it's a wonderful invention. All your inventions are so thorough, Eustace." He carefully wraps his knitting needles with yarn so that no stitches will be dropped, and sets them on the throne as if they might stand in for him in his absence. He waits while the others approach, and then he links arms with Sigmund (more to keep the wizard with them than out of any special favor) and walks with them toward the tall, open windows that lead to the terrace.

Which leaves Queen Hortensia to herself, consumed with emotion. Her song pours out of her, mournful and sticky.

> "Alas, alas the tragic day I never thought to see
> My sweetest babies, unaware, are being reft from me;
> And leave me here alone, alone, with just this simple
>   song:
> Oh, won't somebody tell me where, where did I go
>   wrong?
>
> "It is a mother's cruelest fate to be deserted so,
> And every mother bows her head to what all mothers
>   know,
> And so I'll languish all the day and all the nighttime
>   long:
> Oh, won't somebody tell me where, where did I go
>   wrong?
>
> "As flowers in a garden grow with tender loving
>   care
> I thought to raise my children so, and now to my
>   despair—
>
> "The time has come for us to part, and more, to say
>   good-bye!

*I'll bravely hold my head upright and fight the urge to
   cry,
While in my heart a doleful dirge will ring with bells
   ding-dong:
Oh, won't somebody tell me where, where, where did I
   go wrong?"*

There is no satisfactory answer to this question, and so
Queen Hortensia gives herself up to her suffering, and retires
to her chambers, where she can indulge herself completely.

Prince Andre Prepares

PRINCE ANDRE'S QUARTERS are done in the princely spartan
style, which is to say that whatever he has is in the best of
taste, and he does not have too much of it. His gear is all
properly stowed. In one cabinet, his boots are set out, rank on
rank, toes lined up, and flawlessly glossy. In a closet, everyone of his coats hangs wrinkleless, arranged by color so that
they form a sartorial rainbow. Beyond the coats, the waistcoats and shirts are displayed, shirt rack over the waistcoats.
Lace jabots and cuffs are set meticulously in drawers that are
just the right size for them. All his underthings are discreetly
folded and tucked away.

It is rare for Prince Andre to notice this. He takes such
things as order and valets for granted, as well he should. This
occasion is typical: he bursts through the door with an expan-
sive gesture and calls out "Armand!" before the echoes have
died in the hall.

Armand, who is as neat and as fussy as the well-cared-for
clothes, hastens to answer the call. He bows so very gracefully that a less magnanimous Prince might be jealous. "Your
Highness?" he says, able to imply that he is waiting breath-

lessly for the very least request Prince Andre might make, so that he can have the honor of fulfilling it at once. He is a trifle overdressed for a servant, but this is not unusual in princely valets.

"Pack a case for me, Armand. I'm going dragon hunting!" He smiles with ferocious delight. "Royal Papa said yes."

"Dragon hunting?" Armand says, his suavity deserting him as his voice breaks.

"Yes; isn't it wonderful?" He pulls off his brocaded coat and tosses it nonchalantly to Armand. As he removes his lace cuffs and rolls up his silken sleeves, he expresses his aspirations in song.

> "Bravery! that's the thing
>   Turns a Prince to a King!
> Teaches fools to be wise!
>   Cuts a brute down to size!
> Valor! that's the way
>   To forge on every day!
> Girds your loins with great might
>   When it's time for a fight!
> Courage! noble thought
>   When a dragon is fought!
> Makes a Prince free from fear!
>   But it won't, no it won't happen here!
> It can never, never, never, never, never, never, never,
>   never, never happen here!"

"Very profound, Your Highness," Armand remarks, struggling to make a recovery. He is staring into the closet, trying to determine what is proper for Prince Andre to wear while he is hunting (shudder) dragons.

"Is it?" Prince Andre asks, begining to feel that he might at last be coming into his own.

"Very," Armand promises him, mentally ruling out the rose-colored silk and turning his attention to a coat of delicate mauve.

"Then it's probably a good thing for me to go on this dragon hunt, if it can teach me to be profound. I'll probably have need for a little profundity when it's my turn to rule." Some reticence comes over him, as if he has committed a social solecism. "Not that I expect to rule for years and years and years. All the same, it's best to be prepared."

"Indubitably," Armand murmurs; he has been saving up "indubitably" for weeks and is thrilled to be able to use it at last.

"Still, dragons are . . ."

When Prince Andre does not go on, Armand suggests, "Fierce? Dangerous? Intriguing?"

"A bit of all that," Prince Andre allows with a self-effacing smile. "I think that's part of the challenge. I know about quests and all the rest of it, but dragons, well, they're in a class by themselves."

"It sounds likely," Armand says, finally taking a beige coat from the hanger. He scrutinizes it, and fingers the fine wool crepe, hoping silently that nothing happens to the material. He decides that an ecru shirt would be the best choice to go with it.

"Yes," Prince Andre goes on, warming to his subject. "It is certainly a good thing to hunt dragons. There's nothing like it." He has got both his sleeves rolled up and he now tosses his frothy lace jabot aside. "I'll need something more severe. Not silk shirts, but linen. Not brocade coats, but woolen ones. And the waistcoats ought to be plain. Nothing fancy except the quality of the fabric and the cut. You'll know the right thing, Armand. You always do." His laughter is warm and eager. "I want to set out in perfect form. I want everyone to remember that I went about my dragon hunting in proper attire."

"Naturally," Armand agrees, horrified at what is coming.

"This is a bit awkward," Prince Andre goes on with less verve than before. "You see, Armand, I'm really very much afraid that . . . well, that I won't be able to take you with me."

"No?" Armand asks, turning to Prince Andre, hardly daring to trust his ears. "Not take me with you?"

"I'm sorry." Prince Andre comes and lays his hand on Armand's shoulder in consolation.

"But . . ." Armand begins, then has the good sense to stop himself. "Why?"

Prince Andre does not give a direct answer. Instead, he strides about his chamber, one hand on his hip as if touching a sword. "You see, Armand, you're a most superior valet. You're irreplaceable. If anything happened to you, I'd never find anyone half as accomplished as you are, or as conscientious. I can't ask you to risk so much on a venture like this one. If it were a diplomatic mission or a ceremony or even a reception, then I wouldn't hesitate to say you must come. But we're going to the Woebegone Wood."

Armand quivers at the mention of the place. "Your Highness, you're very brave."

"If I'm not, I'll be sure to find out soon." He favors his valet with a hearty smile. "And that's an essential thing for a Prince to know."

"Yes," Armand mutters, still reeling inwardly with relief. He has to control the giddiness that threatens to burst out in giggles.

"But you, Armand, you need no such test, and I simply cannot bring myself to ask you to take that risk." He regards his valet steadily. "You always render the most excellent service. I know that without you, I'd never get the right shirt with the right breeches and coat. But I'd never forgive myself if you came to harm because of my ambition to hunt dragons. You do understand, don't you?"

"Of course," Armand says at once, not caring for anything but the reprieve he has been granted. It matters not a jot to him that Prince Andre is concerned about his conscience—all that matters to Armand is that he will not have to go to that unspeakable place. "Your Highness is most considerate."

"Not at all," Prince Andre demurs with a wave of his hand. "You certainly realize that it would be very bad policy for me to demand that my servants do risky things for me. It isn't good ruling to behave that way."

"Quite," Armand agrees, wanting to encourage Prince Andre in this vein of reasoning.

"So." He resumes his bracing manner. "I don't know how long I'll be gone, and that might be something of a problem for you. Still, do your best, and I give you my word that I'll try not to disgrace you."

Armand manages to give an appreciative bray of laughter. "As if that were possible, Your Highness."

"I can't be as confident of that as you, Armand," Prince Andre says in a thoughtful tone. "Who is to say what might transpire in the Woebegone Wood? There's always a risk when you're hunting dragons, no matter what you may hear about it."

"Indeed," Armand says, swallowing hard.

"But you need not worry, Armand," Prince Andre assures him, his manner as gracious as possible. "You are going to remain here, away from the dangers and the risks. If we're fortunate, there can be glory for the work, but it's wrong to count on it." He achieves a modest smile.

"You're very good, Your Highness," Armand declares, with a bow for emphasis. It is hard for him not to admit that the last thing in the entire world he wishes to do is to court glory by hunting dragons. He would rather volunteer for one of Eustace's experiments than trek off to the Woebegone Wood.

"Ah, Armand, you are a valet of impeccable tact." There is a twinkle in his eye as he says this, and a moment later, he begins to unbutton his shirt. "I'll need something neat but sporting, I think. I'll depend on you to select the right thing for me. Be sure to pack something I can change into when I return with the dragon."

"Something with a festive touch?" Armand recommends, once again staring into the closet and studying the contents.

"It sounds ideal! Have the bags ready in an hour, will you? I know you can do it." In the next moment, he is gone into his bedchamber, pulling the door closed behind him to leave Armand to the business of preparing his luggage for his dragon hunt.

Very briefly a sour expression flits over Armand's tranquil features. Then it is banished, and unruffled calm once again composes his countenance as he takes several items from hangers and begins the packing he has been ordered to do.

Princess Felicia Prepares

EVERYTHING IN PRINCESS Felicia's quarters is silver and rose. The mirrors—and there are lots of mirrors—are all caught up in frames of silver with pale jeweled inlays that sparkle more than the glass. Her chiffonier and armoires are of cherry and rosewood, and carved so extravagantly with flowers and vines that the whole place feels like a bower frozen by art.

Blanche, Princess Felicia's maid, is as pretty as the room: her light auburn hair curls naturally around her very pretty face, she wears her white-and-rose-striped dress with flair, and she moves light as thistledown through the chamber. She is sublimely unaware of the Princess's petulance and boredom.

Princess Felicia herself comes into the room, her lovely head drooping. She lifts her eyes and regards the charming apartment with a look that approaches loathing. She sighs.

"Good afternoon, Your Highness," Blanche says, making a perfect curtsy. "Is there anything you require of me?"

"Yes." Princess Felicia crosses the room to a bench in the window embrasure. She settles onto it, plucking idly at her silver lace petticoats.

Blanche picks up her amazingly floofy featherduster and sets to work on the already pristine furniture. "Is it anything immediate?"

"Yes," Princess Felicia says, her perfect lips set in a moue of dissatisfaction.

Bright and bouncy and obliging, Blanche continues her dusting. "Will it take very long?"

"Perhaps," Princess Felicia answers remotely. "I am going with Prince Andre to hunt dragons." The way she says this suggests that she is being sent to the dungeons without her supper.

"Dragons! Gracious! How exciting!" Blanche has stopped her dusting and now clutches her featherduster to her bosom. "Aren't you thrilled?"

Princess Felicia does not deign to answer.

"When do you start, Your Highness?" continues Blanche, who is used to Princess Felicia's silences.

"This afternoon," Princess Felicia says, staring down at the toe of her rose satin slipper.

Blanche is too well-behaved to screech, or she certainly would have at this announcement. "This afternoon, Your Highness?"

"That is what Prince Andre wishes to do," Princess Felicia says listlessly. "But Andre is like that. He's always wanting to rush out this way. It's one of the most boring things about him."

It is not Blanche's place to agree or disagree, and she is a good, sensible maid. "And you are going with him?"

"Yes. Royal Papa gave his permission just now. I suppose I'd better get ready, and you'd better pack for me."

"Of course," Blanche says, starting to do what on anyone less graceful and pretty might be called bustling. "How long will you be gone? Where are you going?"

"Days and days, perhaps. But days are all the same, so it hardly matters." She looks up, her eyes fixed on some distant place that none of the mirrors reflect and the windows do not reveal. "Isn't it dreadful, the way everything is always the same?" And she continues her complaint in song.

> *"If only the sky were other than blue*
> *Or the trees were other than green*
> *Then I wouldn't care much if the weeks ran through*
> *All the months in the order they've been.*
> *If only the clouds weren't whiter than sheep*
> *Or the brooks didn't sing the same song*
> *Then I wouldn't care much that the mountains are steep*
> *Or the hours are equally long.*
> *If only each day weren't followed by night*
> *Until they add up to a year—*
> *Even if it could change, and I think that it might*
> *It could never, never, never, never, never happen*
> *here.*
> *It can never, never, never, never, never, never, never,*
> *never, never happen here."*

"What does a Princess wear on a dragon hunt?" Blanche wonders aloud as soon as it is polite to speak.

"Clothes," Princess Felicia exclaims in despair. "Clothes."

"But which ones, Your Highness?" It is a reasonable question, and any other Princess might have a reasonable answer for it, but Princess Felicia looks up, her enormous eyes awash with tears.

"Does it matter, Blanche? They're all beautiful and fit perfectly, and none of them have a single surprise about them. Every dress is like every other dress, with sleeves where the arms are. Why are dresses like that? Why must the skirts fall from the waist? What if they were sewn on at the cuffs?"

During this outburst, Blanche has opened two closets and

an armoire, staring thoughtfully at what she finds. "Your Highness will want your riding habit, won't you?"

"We *will* ride, I suppose. It has to be done. We will not fly, or sail, or burrow. Always, we ride to cross the land, or are drawn in coaches. It's the same every time." She fixes her tragic gaze on the windows. "We never do anything new."

"Hunting dragons is new," Blanche carefully points out as she selects three ravishingly beautiful riding habits and starts to lay them out for packing.

Princess Felicia shakes her head. "Hunting is not new. Dragons, that might be different, but the chances are that we'll chase after it while it tries to get away, and either it will get away or we will catch it, since that's the way hunting goes." She gives her head a shake and her pale ringlets bounce and shine delectably. "Still, the dragon might turn on us. That would be different."

"Oh, Your Highness!" Blanche protests, visibly shocked.

"It would be something new, to fight a dragon." She gets up and looks wistfully around her. "I wish it weren't all so boring."

"Your Highness," Blanche says, to let Princess Felicia know she is listening (though, in fact, she isn't).

"Spring, Summer, Autumn, Winter: you'd think that there was another order that might come up." She trails her fingers along the leading of the glass panes. "The days of the week are always the same, and the months."

"I expect that it's easier for most people that way," Blanche ventures as she begins to fold one of the riding habits. "Would you like to wear this one when you depart?" She holds up a linen habit in the palest, rosiest pink with military lacing and epaulets in silver.

"It's as good as any of them," Princess Felicia allows in a dispirited way. "And the hat as well, perhaps. Royal Mama will probably insist on the hat."

Queen Hortensia would *undoubtedly* insist on the hat, thinks Blanche, but she says, hardly pausing in her folding, "Whatever you prefer, Your Highness."

"I would prefer to put a pillow on my head, or a gosling, or blueberry tarts, anything but a hat. Everyone wears hats." She is making circles on the glass with the tip of her finger. "If I did that, everyone would think I'm peculiar, because they don't know how bored I am."

"A difficult problem, Your Highness," Blanche declares, not bothering to look up.

"How easily you say that," Princess Felicia chides her gently. "I wonder: are you ever bored?"

This time Blanche does give Princess Felicia her attention. "Sometimes, I suppose, when I've time on my hands and no way to fill it. An afternoon can be boring, or a rainy day, but it never lasts long, do you see? There's always something new going on, and then I'm not bored anymore. Folding clothes can be boring, but I don't have to do it all the time, and so it's not."

Princess Felicia gives a soft, heart-rending sigh. "That's the difference, I suppose. You can go on, you can banish your boredom because you are bored by trivial things. *I*"—she continues with a fleeting hint of satisfaction—"am bored by greater things than that."

"Yes, Your Highness, I know." Blanche tries to make her tone commiserating, but it comes out a trifle too briskly for that.

"And now you're getting bored with *me*," Princess Felicia observes with an air of fatality. "That was how it began for me. I was only bored by little things, and then I saw that there was more to it than that." She comes over to where Blanche has started folding the second riding habit. "Do you always fold them the same way?"

"Yes, Your Highness," Blanche assures her.

"How can you bear it? Wouldn't you rather do every one a different way?"

Blanche is able to laugh this time. "Goodness, no. That wouldn't suit me at all, and Your Highness would look a perfect quiz when you dressed."

"A quiz? Being a quiz now and then might be interesting. If I did it regularly, it would be boring, of course," she adds.

"Naturally," Blanche says, doing her best to keep from giggling. "There, Your Highness—that's two done. Why don't you leave me to finish the packing. It's a beautiful day. Why don't you walk in the garden for an hour or so?" With Princess Felicia out of the room, Blanche is sure that she can get much more of the packing done.

"It's always a beautiful day," Princess Felicia mourns. "Still, a walk is better than waiting. Perhaps I'll find something new."

As Princess Felicia wafts forlornly out the door, Blanche gives a sigh of relief and gets on with her packing.

Meanwhile,
On The Terrace...

GOOD AS HIS word, King Rupert has taken Eustace, the fifteenth Official (and Hereditary) Torturer; Professor O. Ambicopernicus, his astrologer; and, naturally, Francis (or Frances) out onto the terrace. It is done in marble with a Rococo railing around it, like the very best cake decorations. Beyond that is the garden, vast acres of perfectly kept beds of lavishly blooming flowers. King Rupert has sent word to the kitchen that he and his companions would like a snack, and requested that Leander the crumpet-baker should be the one to bring the snack—King Rupert wants to tell him about the dragon hunt himself.

Eustace, persistent as always, has brought his model out with him and has set it in the center of the table where he, the Professor and the King are seated. "I've spent years perfecting this, Your Majesty," he is saying urgently. "*Years*. It's by far the best design I've ever come up with. No one anywhere has anything like it. With this device, no other ruler would be able to torture half as well as we could."

"Um," King Rupert muses, trying to find the best way to keep from hurting Eustace's feelings. "I can tell that it is... innovative."

"It *is*. Yes, it *is*," Eustace says, beaming.

From somewhere off in the garden where he has wandered, Sigmund can be heard making an exclamation of discovery. It is unrealistic to assume his attention will last long enough for anyone on the terrace to learn more about it. King Rupert, who is used to this, waves in the direction of the sound in vague encouragement before addressing Eustace again.

"I can understand your enthusiasm for the design, but, regretfully, I can't possibly let you try it out on anyone. From what you describe, it would be quite painful."

"That's the *point* of torturing, Your Majesty: it's *supposed* to be painful." He looks at the Professor, hoping he will say something in support of this new device. "And this would do it very well."

"It certainly seems so," King Rupert agrees, putting the tip of one finger very gingerly on the most prominent spike. "Gracious! It's sharp."

"It has to be sharp, Your Majesty," Eustace says, knowing that King Rupert is not likely to approve of that.

"Um," says King Rupert again, this time more remotely.

"I promise I'd only use it on an enemy," Eustace vows, making a last-ditch stand for his invention.

"I understand that," King Rupert tells him. "You'd hardly want to use this on a friend. But it would be a guarantee that the enemy would always be your enemy, and you might never learn to like one another. No, Eustace. I hate to disappoint you, but I doubt that you'll have the chance to use it. I'm very sorry. I know how sincere you are, and there's no doubt that you have the greatest skill. I do recognize your abilities, and I value them. That's why I truly believe that I must not let anyone use your invention."

Philosophically downcast, Eustace takes the model off the table and sets it beside his chair. "As you wish, Your Majesty."

It always troubles King Rupert to see his courtiers dispirited. "Come, come Eustace. Don't let this upset you. Why, you're an excellent torturer, you know. I have no doubt that you're the finest torturer in the entire history of Alabaster-on-Gelasta."

Somewhat soothed by this, Eustace still cannot keep from reminding King Rupert, "But, Your Majesty, I've never tortured anyone—how can you be sure?"

"There *is* that," says King Rupert, who has anticipated this protest. "But you're always ready to, and you are certainly *prepared;* goodness, yes, no doubt about that. And that's very important, you know. Yes, indeed. Preparedness is everything when it comes to torture."

Professor Ambicopernicus includes his own commiseration. "And the art, these days, is much neglected."

Eustace nods. "Times have changed. In my grandfather's day, now, that was the time for torturers." He smiles in fond reminiscence, for he has heard the stories since he was a toddler and has passed them on to his own children. "If it wasn't the Warlocks in the Woebegone Wood, it was one of the Humgudgeons or Truculins over in Addlepate. Quick as a whisker, they'd be on the rack. Or laid over a hurdle. Or spread out on a grill. Snap! Crunch! and neat as a pin." He sighs. "Those wonderful days have gone forever."

"It's a lost art, I fear. You do well to recall—" Professor Ambicopernicus begins, but is interrupted by Francis (or Frances), who becomes suddenly alert.

"An Ounergoth Mercenary, Your Majesty," he (or she) announces, and then finds a comfortable spot on the terrace railing where he (or she) can relax in the sun.

As soon as Francis (or Frances) is out of the doorway, the Ounergoth Mercenary strides onto the terrace. He is ferocious: he is encased in heavy armor and he fairly bristles with weapons. His long mustaches quiver with importance. He bows, clanking, before King Rupert. (In fact, this is really Humgudgeon's Spy, doing his best to follow his master's orders.) "King Rupert, legendary hero of Alabaster-on-Gelasta, your fame is spread far and wide!" he declares in stentorian tones.

"Has it?" King Rupert responds politely. "Well, that's most interesting. My fame, eh?"

"It was inevitable," Professor Ambicopernicus says ponderously. "The stars reveal that it could not be otherwise."

Sigmund has wandered back to the terrace, and now he peers at the Ounergoth Mercenary. "What is . . . I don't think . . . I know him . . . do I?"

"None of the rest of us do, Sigmund," King Rupert says to his wizard. "That is not to say you don't."

"No," Sigmund agrees vaguely. "It isn't . . . is it?"

Realizing that this might lead to embarrassment at best and disaster at worst, the Spy blunders on. "The peace and prosperity of Alabaster-on-Gelasta is the marvel of all the world. Rulers everywhere seek to emulate your success."

King Rupert's expression remains unruffled and cordial. "If you say so, I'm sure it's true and I am flattered."

Seizing the opportunity, the Spy sinks down on one knee, his weapons jangling around him. "But this is not flattery, Your Majesty. For there are those who are envious and greedy"—unbidden, the image of Humgudgeon comes to his mind, and he suppresses a shudder—"and they covet your wealth and the gracious land you rule. Even now, they plot to mass and march on your borders, to pounce! on you and your happy and fortunate subjects."

"Do you know anything about this, Sigmund?" King Rupert inquires.

"Pouncing? . . . I . . . no . . ." He has been staring at something that might be a large, dark butterfly sailing over the garden.

Desperately the Spy goes on. "There is danger, great danger."

"If so many of my neighbors are distressed, I suppose there is," King Rupert says thoughtfully. "I'm surprised they haven't spoken up. It's what they usually do. We exchange missions and after a while, we work matters out."

The Spy continues, "Diplomacy!" he scoffs. "When there is so much to lose, diplomacy is not sufficient." At last he is back on his theme. "That is why I have come. I offer myself as the leader of your armies against the foes of Alabaster-on-Gelasta."

King Rupert reaches out and pats him on the shoulder. "That's really very kind of you—you're most considerate—but I'm afraid I haven't got any armies."

Doggedly the Spy persists. "Your reserve soldiery, then," he recommends, telling himself that such an army would more easily be subverted to his purposes and the will of Humgudgeon IX.

"I'm sorry, but I haven't any of those, either," King Rupert apologizes.

"None?" the Spy asks, his voice cracking. "Not even a Palace Guard? You *must* have a Palace Guard."

Seeing how distressed the Ounergoth Mercenary is, King Rupert tries to offer some comfort to him. "Well, there is Francis, of course."

"But this is dreadful!" the Spy cries out, baffled and for once quite sincere. "You are unprotected and naked to the blows of your enemies."

King Rupert looks around him, as if to locate enemies,

then tells the Ounergoth Mercenary, "I have Sigmund and Professor Ambicopernicus, and of course Eustace. They help out occasionally."

"Your magicians. Your torturer!" It is the Spy's turn to look about, in case he requires an escape route. "I had forgot about them. They will keep you safe. Naturally."

"If that's what I need them to do, I imagine they will," King Rupert says almost merrily.

"I never thought of that," the Spy admits, already fearing Humgudgeon's *consequences*.

"If you want to help me, as you say, you might go along to those enemies of mine, the ones that want to mass at the borders, and remind them about the Professor and Sigmund and Eustace. I'd really appreciate that." He beams at the Ounergoth Mercenary.

The Spy, who is more used to Humgudgeon than to King Rupert, reads all sorts of sinister intent into that congenial smile, and he lurches to his feet. "Yes. Naturally. I surely will." He beats his retreat, calling out as he attempts to make one last bow, "I'll tell them about the magicians and the torturer."

As soon as the Ounergoth Mercenary has floundered off through the garden, King Rupert permits himself a mild frown. "Enemies at the border. Dear me."

Seeing an unexpected opportunity in this, Eustace leans forward. "I could go along with the Ounergoth Mercenary and find a few of them, Your Majesty. I could try out my new device."

"Don't be silly, Eustace. There's no point in making them angrier than they already are. Sigmund will come up with something." He raises his voice. "Won't you, Sigmund?"

From his place near the railing, Sigmund answers. "Hum? Oh . . . yes. Come up with . . . something. . . . But it's . . . you know . . . a secret. Yes. That's . . . *it* . . . secret."

"There. You see? Nothing to worry about. You know what these rumors are like, Eustace. Some traveler sees two or three men with swords—bandits or hunters, perhaps—and tells another traveler, who tells another traveler, and by the time the word reaches here, the few men have swollen into an armed tide of enemies when it was nothing more than a mistake." He nods to himself with satisfaction.

"But perhaps Humgudgeon—" Eustace begins.

"Oh, Humgudgeon," King Rupert says shaking his head. "No doubt he's itching to go to war with someone. He's like that, you know. They all are, over in Addlepate. All of them, Humgudgeons and Truculins, have been like that. Nothing seems to change them. They're jealous and spiteful, but they have such trouble with their people and their court that they rarely can do more than try to hang on to Addlepate, let alone war with their neighbors. The current Humgudgeon is no different than the rest. And his people trust him no more than they'd trust his ancestors or a weeping crocodile."

"But that would mean that he might actually attempt to . . ." Eustace pauses, at a loss for words.

"He might *want* to," King Rupert corrects him gently, "but gracious me, wars are expensive! And I can't see Humgudgeon sacrificing even the smallest of his amusements to pay for a war."

Francis (or Frances) does not move from his (or her) place on the wall, but announces, "Leander the crumpet-baker."

An astonishingly handsome young man comes through the door bearing a large tray that has many tempting edibles set out on it. He bows incredibly gracefully, in spite of his burden, and then speaks in a voice resonant and plaintive as a viola da gamba, "Where would Your Majesty like me to put this?"

"Oh, here on the table, Leander. That way we can all share it." He motions to Professor Ambicopernicus and Eustace to move a bit closer. "It looks quite splendid. What's this? Candied violets in whipped cream! My favorite."

Leander does as he is told, with elegance and deference that would be enviable in a favored knight, let alone a humble crumpet-baker. His golden locks shine where the sun strikes them, his large blue eyes are framed with lashes so long and thick that most girls and a few horses might weep with vexation to have them. The only thing that mars his beauty is a small smudge of flour, but since it subtly emphasizes the attractive cleft in his noble chin, it can hardly be called a flaw. As soon as the tray is in place, Leander steps back and waits in respectful silence.

"This is grand, Leander," King Rupert tells him as he surveys the array before him. "And strawberries, too, at this time of year. The Knights of the Golden Trowel do a remarkable job, don't they?"

"That they do," Professor Ambicopernicus agrees as he reaches for one of the mushroom-shaped pastries that is filled with brandied custard and dusted with nutmeg and sugar. "Delicious," he says around the goodie.

"Is there anything else Your Majesty would do me the honor of commanding?" Leander asks as King Rupert motions to Eustace to pour the tea into the porcelain cups as beautiful and fragile as petals.

"Yes, yes. Now that you mention it, I believe there is." He is about to explain when Sigmund appears at the terrace railing again, his periwig even more askew, and an expectant twinkle in his eyes.

"Ah!" Sigmund exclaims. "Pomegranates and kumquats! Wonder . . . ful." With amazing agility, he vaults the railing and hastens over to the table, drawing a chair behind him.

"Fine, Sigmund. Join us, yes, by all means, join us." King Rupert gestures to his wizard, although such invitation is unnecessary and unnoticed by Sigmund. "Now, then, Leander. What have I told you?"

"That there is something you wish to commission me to do, Your Majesty. I am eager to know what honor you are willing to bestow upon me."

King Rupert pops a candied violet into his mouth, then says, chewing his way through the words, "You may change your mind about the honor when you know what it is. Nevertheless, I will tell you that my son Prince Andre has decided to hunt dragons."

"What estimable enterprise!" exclaims Leander, his blue eyes alight with admiration.

"Um," King Rupert says. "And since his valet is not a man to enjoy treks through the Woebegone Wood, Prince Andre has designated you as the man he would like to have accompany him." He reaches for another candied violet, holding one hand under it to catch any drips of cream.

"Prince Andre has requested me?" Leander cries out, one hand rising to his chest. "Oh, how overwhelming."

"It is, isn't it?" King Rupert nods. "You, being a crumpet-baker can tend to the food for the Prince and the Princess."

"The Princess?" Leander repeats in hushed accents.

"Yes. Why, Princess Felicia has said that she wishes to accompany Prince Andre. She seems to think she would enjoy dragon hunting. Marvelous, isn't it, the way that young people spring at the chance to do great deeds." King Rupert looks at the other men gathered around the table for their confirmation.

"It is to be expected," Professor Ambicopernicus says in a portentous tone. "The stars indicate it."

"And . . . there's the secret," mumbles Sigmund as he inspects another kumquat.

"The Princess is to accompany the Prince?" Leander asks, as if not believing what he has heard.

"That's the ticket!" King Rupert says, merrily selecting a candied tangerine for variety.

"What courage! What sterling character!" Leander insists.

"Just so," King Rupert says. "Well, that is how things are. Prince Andre wants to be off this afternoon, so you'd better run along and pack. Don't forget the crumpets. And you might want to include a few of the candied violets. They're simply delicious."

Leander bows deeply, clearly much moved. "Sire, it is my greatest aspiration to serve you in all things. To permit me to participate in this royal adventure fills me with such emotion that mere words do not suffice. My being is suffused with a gratitude and an appreciation so total that every breath I take while on this expedition will be to utter silent thanks to Your Majesty for this great favor you have deigned to bestow upon me."

King Rupert listens to about half of the effusion, then directs his attention to the garden, where Princess Felicia has just arrived in the company of three of the Knights of the Golden Trowel. He waves, saying, "Why, there's Princess Felicia now. Hello, Felicia!"

All turn toward her, and so no one sees the look of adoration that crosses Leander's glorious features.

"Hello, Royal Papa," Princess Felicia answers. "I thought I might pick some flowers, but they all look the same. Petals and leaves, all of them."

King Rupert claps once with enthusiasm. "That's a real challenge for you, then, Felicia. You keep looking. You'll find something, I'm sure."

"Ah, Princess Felicia," Leander breathes as he stares after her, "could I but long for you."

"Princess Felicia's Venus is in Cassiopia," Professor Ambicopernicus announces. "She will succeed. It is predestined."

"You hear what the Professor says, Felicia?" King Rupert calls to her. "You keep at it. It's in the stars."

While Leander gazes at her and the party on the terrace tastes and munches, Princess Felicia at last finds a particularly fine daffodil, and points it out to the Knights of the Golden Trowel. "I think I like this one. It looks different than the others, at least a little bit."

The First Knight bows to her, saying, "Why, yes. It is the perfect thing for you. Only the loveliest of flowers are fit for Your Highness."

The Second Knight drops to one knee before her. "Quite, quite right. Only the most perfect are fit for Princess Felicia."

The Third Knight holds out his arms in a gesture of total abandonment. "And nothing would give us more pleasure than for you to have it; you must believe us, but . . ." And since what is coming next is bad news, the three Knights hum notes to each other so that they can soften the blow with song.

"But it's much too pretty to cut."

Princess Felicia has good enough manners not to sigh too obviously. "Never mind, then. I'll see if I like something else better." She turns her head and says, more critically, "How tedious; all those roses look like roses."

On the terrace, Leander dares to speak to King Rupert. "Your Majesty, I wish to beg a boon of you." He has gone back on his knee again.

"A boon? Goodness, it's been months since anyone's wanted a boon. What is it, Leander."

"It is not for myself," Leander vows. "Danger and hazard mean nothing to me if they are endured in your service. But for so exquisite a Princess as Princess Felicia is, the mere thought of risk must be tantamount to the greatest terror. How can I serve Your Majesty if I cannot promise with my life's blood to guard her from all unpleasantness. For that reason, and that reason alone, I beseech you—"

"Beseech as well?" King Rupert says, astonished.

"Yes, beseech," Leander says with growing fervor. "You have in your court wizards and magicians of great power. Surely one of them could find a way to perform a spell that will guard the Princess Felicia from any and all dangers that might beset her upon this quest."

"Um," King Rupert says, considering. "Sigmund, what do you think?"

Sigmund looks up from a little plate of jellied rosehips in honey. "Spell? The Princess . . . the Wood . . . But . . . not at all possible . . . no . . . after all, the Woebegone Wood . . . you know . . . not possible . . . to . . . to . . ."

"Throw a spell over it," King Rupert finishes for him. "Well, I think it might be better the way it is. No sense in facing danger if it isn't real, is there? Eh, Leander? That means that I'll depend on you to see that nothing happens to her. You'll do that for me, won't you?"

"Oh, Your Majesty, yes! though it cost me my life!"

"Excellent," King Rupert says, adding, "Since you're leaving soon, you might want to tend to your packing."

"Of course," Leander vows with a flourish of his right hand and a bow that nearly causes his bright hair to brush the marble marquetry of the terrace.

"Grand, simply grand," King Rupert says, leaning back in his chair, content with himself and the world. The only thing he lacks to make his pleasure complete is his knitting. He looks from Sigmund to Professor Ambicopernicus to Eustace and back again. "Does your heart good, doesn't it, to see the young people in such fine fettle. Why, to see Princess Felicia among the flowers is enough to make anyone pleased. Prince Andre is turning out to be a model Prince, which bodes well for Alabaster-on-Gelasta."

Francis (or Frances) stirs on the railing. "There's a Plaid Friar in the garden, Your Majesty."

King Rupert rubs his hands delightedly. "A Plaid Friar? Send him over."

"King Rupert wishes to see you, Friar," Francis (or Frances) calls out, yawning the last bit.

A moment later, in answer to the summons, the Friar appears. He is in a plaid habit, of cerise and mustard. It is a vulgar plaid, but it is the best the Spy (for it is the Spy, back again for another try) could manage on short notice. He moves toward the terrace, almost tripping over the hem of the habit, which is slightly too long for him. He makes what he hopes is a proper religious gesture and says, "May the blessings you deserve fall squarely upon Your Majesty's head."

"Well, thank you," King Rupert says at his most benign. "That's very kind of you."

There is an awkward pause while everyone stares at one another, and then the Spy gathers his wits and begins. "I am making a pilgrimage to . . . to the unfortunates in Addlepate. I thought that in order to prepare myself for the ordeal, I would gather inspiration here in Alabaster-on-Gelasta.

"Fascinating," King Rupert says, then nudges Professor Ambicopernicus. "Isn't it fascinating?"

"Anything that fascinates Your Majesty is deserving of great attention. There are stellar precedents for it." He has not lifted his turbaned head from the array of succulent cheeses he has been consuming, but that apparently bothers neither King Rupert nor himself.

"Yes," the Spy goes on with great determination. He is not about to be sidetracked again. "Ordinarily I would regard Alabaster-on-Gelasta as an example to shine in the world, but as soon as I came into your previously perfect kingdom, I realized that a terrible change had occurred."

"A change?" King Rupert interjects, adding to the others. "This ought to interest Felicia."

"A terrible change," the Spy continues. "Everywhere there is doubt and mutterings. The people are in a furor of worry."

"It is not the proper time for worry," Professor Ambicopernicus advises both the Plaid Friar and King Rupert. "There is nothing of worry in the stars."

"Could it mean an uprising, do you think?" Eustace asks, his expression hopeful.

"There can be no doubt of it," the Spy says, taking full advantage of Eustace. "I was much disconcerted—in my heart of hearts, I was troubled—to hear these sentiments in your kingdom which has ever been a haven to those who love the happy life. Since there can be no questioning the prosperity around you, Your Majesty, it appears to me that what has failed is spirituality. You have no idea how much happiness can undermine spirituality."

"Oh," cries Eustace in gleeful anticipation, "there may be doubters in that case. Do you think they might need my . . . guidance?"

"I'm sure it won't be necessary, Eustace, though it was good of you to think of it," King Rupert responds. "Heartwarming, isn't it?" he asks the Plaid Friar, "having a torturer who is as eager as Eustace?"

"Yes," the Spy squeaks out.

"But, Your Majesty," Eustace objects, pulling his new-design thumbscrews from the capacious pocket of his wide-skirted coat, "I could use *these*. They're ready to go."

The Spy makes a sound that is close to "Yipe!"

"Eustace, Eustace, put those away. You're upsetting the good Friar, who has done us the compliment of letting us share his company. That's hardly the way for a courtier to act. Remember, he is a spiritual man and his Friar's mind is on other things." He smiles at the Friar. "Isn't it?"

By this time, the Spy has conjured up all sorts of unpleasant visions. He is convinced that the Official Torturer is on to him and prepared to pull and pinch the truth out of him at any cost. He is certain that behind King Rupert's bland exterior lurks a soul as ruthless as it is devious. The magicians only serve to make the whole impression worse. "I . . . You . . . that is—"

"Men in Orders don't wish to know about the realities of the world. That's why they're in Orders, you see. It isn't kind of you not to respect that, Eustace." He gives his attention to the Friar again. "It must have been difficult, even distasteful for you to come here. And I appreciate your efforts, Brother. You have shown great persistence, and that is a virtue, isn't it? It is a credit to you that you're willing to come to me with your concerns, but I'm sure that the situation isn't nearly as bad as you fear it is."

The Spy is at a loss once again. "Perhaps—"

"Men who have devoted their lives to the study of religion often forget that most of us aren't able to measure up to them, and so are often bewildered and puzzled by the way that their lives unfold. No wonder that they ask questions that for a more enlightened man would seem dangerous and seditious. But, you see, I have no desire to keep my subjects from speaking their minds. No doubt you, from the advantage of your learning, misunderstood."

"But—" the Spy protests.

"To one unused to our customs, I daresay we seem very harum-scarum to you, lacking dogma and orthodoxy as we do. Still, we do get along in our own way. There's no point in disturbing the people now. Gracious, what a time we should have of it if we tried." King Rupert laughs at the notion. "No, Brother, we're probably not capable of your level of advancement."

In the garden, Prince Felicia has discovered a hydrangea that is slightly more perfect than the others. "What about that one?" she asks the Knights of the Golden Trowel.

The Spy attempts to avoid the distraction. "It's not a—"

King Rupert regards the Friar with sympathy. "I *am* sorry that our ramshackle ways disturb you. You must admit that everything you have been trained for is more stringent than what we have here, and that must make it hard for you to understand us. Let me assure you that there is nothing to be concerned about. Good Friar, we're always like this."

"No, not that one," Princess Felicia instructs the Knights, "the other one. The tallest one."

The First Knight touches the stem of the hydrangea reverently. "This! The most beautiful!"

The Second Knight bows to Princess Felicia. "It is almost as beautiful as a Princess."

"I don't understand," wails the Spy.

The Third Knight lowers his head. "The only one you should have, dear Princess, but . . ." He signals the others and they make a preparatory hum for a more elaborate musical disappointment.

"But it's much too pretty to cut!"

The Spy, now thoroughly confused, demands "What was that?"

"Why, just my daughter and the Knights of the Golden Trowel. They look after the garden for me, and they have done so for quite a while now. It didn't seem fair to keep them about with nothing to do, and Alabaster-on-Gelasta has been at peace for so long now that . . . well, you see my problem." King Rupert beams with resignation.

"Knights!" the Spy yelps.

"Don't let them bother you, Brother. Members of your Order must sing about things from time to time."

"Are they deranged?" the Spy asks, lowering his voice to do so.

"They are picking flowers. Surely you can see that for yourself." King Rupert selects an untouched dish on the tray and holds it out. "Cherries jubilee?"

"Picking flowers?" the Spy asks, the words coming out higher and higher as his panic increases.

"Why, yes, it gives them something to do. Would you prefer apricots?" He waits, his face solicitous.

"I . . . see . . ." the Spy says, in an effort to steady his nerves. "Knights who pick flowers."

King Rupert is delighted that the Friar has understood at last. "Precisely! Quite so, good Brother."

"You do . . . see?" Sigmund marvels as he stares out at the garden. "I can't . . . not from here. . . . Out of sight . . . the Princess. . . . Very odd. Very . . . odd."

The Spy feels what little control he possesses slip away from him, and he realizes that if he does not retreat at once, he will be undone. The vivid impression that Eustace's thumbscrews made is quite fresh with him, and it takes almost no imagination to feel them digging into his flesh. He makes another odd gesture that might be a benediction, and steps back from the table. "I must thank Your Majesty for this audience. It has been most . . . informative. But I believe that it is time for me to continue on my way to Addlepate to comfort the afflicted there."

King Rupert half rises. "Oh, gracious, Friar, you needn't leave at once." He is reaching toward the tray to offer another of the comestibles.

"No, no. Your Majesty is most kind," the Spy insists desperately, "but I must. Truly, I must."

With good grace King Rupert accepts this. "Well, you know best, I'm convinced of it. Religious men are always more in tune with their actions, or so I've been led to believe. Addlepate. That certainly shows heroic devotion on your part, Brother. I hope you'll be good enough—but that's to be taken for granted, you being in Orders as you are—to give my regards to Humgudgeon when you see him."

"I?" the Spy starts guiltily. "See Humgudgeon?"

"Come now," King Rupert admonishes him gently, "you really ought to call on the ruler of the place you visit. After all, you've been willing to visit me, haven't you? And it's only courteous to do the same in Addlepate. I admit that Humgudgeon is occasionally a trifle"—here he pauses while he searches for the most tactful word—"unpredictable, but he will receive you, Brother."

Completely nonplused, the Spy bows again. "Oh, I will call upon him. You're right, Your Majesty. It's part of my duty. I will make every effort, since you wish it."

King Rupert looks disappointed. "Gracious, you make me sound a tyrant. If you prefer not to meet with Humgudgeon, I'm the last man in the world to compel you to act in a way contrary to your conscience."

"Very . . . commendable," the Spy blurts out, showing more of the whites of his eyes than is normal. "Humgudgeon. I'll make a point to call on Humgudgeon. I'll bear a message to him, if you wish."

King Rupert considers this carefully, then shakes his head. "I don't think I'll trouble you with such a task. Dealing with Humgudgeon is awkward enough without reminding him that his Protectorate is not as thriving as it might be. He and I haven't a great deal in common, you know, and he sometimes takes the most cursory inquiries amiss. It would appall me if you had to endure any unpleasantness for my sake. You're too kind to suggest it."

"As you wish," the Spy blathers, seeking for the chance to leave.

"Thank you very much for calling on me." King Rupert lifts his hand to wave at the Plaid Friar as the Spy bolts for the door, the skirts of his habit gathered untidily in his hands.

"Not at all. Blessings and joy fall from heaven squarely on Your Majesty."

King Rupert accepts this with delight. "Why, how good of you, Brother. I'm most appreciative."

As the Spy rushes through the Throne Room, he almost collides with Prince Andre, who has changed into his most noble riding habit and is now coming in search of his father. He looks after the fleeing Spy and then tucks his tricorn under his arm and bows to King Rupert. "I have just been to the kitchen, Royal Papa. Leander is preparing for our departure. He was full of praise for your allowing him to come with Felicia and me."

The Spy, who is almost out the door, halts in his tracks. He has overheard enough to gain his attention. Whatever is going on might be sufficient to return him to Humgudgeon's good graces (such as they are) once again. Carefully he moves back across the Throne Room toward the terrace.

"A most industrious crumpet-baker," Professor Ambicopernicus states with obvious approval.

"He's a good fellow," Prince Andre concurs. "It's much better that he's going with us than Armand."

"Pardon me," the Spy interjects as he insinuates himself back onto the terrace, "but what is this endeavor that has you all so excited. It would be a pleasure for me to add my blessing to the undertaking." He considers the last word especially apt.

Prince Andre, who has paid little attention to the Plaid Friar, declares, "If we are underway this afternoon, we should be in the Woebegone Wood by this time next week."

"Splendid!" King Rupert exclaims. "Simply splendid. How marvelous for you, Andre."

"The Woebegone Wood?" the Spy asks of no one in particular.

King Rupert turns toward the question. "Oh, this is no concern of yours, Brother, though it is kind of you to inquire. Just what I would expect of so spiritual a man. Andre here is going after his first dragon. Isn't that exciting?"

"Then many, many blessings on the venture. May you triumph over your adversaries and bear yourself with courage and . . . succeed." He makes his spiritual gesture again, then rushes away, plotting to get more information before he returns to Addlepate.

"Wasn't that good of him?" King Rupert asks the others, not expecting an answer. "Coming back to offer his blessing for the dragon hunt. Now, that's not the way most Friars behave. This was most courteous." He has eaten all the candied violets and now has started on the scones with ginger marmalade. He eats carefully, almost daintily, so that he will not get sticky goo all over his red damask coat.

Out in the garden, Princess Felicia has come upon a bed of spider mums, the great big kind, and she points to the most exuberant of them. "This one, then, if you don't mind. It looks all right."

The First Knight nods vigorously, his eyes alight with pride. "A superb choice, Your Highness. What impeccable taste you have, what sensitivity and aesthetic standards."

"Truly, impeccable taste," seconds the Second Knight as he bows to Princess Felicia. "It is quite the best flower here, Your Highness, and it shows how keen your eye is, that you selected that flower over all the others."

Once again the Third Knight drops to his knee. "The only one in the entire garden truly worthy of your notice, the only one grand enough to bloom in your presence, and it would be the finest flower to give to you, but..." There is another round of humming and establishing of pitches, and then they are at it again, in a very elaborate apology, singing with energy and artistry in order to make Princess Felicia feel better.

> *"But it's much too pretty to cut!"*

Princess Felicia endures this with the best humor she can manage, which is to say that she looks faintly more bored than she did before. She motions to the Knights of the Golden Trowel to follow her, saying to them as they disappear in the vicinity of the Nile lilies, "Never mind. I'll jut look at them."

King Rupert, who is munching on his second scone, motions Prince Andre closer to him. "Make sure you take plenty of crumpets. It wouldn't do to run short. Scones don't travel nearly as well as crumpets. The crumpets are your best bet."

"Leander will take care of the crumpets, Royal Papa," Prince Andre says, helping himself to a pickled baby beet. "He told me to leave all that to him, so I have."

Professor Ambicopernicus, who is investigating an aromatic cheese, remarks as he has done before, "Leander is a remarkable fellow. His stars reveal a noble nature."

Sigmund nods in agreement. "Good thing in a crumpet-baker... nobility, that is... nobility... not stars... no..."

Prince Andre glances back toward the Throne Room, saying reflectively, "Did you say that the Plaid Friar is going to Addlepate?"

"Yes, so he told me," King Rupert replies. "He is on a pilgrimage to Addlepate and was kind enough to stop and visit."

"Who'd want to go to Addlepate?" Prince Andre wonders aloud, as well he might.

"Want to... go there?" Sigmund responds unexpectedly. "No one wants... to go to Addlepate.... Not the thing to do... not at all... after all, Humgudgeon... not the thing..."

Since no one is ever sure when Sigmund has actually finished speaking and when his attention has been diverted, no one worries about interrupting him. Professor Ambicopernicus says, "The stars are afflicted in Addlepate."

"Dear me," King Rupert says, his third scone halfway to his lips. "How very unfortunate. Humgudgeon *and* afflicted stars."

Prince Andre takes a decisive stance. "When I am King, I will arm the kingdom and destroy Addlepate. That won't be for a long time," he adds hastily, "and that will give me years and years to prepare."

"Oh, gracious!" King Rupert protests. "No, Andre, you mustn't. Believe me, it is folly. If you destroy Addlepate, there are those who are bound to object. It never fails. Even those who absolutely detest Humgudgeon will not like you if you arm against him. And then, if you managed to destroy Addlepate, there would be someone else you might have to destroy because they might want to destroy you, and then where would you be? It's a spiral, my boy, a spiral. Forget about fighting Addlepate. Think about a hobby. Content yourself with catching dragons. You might want to rescue a maiden or two. That's a much better way to live. Oh, yes. Far better than battling Addlepate."

Sigmund raises a finger to get Prince Andre's attention. "Not so . . . you know . . . hectic. . . . Dragons are much better . . . much better. . . . Know where you are with a dragon."

"But think of the way that Humgudgeon behaves! Of the abuses he has commited on his people! It galls me to hear of it." Prince Andre is not as easily persuaded as some Princes are.

King Rupert puts his scone down. "That's the problem with rulers like Humgudgeon—to do something about them, you almost always have to make yourself worse than they are, and where's the point to that? Knitting may not solve many ills, but it creates few of them. Consider that, Andre. You find a hobby that pleases you, that's the answer." He picks up his scone and gobbles it.

"Still," Prince Andre insists, his fine jaw thrust out a trifle farther than usual.

"There's plenty of time yet. You catch that dragon of yours, and you try out a hobby or two, and by the time you're King, you'll know what's what." He looks at the tray. "We seem to have run out of scones."

Eustace, who has been listening to Prince Andre with rapt attention, shakes himself and has the presence of mind to say, "Shall I go to the kitchen and bring some more?"

King Rupert turns the idea over in his mind. "No," he says

reluctantly. "They're probably all busy helping Leander prepare for the departure. Hardly the time to bother them with scones. They'll make more tomorrow, with currants if I remember to send word in time. There are two custards there, and a jelly with marzipan. That ought to suffice until supper, don't you think?"

"As you wish, Your Majesty," Eustace says, most of his attention once again on Prince Andre. He wants very much to give his own opinion of Prince Andre's ambitions, but is worried that they might offend King Rupert. The dilemma makes him slightly queasy, the way a moth must feel after one too many assaults on a lamp.

"Goodness!" King Rupert exclaims suddenly. "I've quite forgot to tell the court consort that you are to depart. They aren't ready. They haven't a new fanfare to play for you." King Rupert is already halfway to his feet and looking about for Francis (or Frances).

"I'd rather have a new fanfare for my return," Prince Andre says, trying very hard not to sound smug.

The appropriateness of this strikes King Rupert at once, and he sits down as abruptly as he rose. "Of course! Your return!" He chuckles. "Very sensible of you, Andre, and tactful, as well. Less likely to distress your mother, and that"— King Rupert does not actually sigh, but there is a movement to his shoulders that is not a shrug—"is something that is wise to do. Don't you agree?"

"Yes," Prince Andre says baldly and with great feeling.

"Then that's settled. You depart with the same old fanfare. You return to something new. I'm certain that Horace will be glad of the time to prepare. He always likes a few days, Horace does, to work out a new piece and run his trumpeters through it." He picks up a beautiful little bowl filled with smooth, golden custard. "The stables? You've talked with them, my boy?"

"Immediately after you gave me permission to hunt the dragon," Prince Andre says. "They are readying the horses now, and a mule to carry things."

"What a grasp of the problem!" King Rupert rejoices. "Not like me in that way at all. All you have to do is tell me that I must leave by a certain time, and I'm in a muddle. Make sure to take your weapons. No saying what you might need when hunting a dragon."

Francis (or Frances) gets up and ambles over to the door of

the Throne Room. After a moment he (or she) says to King Rupert, "This time he says he's a parapatetic philosopher, Your Majesty."

And sure enough, it is the Spy back again. He wears a long robe that might once have been scholastic, and carries an enormous and ancient tome entitled *One Hundred Seventy Things to Do with Dead Fish*. He bends low before King Rupert, his robes fluttering around him and his mustache all but falling off. "King Rupert of Alabaster-on-Gelasta, it is a privilege for me to meet you at last, philosopher that you are known to be."

King Rupert greets him with a slight, familiar wave. "Back so soon, eh? Most enterprising of you, really. I am impressed. Well, what may I do for you this time? I already know about the enemies at the borders and the uprisings and doubts of my subjects. What more has happened to distress you?"

The Spy might lack good sense, but he is pluck to the backbone. He shakes his head mournfully, *tisk*ing as he does. "I will not remonstrate with you, Your Majesty, because that would not be philosophical."

"Not at all," King Rupert agrees amiably.

"Still, as one who has studied much, I can't keep all my ponderings to myself, which is why I have come." The Spy looks uneasily at the other men seated at the table, as if he expects one of them to explode.

"And very good of you. What do you wish to be called? It is so hard to think of a title that a philosopher might like." He pauses expectantly, and when he has received no answer, he says, "Perhaps it's just as well not to bother, wouldn't you think so?"

". . . Yes," says the Spy when he has decided that it is not a loaded question. He clears his throat. "It is appropriate for monarchs to take stock of the state of their kingdoms. Every teaching available can be put to good use by a monarch, if he is willing to improve his mind."

"True; very true," Professor Ambicopernicus says.

"And. . . ." the Spy says, wanting to keep some semblance of control of the discussion this time, "and without such reflection, a monarch can take the wrong view of things. He can find himself in very hazardous circumstances because he is not able to perceive what the realities of his position are in a philosophical light. There are aspects of ruling that require a philosophical approach—no doubt you agree, Your Majesty."

"Most certainly," King Rupert declares. "And there are some situations that are more . . . philosophical than others." He has taken his teacup in hand and has added milk, lemon and sugar to it. He regards the peripatetic philosopher over the rim and adds, "Is that all you wanted to say to me?"

The Spy recovers quickly, determined to make the most of this opportunity. "There are many things that have occurred to me, and that I would like to discuss with you. Foremost in my mind is my concern for your apparent disregard for potential disasters. In your view, it would seem that you believe that a King is most effective if he is inactive."

"It is a sensible way of ruling as any," King Rupert says with an amused shrug that nearly oversets his teacup.

"No, no," the Spy protests. "There is no point in ruling if you do not rule."

"What a peculiar attitude for a philosopher, peripatetic or otherwise," King Rupert muses. "I'd imagine you'd be the one most likely to agree with what I do. Or don't do, as the case may be."

"Yet consider your activity. If you were to be a stronger presence, you could bring about changes!" The Spy makes an extravagant gesture that sends the dags of his sleeves flapping like a scarecrow in a stiff breeze.

"Why would I want to do that?" King Rupert asks in amazement, and explains in song:

"I suppose that if I listen to your sage advice and council,
I will rapidly perceive that all my kingdom is a mess
But if I hasten to ignore you with your words of worldly wisdom
There's a chance that we'll continue in our blissful happiness.
Since you tell me of the forces and the evils all around me
Let me instantly inform you that I've never cared for war
If perhaps I took an interest in my armies and my taxes
I might find it to my liking, but right now it's just a bore.
So you really must forgive me if I still prefer my knitting

> *No doubt I'm ev'ry bit as simple as my hobby would*
> *appear*
> *But the thought of waste and pillage turns my royal*
> *bones to sawdust*
> *And though such things have surely happened, they*
> *can never happen here!*
> *They can never, never, never, never, never, never,*
> *never, never, never happen here!"*

The Spy, now almost wholly demoralized, cries out, "What's going on?"

Sigmund answers him. "Singing, you know . . . very good thing . . . singing . . . good . . ."

The Spy, aware of Sigmund's reputation, stares hard at him. "What do you know about this?"

"This?" asks Sigmund, apparently trying to sort out which "this" the peripetetic philosopher means.

"This!" the Spy insists, then goes on in a more courteous manner. "You're said to be a wizard of ability. We must have much in common. Surely King Rupert isn't the foo—innocent he seems?"

"Good King . . ." Sigmund says with as much decision as he ever says anything. "You know, good . . . subjects happy, kingdom prosperous . . . whatever else are Kings for? . . . Kings . . ."

"It must be your doing!" the Spy says, because he has come to this conclusion himself. "Since you're a wizard, and very powerful from all I've been told, you must be the one who is protecting this kingdom and that simpleton"—he nods in the direction of King Rupert, who has almost finished his tea—"and assuring the prosperity."

"Powerful?" Sigmund repeats, paying little attention to the rest of what the peripetetic philosopher has said. "Oh . . . I suppose I must be . . . if I keep the kingdom . . . that is, protect is . . . takes powerful wizardry to do that . . . you know? . . . to keep . . . that is . . ."

"What have you done?" the Spy interrupts, thinking that Sigmund is trying to get him off the track deliberately. "You can tell me, for I haven't any magical powers."

Sigmund beams at him. "Could I? . . . Really? . . . But it's . . . you know . . . a secret. That's it . . . a . . . secret."

"Andre, my boy," King Rupert calls out, "shall we plan

your departure for an hour from now?"

"Fine!" Prince Andre replies. "Everything should be ready by then. An hour is plenty of time."

"It is an auspicious hour," Professor Ambicopernicus interjects.

The Spy is still attempting to get information from Sigmund. "What have you done for King Rupert? What protects him? A spell?"

"I enchanted it!" Sigmund says with delight.

"What? The kingdom? King Rupert?" If the Spy can worm this one bit of intelligence out of Sigmund he will be able to return to Humgudgeon without disgrace (and without *consequences*).

"I can't remember..." Sigmund admits cheerfully. "And besides... it's a secret."

"Well," says King Rupert as he puts down his teacup and gets up from the table, "I can't spend the whole day in jollification. I really ought to get back to my knitting. Come, Francis." He waves to the Page and to Prince Andre and Princess Felicia. "Come by the Throne Room before you leave, children. We'll have that fanfare then."

"Yes, Royal Papa," Prince Andre and Princess Felicia answer in unison.

"Wonderful!" King Rupert exclaims. "How exciting." He adds to the others, "Finish up without me. No need for you to stop on account of me." He saunters toward the Throne Room, whistling the refrain he had been singing earlier to "never, never, never, never" (et cetera).

The Spy is greatly confused, but determined not to lose his opportunity with Sigmund. He knows now that he is close to the secret, and it fires him. If he had antennae, they would be quivering. Taking the chair that King Rupert has vacated, the Spy draws in close to Sigmund, their knees almost touching as he says, "You've arranged something, haven't you? You're planning something that the rest know nothing about."

Sigmund considers this in a pleasantly vacant way. "I may be," he allows finally. "I suppose... I could."

"What is it?" the Spy demands.

But Sigmund's attention has drifted to other things. "Must go..." he says as he rises. "Have to... make something for ... the dragon-hunt.... The Prince... the Princess... Must go." He starts across the terrace, but the Spy pursues him.

"The dragon hunt. That's not what's really going on, is it? There's more to it than that, isn't there? What are they really doing? You can't make me believe that all they're after is a dragon—in this day and age!" His scoffing gains a bit of Sigmund's attention.

". . . No-o-o-o-o," he says, very slowly. "Not all."

"Then what are they actually doing?" What are they hunting?" He has taken hold of Sigmund's arm and is shaking it, as if the information might fall out of him.

"Can't . . ." Sigmund says, his attention once again drifting away, though he does have one last, provocative hint to add. "That would . . . be telling."

As Sigmund wanders off, the Spy is left, aggravated, trying to come up with an excuse for detaining him again. He scuffs his foot on the complicated inlaid pattern of marble and shakes his head slowly.

Professor Ambicopernicus, who is finishing up the last of his snack and watching the Spy, speaks up. "It must be a very trying day for you."

"What?" asks the Spy, caught off-guard.

"Your tenacity. Most remarkable. No doubt your stars are very fixed. And all those costumes. It shows great persistence and invention to manage so much in so little time." He taps his turban. "Permit me to say that I find your versatility amazing."

The Spy takes two steps back, as if he had been offered a nest of scorpions instead of a compliment. "I . . . don't understand," he says lamely, trying to hold on to the few shreds of dignity and professionalism left to him.

Professor Ambicopernicus apparently does not realize the shock he has caused the Spy, for he continues in the same unctuous tone. "I know I haven't the ability to do so much myself. I'd be reluctant to attempt it. And you, you appear and show us all how it's done. A great achievement, sir, believe me."

"You know?" shrieks the Spy, all trace of control leaving him. "You let me trap myself!" He looks about wildly, expecting to find guards or some other armed officer coming for him. He blunders toward the table and his foot catches on something. He bends down to look and his heart goes leaden in his chest.

"You haven't seen this, have you?" Eustace, the Official

Torturer asks in delighted innocence. At last he has found a new and appreciative audience for his invention. "Will you let me show you how it works? I haven't had the chance to test it out on anyone, but I'm sure you can—"

The Spy lurches toward the terrace railing, all but falling over it in his haste to get away. He can already feel the pincers and pullies and teeth doing their work on him. "What is that?" he croaks.

"My new rack. It has many features never included before, if you'll only let me show you."

"New rack!" the Spy bleats.

"The design is superb, I give you my word. But I haven't found anyone to help me perfect it." He gets up from his chair and advances, holding out his hand.

This is too much for the Spy, who flings himself over the railing and goes careening through the garden, wailing. *"No. No, no! You can't do this to me!"*

Watching his erratic progress between the roses and the bougainvillaea, Professor Ambicopernicus offers his opinion. "Wrong rising sign; it's obvious."

Eustace stands by the railing, his attitude downcast. "It's such a *good* rack, too. The best I've ever done."

Professor Ambicopernicus is willing to commiserate with him. "You persevere very well. We all have our trials to bear. Every one of us must deal with one great disappointment in life. Even I: I lost my one true love many years ago, and have had to live with the heartbreak all this time. It remains as acute as when we first parted."

"That *is* disappointing," Eustace agrees, then brightens, as a new notion occurs to him. "If you're suffering, maybe *you'd* like to try my rack?"

Although Professor Ambicopernicus pretends not to have heard this offer, he finds an excuse to go back into the Throne Room, leaving Eustace to solace himself with the rest of the custards and jellies while waiting for the ceremony to mark Prince Andre's and Princess Felicia's (and Leander's) departure on the dragon-hunt.

The Departure

PRINCE ANDRE WEARS a wide-skirted riding coat of tooled burgundy leather, a simple waistcoat of plum-colored satin, a linen shirt with a lace-edged cravat tied in the least extravagant manner. His fine wool britches are the same shade as the coat, caught below the knee with plain brass buttons. His boots, so polished that they look more like jet than leather, come just to the buttons. His spurs are steel, glittering. He carries his sword and tricorn in the same hand.

Beside him, Princess Felicia is rigged out in a linen riding habit of a white that approaches blueness. There are rose buttons (dozens and dozens of them) in a double row up the front of the jacket. The skirt is voluminous, sweeping around her like the froth of a wave. Her chamise is of pale rose pink, and a bit of its ruffle shows at collar and cuff. She carries a riding crop and the most adorable white hat with a tall pink ostrich plume, which perches on her fair curls. She is quite dashing, from the tip of the plume to the toe of her white kid boots.

"Well," says King Rupert with satisfaction as his children bow and curtsy before him. "This is fine, very fine. You're both a marvel to the eyes."

"Thank you, Royal Papa," they say in unison.

"A pity I haven't an Order of Knights—I might send one or two along with you, just in case. But it's been so long since we've needed them; generations, in fact. And the Knights of the Golden Trowel can't be turned into fighting men at this late date." He is knitting again, the strange, shapeless mass of stuff gathered near his feet like a very shaggy dog.

"It's better this way, Royal Papa. I wouldn't want help catching my dragon." Prince Andre stands very straight. "It is proper for a Prince to hunt his dragon alone."

"Precisely so . . . yarn over, knit two." King Rupert smiles warmly at his children. "Well, then, off you go. Your mother is too overwrought to bid you farewell. A pity, but . . ." He shrugs.

"Give her my duteous greetings," Prince Andre says very carefully.

"And mine," adds Princess Felicia.

"The very best of luck to you. Horace is waiting in the courtyard with his musicians to see you off. Good fortune. Good hunting." He pauses. "And to you, as well, Leander."

Leander goes down on one knee to King Rupert. "Oh, Your Majesty, I cannot thank you enough for this opportunity to serve you, and to devote myself to the welfare of the Prince and the Princess, no matter how humble the office I fill. To have this responsibility cannot be a burden, but the rarest privilege that anyone could aspire to attain."

"Um," says King Rupert, peering at Leander over his knitting needles. "See to it that they have plenty of crumpets; that's the ticket." He pauses again. "Is there anything else I've forgot to do?"

"Well," Prince Andre says, blushing faintly and furious with himself for blushing, "I thought that a Kingly blessing . . ."

"Of course, of course!" King Rupert cries. "You're quite right Andre. And to think it slipped my mind entirely. Consider that you have it. It goes without saying." He puts his knitting aside and comes down from the throne and the dais. He clears his throat, then kisses Princess Felicia on both cheeks, and then, more awkwardly still, Prince Andre. "That should do it, don't you think?"

"Thank you, Royal Papa," his children say in unison.

Not certain how best to speed Leander on his way, King Rupert approaches him (Leander is still on his knee) and holds out his hand. "Good fortune, Leander."

To King Rupert's profound embarrassment, Leander seizes his hand and kisses it, vowing, "I will give everything, even my life, to discharge Your Majesty's commission."

"That's fine, Leander; fine," says King Rupert, tugging his hand away. He had not intended to do more than shake hands, and Leander's display leaves him perplexed. He motions to Francis (or Frances), saying, "Escort them to the courtyard, there's a good fellow. Wave to them for me. I'd come myself, but I'm so behind on my knitting . . ."

"Good-bye, Royal Papa," Prince Andre and Princess Felicia say together, bowing again before leaving the Throne Room.

King Rupert watches them go, his expression a trifle wistful, as if he might once have wanted a more enterprising hobby than knitting. Then he picks up the needles and counts the stitches to remember where he was before he sets the next loop of yarn in place. All in all, he tells himself, a very satisfactory day.

An Audience With Queen Hortensia

THE TORMENTS AND agonies of the day have driven Queen Hortensia to her chambers, and she lies there now, sprawled on her chaise longue in an enveloping robe of golden tissue, with so many ruffles and flounces that she looks more as if she should be hung in a window than left on a bed. Her two chambermaids, Magnolia and Pansy, are within reach, but not so close as to give the Queen occasion for another outburst.

From somewhere below, there comes the sound of a fanfare, nothing remarkable, but competently played. This is followed by a muffled cheer.

"Ah!" cries Queen Hortensia, clasping her hands to her bosom and wriggling as if impaled. "So soon they are gone!"

Magnolia tiptoes toward the door, hoping to have a few minutes' respite in the outer room, but it is not to be.

"I cannot bear it," Queen Hortensia sobs stentoriously. "I cannot! My soul is rent!" She flings up one of her hands. "How can I bear it!"

Pansy, who has been holding several vials in her hands, sighs in what might be sympathy but is more likely exasperation. She looks at the various concoctions she can offer and tries to settle on one that would be appropriate.

"They are being sent into the most ghastly danger, where they are sure to find ruin and degradation and death. That my precious buds should come to such a pass!" She wallows onto her side. "Nothing can calm me," she threatens. "There is no surcease, no succor for me."

"Very sad, Your Majesty," Pansy says softly, hoping to distract the Queen.

"Sad!" she expostulates. "That is a puny word for this calamity, this disaster, this catastrophe!" Her emotion brings her almost into a sitting position, then she collapses back onto the daybed with a moan.

Magnolia and Pansy exchange glances, but remain prudently silent.

"What is a mother to do?" Queen Hortensia demands of the air in the most tragic tones. "I have carried them under my heart, I have nurtured them and tried to guide their footsteps, and then this! They are gone from me with no more feeling for the suffering I endure than if they had trod on an insect in the garden."

Both chambermaids have been with Queen Hortensia long enough not to be unduly alarmed by these dramatic protestations, but neither of them is inclined to indulge Her Majesty any longer than necessary. Pansy, being more forthcoming than Magnolia, approaches the chaise. "Your Majesty," she begins, and hardly draws a breath for fear that Queen Hortensia, given the least chance, will be off on another tirade. "Perhaps if I send word to His Majesty..."

Queen Hortensia waves her away abruptly and mumbles into the cushions.

"Surely someone must be able to help you?" Pansy persists.

"No one!" Queen Hortensia declaims in her more histrionic manner. "I am deserted and alone in my travail!"

"Your Maje—" Pansy begins, hoping to head off the flood, but to no avail.

"I have never questioned the demands of fate. It cannot be done. But I am prostrate with grief that so drastic a misfortune has been visited upon me. If I had not been given the sensibilities that plague me, no doubt I would be as the others, laughing and singing and smiling as Prince Andre and Princess Felicia ride off to certain destruction, all on a whim!"

Unwisely, Pansy points out, "They might be fine, Your Majesty. There's no saying that Prince Andre *won't* catch the dragon. He may be the victor."

Queen Hortensia turns to her with an expression of loathing. "How can you think that, you idiotic girl? He's a Prince, gently, carefully raised, guarded and protected from every mischance. What can he possibly know about hunting dragon? You have heard, I trust," she continues with icy sarcasm, "that dragons are dangerous, that they have long, pointed teeth and breathe fire. You are aware, aren't you, that such creatures have been known to ravage whole countries and to destroy nations? What can a kindly, good, noble Prince like my darling Andre do against such a monster?" She puts her soggy handkerchief to her welling eyes. "He is lost to me, completely lost. I will next see him on his bier, and the rest of my life will be blighted. Doubtless the terrible monster will take Princess Felicia captive and keep her for its vile amusements, and when she is beyond madness and pain, it will dispose of her. My treasured little flowers will wither before they have fully blossomed. I am overcome with grief." This last assertion is hardly necessary, but it provides an excellent opportunity for more lamentation.

"Oh, Your Majesty," Pansy commiserates, "you must not give up hope. Prince Andre hasn't been gone for more than half an hour. He and Princess Felicia are not yet beyond the banks of the Gelasta. No matter what dangers they face, they do not face them yet."

"Ah," Queen Hortensia sighs, saying in her darkest tone, "to have less acute sensibilities. To be less afflicted with a sensitive nature. I have often thought that those with blunted sympathies and cloddish nerves do better in the world than those of us with more finely tuned temperaments." She regards Pansy with curiosity and distaste. "How can you stand there, fresh and neat, while the Heir to the Throne departs on his last journey? Why aren't you prostrate with misery?"

"Your Majesty is prostrate with misery already, and we would not serve you as we ought if we were as overcome as you are." Pansy dips a crisp little curtsy.

If there is impertinence in this, Queen Hortensia is too caught up in her own emotions to be aware of it. Her lower lips trembles. "Such loyalty. I had not realized . . ." She makes a halfhearted attempt to stifle a sob, then gives way to yet another torrent of tears.

"Your Majesty..." Pansy says after a bit, leaning forward. "Let us bring someone to you. Tell us who can aid you."

"No one!" the Queen exclaims comprehensively. "I am wholly bereft!"

"Would Professor Ambicopernicus help?" Pansy persists. She looks quickly at Magnolia, who still hovers by the door. "Would you like to talk to Sigmund?"

"They cannot help me. They cannot return my children to me. They cannot save them from the disasters that await them on every hand."

"Your Majesty..." Pansy says, a bit of her exasperation creeping into her voice now. "You cannot let yourself be cast down this way. You must keep a good face, for the sake of the King."

"The King!" jeers Queen Hortensia with a great sneer. "He is the one who has permitted this to happen. He gave my precious babies permission to hunt the dragon. Every misfortune that comes of this ill-conceived adventure is on his head. Why should I do anything that would permit him to forget for an instant that he has condemned his own exquisite offspring to a hideous death."

"You are harsh with him," Pansy says, and wishes as the words are uttered, that she had bitten off her tongue.

"Harsh with Toby? Ridiculous! He is the one who is heartless and cruel. He has doomed his children and me to untold agonies." Queen Hortensia let out a long, undulating wail that lasted a remarkably long time. "What has he done to me, the monster that he is? What has caused him to feel this way, to neglect every aspect of parental authority, to show himself callous and pitiless, ruthless, scheming, conniving, unmoved by uxorial woe."

Pansy knows from the past that when Queen Hortensia starts using words like *uxorial* the situation is critical. She straightens up. "I am going to bring Professor Ambicopernicus to you, Your Majesty. He will read the stars for you, and show you that the fate of your children may not be as dire as you fear."

"That cannot be," Queen Hortensia sniffs, "but it is good of you, and you are a good, simple girl, aren't you? You cannot begin to comprehend the depths of despair into which I have plummeted. Still, I will listen to the Professor if he will wait upon me. That much is possible."

Relieved and satisfied, the chambermaid curtsies and

makes for the door with dispatch. "Find the Professor, will you, Magnolia?" she whispers to the other. "I'm hoping I can find Sigmund. Someone has to talk some sense into the Queen before she works herself into one of her states again."

Magnolia nods. "I'll do it, but I think it will take more than an astrologer and a wizard to keep Her Majesty from strong hysterics." The two chambermaids sigh together, and Magnolia says, expressing both their sentiments, "Most of the time she's easy enough on us, and we're fortunate to have the rough side of her nature as rarely as we do. The King, poor dear, gets more of this than we."

Once they are outside the door, Pansy ventures to ask, "Do you think that anything *will* happen to the Prince and the Princess?"

Magnolia considers it. "I doubt it. If there were real danger, or too much danger—dragons must be a bit dangerous, I'd think—I don't think the King would have permitted them to go off as they did."

By now they are at the top of a wide marble staircase. "Well, good luck to you. Sigmund might be anywhere; the Professor is undoubtedly in his study." Pansy waves to Magnolia and starts along the gallery toward the Wizard's Tower while Magnolia goes down the stairs and across the hall where Professor Ambicopernicus has a private study on the far side of the library.

Of course, Magnolia returns to Queen Hortensia's apartments far sooner than Pansy. She has a reluctant but determined Professor Ambicopernicus in tow.

"Uncanny!" declares the Professor as he hears the hoots and weeping from the figure on the chaise. "How long has she been like this."

"Hours," Magnolia says in a resigned tone. "Ever since the King said that the Prince and the Princess might go hunting dragons."

"Dear, dear," Professor Ambicopernicus says, touching his turban as if to reassure himself that his head is on properly. He advances across the room and addresses the Queen in a solicitous and hearty manner. "Your Majesty. How do you come to be so afflicted—you, of all women?"

This is the wrong question, as the Professor realizes too late: Queen Hortensia is primed for her favorite subject and she once again is off in full cry. "How easily you say that!

How easily you assume that because I was born to my station in life, that all my sensibilities were relegated to a distant part of myself. How little you understand what it is to be as sensitive as I am and still have to bear the burdens of majesty. Think of how it influences me, this awesome position and power that requires all the magnificence of my birth and all the charm of my manner, but denies me the full expression of my innermost temperament."

"A difficult ordeal, most assuredly," Professor Ambicopernicus says, attempting to recover some vestige of his authority.

This is not what Queen Hortensia wants at all. "You, who have given yourself over to study cannot imagine, in your wildest fancy, what I have to suffer every hour of my waking life. I am buffeted about as a flower in the wind, I am uprooted by demands of state that crush the range and color of my spirit. I have the tenderest of mother's emotions welling in my breast, and they are constrained by what I am expected to do as Queen. I yearn to enfold my most adorable children and to protect them as the tigress does her cubs, yet as every feeling cries out for this, the King abrogates my very just insistences and sends the Prince and the Princess, as exposed and helpless as infants thrown to wolves, to the Woebegone Wood where there is —we have our information on excellent authority—a dragon, perhaps more than one, whose entire purpose in life is to bring the most hideous death and destruction to my treasured darlings!" Queen Hortensia's handkerchief is soaked, her eyes have blushed the same shade as the climbing roses outside her window, and her body quivers and trembles with every complaint. She turns her head away, momentarily exhausted, and weeps her voluminous-though-silent tears.

Now that there appears to be an opening, Professor Ambicopernicus clears his throat and sets about putting the Queen more at rest. He fingers one of his sleeves, as if it might contain a dove or other entertainment, but it turns out that this is just a nervous habit (and the Professor has good reason to be nervous). "Your Majesty," he begins, feeling safe enough with her title, "I have listened to you with great sympathy. You are known to be of a delicate and sensitive nature, and it is not astonishing that one as . . . as refined in breeding and personal proclivity as you are might experience more distress than many others at such a time as this one."

"It is very true," she murmurs, the words partly muffled by the pillow she has lain on.

"Yes. Those of us who are privileged to know you are aware that you have an elegance of person that is only a reflection of the exemplary distinction of your true self." Over the years, Professor Ambicopernicus has learned as much about tact as he has about astrology. As he himself might tell you (if you caught him in a candid moment), the two are often the closest of companions. "Queen Hortensia, let me speak openly with you." This, clearly, is not one of his candid moments.

"Please," Queen Hortensia beseeches him in her autocratic way.

Professor Ambicopernicus clears his throat again. "I have taken the liberty of reading the stars for Prince Andre and Prince Felicia, and I have come to you to tell you what the stars reveal."

"Ah!" Queen Hortensia cries, a picture of dejection and dashed hopes.

"But Your Majesty," Professor Ambicopernicus goes on, "do not be disconsolate. It is true that there are dangers to be faced by your children, but you must recall that they have more than their condition to protect them. It is true that they have never faced such extreme dangers, but . . ." He waits, wanting to be certain he has her attention, for he is hopeful that the ploy he is putting into play might work. "Your Majesty, you underestimate them, for they have not only their highborn life to draw upon, but their breeding as well. If they were the children of peasants, or even most barons, then it would be a near thing, I must agree. But these are not the brats of crofters, they are *your* children. The blood of your family is in their veins, and with so admirable and intrepid a line, how can you think that they are unable to face dangers? It is known that your father was a man of the utmost mettle and one that showed great fortitude in his kingdom."

"True," Queen Hortensia sniffs, listening carefully.

"And I need hardly speak of all your ancestors, for their deeds, their exploits are the hallmark for Kings the world over." This is really pushing it, but Professor Ambicopernicus is certain that he knows Queen Hortensia well enough to pull it off. "You are the flower of that family, and you have achieved a well-deserved celebrity in the world."

"I have some reputation, I understand," Queen Hortensia says coyly, using the pillow to dry her tears.

"It could not be otherwise," Professor Ambicopernicus says with honesty. "A woman, a Queen of such eminence, of so great dignity and grandeur, you are the center of this court. You show how great is your magnanimity in many things, and the concern for your children is not the least of it. In this you reveal the mother in the Queen, a proclivity that is perceived by many with the strongest impression." Professor Ambicopernicus is not above a little sarcasm from time to time.

"Do you really think so?" Queen Hortensia asks, brightening noticeably. "I had not known, I confess, that I had so great a repute."

"Your nature is modest, Your Majesty," Professor Ambicopernicus says smoothly, keeping a straight face. "You are not one to seek out the praise of others or to demand aggrandizement the way that many another has done."

"Yes," Queen Hortensia says darkly, plainly thinking of some of those other over-aggrandized ones Professor Ambicopernicus undoubtedly means. "There are those without an appropriate sense of merit, aren't there?"

"Yes, Your Majesty," Professor Ambicopernicus says, beginning to believe that he has turned the tide at last.

"You are right to remind me of the strength of character that is part of my blood. Toby is a dear, and I am completely devoted to him, for a sweeter man does not breathe upon the earth, but I must admit that he is nothing in dignity to my father and my uncles who had a much better understanding of the responsibilities of their position. They would never have allowed any of their children to set off in this ramshackled way to hunt dragons." There is a warning trembling of her upper lip, and Professor Ambicopernicus hastens to try a more fruitful approach.

"Your Majesty, you know that King Rupert depends upon you utterly, and is always aware of how much he owes you. King Rupert is a man who recognizes the profound debt that he owes to you, his wife and Queen. It is not apparent to those who do not know him, but *your* keen eye has, naturally, seen through his pretense. He is as apprehensive as you are as to the fate of the Prince and the Princess, but it is not fitting for him to reveal it. He is as much a victim of his rank as you are,

Your Majesty, and he is forced to show an untroubled face to the world. Your support and sympathy at this time would mean much to him, but he is not able to ask it of you, for that might give you a greater burden, and it is always King Rupert's desire, because he treasures you, to spare you as much anxiety as possible." Professor Ambicopernicus finishes this in a rush, and waits to see what Queen Hortensia will make of it.

"He *is* a sweet man," Queen Hortensia repeats. "And it does him credit to realize how precarious my nerves are. Those of us who have such fragile nerves are often misunderstood by others, but Toby is aware that this comes from the sensitivity of my nature." She is sitting up now, still holding the pillow, but her expression is less like a bad painting of the Tragic Muse and more like a statue of one of those formidable Roman matrons.

"Just so," Professor Ambicopernicus says by way of encouragement.

"I ought to offer solace to him, oughtn't I? And he could offer his to me." She smiles a bit, her eyes growing moist at the thought of a new audience.

"You know how it pains him to see you overset. When King Rupert is the cause of your distress," Professor Ambicopernicus says hurriedly, "it doubles his suffering, for he blames himself for bringing the least affliction to you." He hopes that this will dissuade her from seeking out King Rupert to show another range of her emotions. "He has as much to bear as you—" This is a major tactical error, and he realizes it as he hears Queen Hortensia give a vehement sob.

"No one—*no one*—is as overset as I am. No one can approach the inexpressible anguish that consumes me! There is no one who can feel the depths of despair that engulf me!" She is proud of this, and her announcement is stentorian and emphatic. "I have endured more than any mother has ever endured. I am riven with grief! My babies are gone from me, and they are doomed!"

"Your Majesty—" Professor Ambicopernicus begins, in vain.

"I must be left alone! Go! The sight of you reminds me of their peril and drives me to the point of madness!" Back she flings herself onto the chaise, her pillow held tightly to her bosom as she weeps and moans.

Professor Ambicopernicus bows and starts toward the door. In part he is delighted to be leaving, but he had wanted to make more progress with Her Majesty then he was able, and he finds the whole encounter galling.

"Aha!" says a voice from the outer door, and Professor Ambicopernicus looks around only to find himself facing the vague and friendly face of Sigmund Snafflebrain. "You're . . . I know . . . who you are."

Professor Ambicopernicus's patience has worn down to the nubbins and he has used up his diplomatic quotient for the day. "If you don't, you ought to," he snaps, and pushes out of the Queen's apartments, leaving Sigmund staring after him.

Pansy and Magnolia take Sigmund by the hands, one on each side, and they lead him in to visit Queen Hortensia, who has worked herself into another semihysterical state. Magnolia says respectfully, "Your Majesty, here is the wizard to talk to you."

"Send him away!" Queen Hortensia orders.

Anyone else would flee at such a moment, but Sigmund seems only mildly curious. He nods to the maids and then addresses Queen Hortensia. "You're feeling badly, . . . are you? Crying . . . I should guess you . . . you know . . . feel badly."

"Leave me alone!" shrieks the Queen.

"Why . . . alone . . . children gone . . ."

This brings for another bellow of woe. "Go!"

"If . . . you like, then. . . . But they're all right, you know. . . ."

"Who?" demands Queen Hortensia, wanting to be rid of Sigmund, but still unable to risist what might be a tidbit of gossip. And who can tell when Sigmund might remember it again.

"You know . . . see them around here . . . young . . . hunting dragons now. You . . . know." He toddles toward the door.

"Prince Andre and Princess Felicia?" crows Queen Hortensia.

". . . No . . . They're not . . . here. Haven't seen them . . . not now." Sigmund regards her in the most kindly and bemused way.

"Of course they're not here!" Queen Hortensia says. "They're hunting dragons."

"They are?" Sigmund is completely enthralled to hear it. "When did they . . . you know . . . do that?"

"Today," wails the Queen. "And you said, or you seemed to imply, that they're going to be all right." She fixes him with her most penetrating stare, which has caught the attention of more distracted men than Sigmund.

"If I said that," he tells her once he has considered her words (at least that is what he appears to do, but with Sigmund you never know), "then it must be so. I don't . . . you know. . . . lie."

"But you didn't say for sure." Queen Hortensia protests, annoyed with herself for becoming embroiled in one of these endless and frustrating go-rounds with Sigmund.

"Then I may not be. Still, I did give them a . . . powder . . . very effective, the powder." He makes another feint in the direction of the door.

"Powder?" Queen Hortensia pounces on the one thing that might be important.

"Um?" says Sigmund.

"What about the powder you gave to Prince Andre and Princess Felicia?" Her basilisk gaze would transfix him if he were the least aware of it.

"Is there something about it . . . I should . . . you know . . . know?" He awaits her answer with rapt interest.

"There is something about it *I* should know," she says formidably. "You will tell me what you have done, wizard, or you will regret your silence bitterly, I promise you."

Sigmund blinks at her, in the slow deliberate fashion of a resting cat. Then he smiles at Queen Hortensia, apparently oblivious to her threatening attitude. "For protection . . . you know . . . powder . . . protection."

"A protective powder? Is that what you gave them?" Queen Hortensia demands. Gone is her languishing and lamenting; in their place is the most militant motherhood. "Are you saying that my precious babies are safe?"

"They have . . . powder," he says in an affable tone of voice.

"A magic powder to protect them?" hoots Queen Hortensia, launching herself off the chaise and advancing on Sigmund with great determination.

". . . Possibly. It . . . might be for . . . protection. I . . . think I might . . . do that." He belatedly remembers to bow to her, and does so now with what passes for a flourish.

"If you can promise me that my adored and adorable offspring are under your care and protection, then all is forgiven."

She almost opens her arms to him, but that would be going much too far. She compromises with giving him her most syrupy smile. "I should have realized that you would not permit my cherished darlings to be lost to me through malice and stupidity."

"Oh?" says Sigmund with interest.

"You, of all the court, have the power and the wisdom to save and protect them. If any harm should come to them, I will be certain who is to blame for it. You will find that I do not readily forgive lapses of so momentous a nature. But it is folly," she goes on in a plummy voice, "to assume the worst, or so you have told me. I have permitted the delicacy of my constitution to overcome me, and you are right to remonstrate with me."

It is useless to speculate how much (if any) of this Sigmund has been able to follow; he beams at Queen Hortensia and says, "Always good to . . . to . . . be of . . ."

"Your service to me is gratifying," Queen Hortensia declares, then she raises her hand and snaps her fingers. "Magnolia. Pansy. I will want my grande toilette in the puce satin. At once."

The two maids curtsy, glad to have something to do and inwardly grateful to this change in mood.

"You will return here within the hour," Queen Hortensia goes on to Sigmund, "then you will accompany me to the Throne Room where I will solace Toby in his despair."

Sigmund bows again; his mind is already on three other things and unless Magnolia or Pansy go to find him, it is unlikely that he will remember to come to the Queen's apartments within the hour or at any other time.

"There, there," Queen Hortensia says to Sigmund, feeling very cordial now. "You may be at ease. Your faithfulness is valued here in Alabaster-on-Gelasta. We are aware of your gifts." Her manner is growing grander by the moment.

"Gifts?" Sigmund asks, startled out of his several reveries. "I didn't . . . think that . . . gifts . . . powder, yes, but . . . no gifts . . . did I?"

Queen Hortensia chortles indulgently. "So clever," she murmurs as Pansy comes and takes Sigmund by the elbow and leads him toward the door.

"Thank you," she whispers as she leaves him in the hall.

". . . You know . . ." Sigmund responds, blissfully unaware of why he is being thanked.

Yet Another Interlude

THE SHAPE WHICH had hovered near Sigmund's Wizard's Tower now flaps away from the dazzling white castle of King Rupert. It curvets on the breeze, sliding now to the north, now to the west, sometimes riding upward, sometimes hurtling down. Looking up, you might think it was a broken kite or an escaped and wayward bit of scarecrow that rides the air, going its vagabond way toward the Woebegone Wood.

Oodles of Adventure

ON THEIR FIRST night of travels, Prince Andre and Princess Felicia (with Leander) stay with Baron Varvel, who has been tathing his fields and thus is in an earthy and festive mood. The resultant feasting, partying and roistering leave his entire company worn and rather fragile the next morning so there are relatively few members of the Baron's household up to see Prince Andre and his pretty, petulant sister (and his crumpet-baker) on their way. This makes it possible for their departure to be fairly swift, with nothing more than a few exchanging of compliments and one or two valedictory speeches before the little hunting party is through the gates and on its way.

By nightfall, they reach the very borders of Alabaster-on-Gelasta, and realizing that hospitality might be a chancy matter once they leave the borders of their kingdom, Prince Andre and Princess Felicia determine to visit the Rapskalion Fort, which is perched on the cliff above the Gelasta. There is a ferry to take them over the river the next day, and as Prince Andre points out, it would be doing the Master of the Fort a favor to show him some distinction for all his years of service.

"Years," marvels Princess Felicia as if hearing of an especially cruel sentence.

"Royal Papa appointed him when you were still a toddler," Prince Andre adds. "Never had any trouble from him about anything."

"He probably withered away from boredom," sighs the Princess, and does not notice the adoring glance of Leander.

Her prediction proves false. "Goodness, gracious me!" cries out the Master of the Fort (King Rupert's great-grandfather did away with the Guard when he did away with the Army, and so Master of the Fort was all the title that remained for the position) as he comes out of the Great Hall to welcome his visitors. He is a small, squat man with a bald pate and merry, penetrating eyes. He bows and calls for his butler to present himself at once.

"We are on our way to the Woebegone Wood," Prince Andre explains to the Master of the Fort when that worthy asks to what he owes the honor of this unexpected arrival.

The Master of the Fort nods sagaciously. "It'd be that dragon, I suspect. As soon as I heard, I said to Horton there" —he cocks his head in the direction of the butler—"that we'd soon see activity. And here you are, as I thought you might be."

Prince Andre finds himself liking this portly, shrewd man. "It's a Prince's duty, after all."

"Very true, but you'd be astonished to learn of the number of Princes now-a-days who pay no attention to such things. Tournaments and festivals, that's all they hanker for. It's good to see that you recognize your obligations."

Since any response would lack humility or be mendacious, Prince Andre merely bows his head, which pleases the Master of the Fort even more.

"Well," he goes on, "I have to warn you that we haven't much fancy to offer you. We set a fair table, and there's more than enough food for months and months, but if you're hoping for more, I'm at a loss. We haven't any troubadours or jugglers or dancing bears for entertainment. I know a few songs and I play the crumhorn, and Horton can balance a dish on his nose, but that's about it."

"It's more than satisfactory," Prince Andre says, for like all Princes, he has been trained to have beautiful manners.

"You're a good lad," the Master of the Fort declares, leading Prince Andre and Princess Felicia into the Great Hall, with Leander following behind. "The grooms will take care of your horses and the mule, and you can have a tour of the Fort, if you want to inspect it. We'll sit down to supper in an hour or two if Horton can get the cooks to stop being flustered long enough to put something in the oven."

Princess Felicia makes a face, but Prince Andre accepts the offer with good grace. "I've never inspected a Fort before," he says truthfully.

The Master of the Fort bows slightly. "Not that there's much to inspect. Long ago there were fortified walls and guard towers, but they were dismantled to make homes for the peasants and to improve the ferrys across the river. About all we do now is examine cargos and keep a record of who has been here. However, Horton and I do what we can to keep the place running."

"You must certainly do an excellent job," Prince Andre remarks while Princess Felicia yawns.

Horton takes Leander to the kitchen to help out.

By the time they all retire to bed, Prince Andre and the Master of the Fort are on very good terms, and Princess Felicia is ready to shriek with ennui. In the kitchen, Leander is racking his brains to think of some particular treat to serve the Princess in the morning.

The Master of the Fort accompanies them to the riverbank and sees them off while giving the transport sum to the ferryman himself. "If you come back this way, we'll try for a little more festivities," he promises Prince Andre, then kisses Princess Felicia's hand. "I am enchanted."

"Yes," Princess Felicia agrees glumly as she steps onto the ferry and looks toward the opposite shore.

"A fine fellow," Prince Andre observes as they begin the crossing. His sister glares at him but says nothing.

Behind him, Leander struggles to keep from speaking; it is

not seemly for him, a mere crumpet-baker to address so illustrious a person as Princess Felicia. He contents himself with staring at her, filling his thoughts with the most delicious and impossible dreams.

This time, when night comes, they are far enough beyond the borders of Alabaster-on-Gelasta that Prince Andre decides it would be more prudent for them to pass the night at the best posting inn they can find. "For you can't be certain," he says in his most adult and regal voice, "that there aren't rascals around ready to do us harm."

"What could harm us?" Princess Felicia asks him with hauteur. "No one would dare to speak to us, let alone touch us." She waits for her brother to contradict her, which he obligingly does.

"If we stumble upon our enemies, then you may be certain that they will want to interfere with us in some way. That is what enemies are supposed to do. If we were simple folk, we'd be left alone, but since we're Royal, it changes everything." Prince Andre cannot conceal his satisfaction in this statement, and for a fleeting instant, he is truly his mother's son.

"Then we'll say we're simple folk. That would be different," Princess Felicia decides with what passes for enthusiasm in her dull, dull world.

"Oh," Leander interrupts, daring to raise his voice to his august companions, "Princess Felicia, no matter what precautions and preparations you made, no one could possibly believe that you are less than you are. Your beauty and your bearing reveal to the meanest intelligence that you are of elevated nature and rank. A streetsweeper need only glimpse the toe of your shoe to perceive your position and rank. There is nothing you might do, though you donned sackcloth, that can alter your innate nobility."

"Leander has a point," Prince Andre says, thinking that their crumpet-baker might have made it in far fewer words.

"But I've never been a peasant, and it is bound to be different from being a Princess," she protests, then sighs. "I didn't think to have Blanche pack anything peasanty."

"Do you *have* anything peasanty?" Prince Andre asks, startled at the notion.

"Well, I do have that charming shepherdess gown, with all the knots of ribbons and the little silk flowers, and the ruched lace all around the corsage. It's quite fetching in a simple way." She hesitates, then adds, "I even had a crook made for it, and tied it with wide ribbands of satin. Royal Mama disliked it, but Royal Papa said it was charming."

"I do not believe that shepherdesses often wear lace and silk flowers, Your Highness," Leander says in a self-deprecating tone. "I have never heard of any that did. It's because they take care of sheep, I suspect. I am told they nibble everything."

"Oh," Princess Felicia says. "It doesn't matter, since I didn't bring it with me. I should have."

"That doesn't bring us to a posting inn," Prince Andre reminds them with rare pragmatism. "The road here is in relatively good condition, and that should indicate that there will be an inn somewhere along it." He pats the snowy neck of his destrier, reflecting that only a really good posting inn would have grooms there who could take proper care of their mounts and their tack. "Keep a sharp lookout, you two."

"I will, Your Highness," Leander says, for once without embellishment.

Just as the sun is blazing down the sky, setting the world aglow with firelight colors, Leander spots a high-walled building, and points it out to the Prince and the Princess. "There is a sign hanging in front of it," he adds. "It shows a knight fighting a dragon."

"An excellent omen!" Prince Andre calls out. "What better indication."

"We have had nothing but good omens," Princess Felicia complains in a listless way. "It might be nice to have a bad omen, for variety."

"No one can want a bad omen," Prince Andre says, going on to say, "Every man setting out on a quest searches for omens, and trusts to their accuracy and fidelity."

"And Prince Andre," Leander joins in, "is of so sterling character and so firm purpose that it is not amazing that the omens are favorable to his project. Enterprise of this scope truly marks the Prince, for it shows him to be aware of the exalted demands of his station in life, and prepares him for the burdens and glory of Kingship, which it is his fate to assume. I am thankful indeed that your illustrious father was willing to permit me to be witness to this most wonderful venture, and to observe the superior wit and strength of this most upstanding young man."

By the time Leander has finished this outpouring, the little party has reached the gate of the inn. Prince Andre raps once on the stout wooden door, and is pleased when the landlord, a saturnine figure with an unctuous smile, appears and bows low to them.

"Welcome, travelers, to the Knight and Dragon. Who do I have the privilege to address, and what am I to be honored to do for them?"

Prince Andre introduces himself and his sister (and, as an afterthought, Leander), and explains that they require lodgings for the night, and a decent supper.

"At once!" the landlord avers, clapping loudly for grooms and ostlers to aid the travelers. "We so rarely see anyone from Alabaster-on-Gelasta." Although this is said with cordiality, it has a sinister ring to it.

"Merchants, surely," Prince Andre suggests.

"We have no merchants here," the landlord informs him with a sniff. "The lowest we permit here are those in the employ of courts. A herald or a page or perhaps a secretary might find lodging here, but never a merchant."

"I see," says Prince Andre, who does not.

"You must be dreadfully bored," sighs Princess Felicia. "Only nobility and royalty."

Thinking that this is a joke, the landlord makes a wheezing sound that is his version of laughter. "Very witty, Your Highness," he tells her, not quite winking.

Princess Felicia looks away, a long-suffering shine in her eyes.

"Where are you bound?" the landlord inquires as he bows them into his front parlor (after making sure that Leander has been started on his way to the kitchen). His smile is as smooth as an undertaker's.

"We're dragon hunting," Prince Andre informs him with justifiable pride. "We're off to the Woebegone Wood."

"Very commendable," says the landlord, signaling to two white-garbed waiters. "I will leave you to peruse the menu, and will return with the port and cheese at the end of your repast." He performs his most servile bow, then withdraws to a small room not far from the kitchen where he hisses into the shadows.

"Am I to leave?" a gravelly voice whispers back.

"It's Prince Andre and Princess Felicia, all right," the landlord says hurriedly in an undertone. "They're going to the

Woebegone Wood. Tell your master I expect my usual reward for this intelligence."

"Yes," mutters the Spy (for it is indeed the Spy, who has been following the little hunting party since they crossed the Gelasta), wondering what reward Humgudgeon would be willing to part with even for reliable intelligence.

"I will make sure they leave late in the morning, to give you a longer start for the capital," the landlord adds. "Their dinner will be lavish—I'll see to that, and I'll tell the cooks to substitute hemp for the parsley." He actually rubs his hands together in anticipation.

"Thanks," the Spy says, worried now about the frugal meal he has already consumed.

"Sleep well, Spy. I want you to be fresh in the morning." Without waiting for a reply, he slams the door.

Left in the dark, the Spy passes his hourlike minutes in endless fretting.

By the end of the meal, Princess Felicia has actually giggled and admitted that the cherries in dark rum sauce taste good. She leans back in her chair, the faintest of smiles on her perfect lips. "I never thought that you could be amusing," she confides to her brother.

"That's because you're such a sour-puss," Prince Andre answers with the teasing asperity he last used when both were a decade younger.

"I am not," she objects, ruining it with a low burst of laughter.

Behind them, there is a faint knock on the door, and a moment later, Leander slips into the room. "Oh, Your Highnesses, I hope that I am not too late to be of assistance to you."

Both Prince Andre and Princess Felicia stare at him, bewildered.

"What's the matter, Leander—crumpets not ready yet?" Prince Andre inquires archly. "You disappoint me, Leander."

Princess Felicia looks at him, gently critical. "Your hair has flour in it."

"I have been at my work. That is how I discovered the perfidy of the landlord and his unprincipled scheme to bring you into danger." He comes nearer the table and bows to the Prince and the Princess. "I am sincerely loathe to tell you that the landlord has shown himself deserving of odium."

"There aren't enough candles, that's true, but that's hardly reason to say he deserves odium," Prince Andre says lazily. "Sit down and have a glass of this excellent port, Leander."

Instead of taking Prince Andre up on this very generous invitation, Leander drops to his knee between the Prince and Princess's chairs. "I fear that I have failed you in your hour of need. I am aware that you are suffering—"

"No such thing," Prince Andre chuckles.

"—without knowledge. And it fills me with chagrin to know that had I been more forthcoming and vigilant, I might have prevented this terrible event." One of his well-shaped hands creates havoc amid his glistening red-gold curls. "Too late did I discover that the cooks were under instructions to prepare your evening meal in an unorthodox way, and to season the dishes with the leaves of a most venomous herb."

"Poison?" Prince Andre asks without a care in the world. "No one would dare to poison us."

"Not poison, as such, but pernicious, nevertheless. The cooks were ordered to put into your seasonings the leaves of the hemp plant, which causes lethargy and lassitude to claim those who eat it." He grabs the hem of Princess Felicia's pale mauve riding habit and kisses it with fervor. "That *you*, dearest Princess Felicia, should be exposed to the vile alchemy of this plant disgraces me more than anything I can possibly imagine. You, who are the most sensitive and elevated of women, ought never to be subjected to this unspeakable affront."

"Tell me, Leander," Prince Andre interrupts, tapping Leander on the shoulder. "Precisely what has happened and why are you upset?"

"I have explained already, but if you insist, I will make the effort to be more specific and concise. I deplore obfuscation." He rises and clears his throat, standing very much the way a misbehaving student might face an irritated professor. "The landlord here is practicing some form of duplicity, for he, beneath his facade of amicability, is preparing to send word of your sojourn to enemies of your father and his kingdom. To further the cause of this agent, the landlord has caused hemp leaves to be added to your food, thereby creating in you soporific good will that reduces your attentiveness as well as imbuing your emotions with a lack of discernment and clarity that can only serve to distort your experiences." He claps his hand to his chest, and a little puff of flour explodes under the impact. "If only I had discovered this treachery sooner, then you might have been spared the ordeal of consuming the leaves, but now that you have, I am determined to make up for your lack of keen observation by doubling, nay, trebling my own!"

"Do you always talk like that?" Princess Felicia asks.

Leander is taken aback. He opens his mouth, blushes furiously, then says, "I always strive to express myself succinctly and articulately, Your Highness. Have I said anything—*anything* at all—to displease you? I would rather wander the world in forgotten ignominy than to cause you one instant of discomfort."

"He *does* always talk like that," Princess Felicia informs her brother, needlessly, since Prince Andre has heard it all, too.

"What have I done to bring about this dissatisfaction in my words?" He looks from brother to sister and then back to brother again. "Has that vile herb insinuated itself into your thoughts so that every perception is distorted and inaccurate?" He snatches up one empty dish and lifts it as if to hurl it into the blazing fireplace. But this would be most improper conduct for a servant, and he recalls himself before he can do anything so inappropriate. He clears his throat. "I must beg the pardon of both Your Highnesses. I am behaving inexcusably."

"Are you?" Prince Andre asks, his tone almost as bemused as Sigmund's.

"I might have done willful damage to the property of the landlord," he admits.

"No harm in that," Prince Andre declares after considering for a moment. "Servants are always dropping things. Royal Mama says so." It is an indication of how far gone he is that he actually quotes Queen Hortensia.

"But the landlord might not like it, and it wouldn't be the least unusual," Princess Felicia says, still looking at Leander with a certain speculative glint in her eyes.

"I should have supervised the cooking," Leander goes on, castigating himself with a will. "I should have lived up to my responsibilities to Your Highnesses and Their Majesties. I should have realized that once beyond the borders of your happy kingdom, there were risks, some subtle, some more obvious. I have failed to defend you after giving your esteemed and Royal parent that I would."

"You had no reason to suspect anything," Prince Andre soothes him. "I didn't think anything would happen here. Not that I know exactly what *has* happened, but actually, I feel uncommonly pleasant." And in proof, he leans back in his chair and props his heels on the edge of the table.

"It is that herb," Leander insists with vehemence. "It is euphoric in its malignity." He watches, aghast, as the chair teeters, and then crashes over backward. "Your Highness!"

"Goodness, Andre!" says Princess Felicia, giggling.

Amid the wreckage of the chair, Prince Andre guffaws. "Royal Papa would never believe this!"

"Royal Papa might not notice," Princess Felicia observes, giggling still.

"Let me help you up, Your Highness," Leander offers, bowing over him with remarkable grace. "It is not seemly for one of your station and dignity to lie there."

"No one can see but you and my sister, so where's the harm?" Prince Andre asks, but being a well-mannered Prince, sits up, tailor-fashion and surveys the ruin of the chair. "Remind me to leave the landlord a little something extra for damages when we leave."

"Little though he deserves it," Leander says with great feeling. "To have subjected Your Highnesses to this humilia-tion—" He grinds his teeth and holds back the tidal wave of words that threatens to break forth. "I will sleep on a mat in front of your doors tonight, so that no further mishap can occur. That landlord should be whipped at the cart-tail for doing this dastardly thing."

Princess Felicia laughs deliciously, her voice low in her throat. She watches Leander with more attentiveness. "And then?"

Since neither Leander nor Prince Andre are privy to her thoughts, both are bewildered by what she has said. "What is it, Felicia?" Prince Andre asks with a great show of concern.

"Oh, nothing, nothing at all." She looks at the two of them and smirks.

"If you're up to your old tricks, Felicia, I warn you that I won't tolerate it," Prince Andre informs her with sudden imperious dignity.

"You're both so funny," she says, and quite suddenly gets

to her feet. "I'm sleepy," she announces to the air.

"Let me escort you to your chamber, dear Princess Felicia," Leander says at once, all but leaping to her side, his eyes luminous with adoration.

"I can find my way. It's where all bedchambers are, isn't it? Upstairs. There's nothing new in that." She wanders toward the door, then stops and looks back at her brother, who has got as far as his knees in the rubble of the chair. "We set out tomorrow morning?"

"At first light," Prince Andre says, although he sounds a bit dazed, as if the shock of falling over backward were only just now affecting him.

"Have someone wake me, will you? I never pay any attention to birds—all they ever do is sing and tweet. If they would roar or bray or roll like a drum I might notice them, but—" She shrugs and opens the door to find the landlord bent over with his face near the keyhole.

"You despicable cur!" Leander expostulates between clenched teeth (no mean trick, when you come to think about it). "Eavesdropping!"

The landlord gives an odious smile, his bow egregiously servile as he attempts to finesse himself out of his predicament. "Your Highnesses . . ." —he looks from Princess Felicia to Prince Andre, hoping for some sign of encouragement, though there apparently is none—"there is a terrible, a most unfortunate misunderstanding here . . . I realize how it *appears*. It *appears* that I was listening to your conversation, and spying on you. If it were true, well, it would be more than reprehensible of me, as your admirable servant implies. But there are other explanations, however unpalatable," he maintains, hoping to think of one while he waffles for time. "A man in my position cannot be too careful, Your Highness. An inn of this sort, catering only to the best travelers, must take measures to be certain that unworthy persons do not take advantages of my esteemed guests. It has happened before, I hate to admit. Do you understand what I am trying to say?" He hardly understands himself, but there is always the chance that they will give him the benefit of the doubt, or be so confused as not to question him.

"This sniveling cowardice is typical of obsequious rogues like you!" Leander bursts out, raising his hand as if to strike the landlord, the epitome of righteous indignation.

"Give him a moment, Leander," Prince Andre recommends. "Maybe he does have a legitimate reason to listen. This *is* his inn, isn't it?"

Princess Felicia folds her arms and theatrically conceals a yawn.

Recognizing a stay of execution when he sees one, the landlord plunges in at once to what is almost the truth. "I often, in my line of work, have to entertain guests who, though well-born, are not really the sort I would choose to stay here. It makes a man cautious, after a time. I . . . I also have a number of obligations to meet—there are those who are willing to destroy the inn and me with it if I don't do them an occasional favor—and a family to support. In these uncertain times . . . And then there are rulers who have shown me some favor, in their ways. For this, they expect . . . they are *entitled* to a few extra services. The Count of Murmoor is one of my occasional patrons . . . from Addlepate, you've heard of him, I suppose. He has a retinue that would better be kept in a kennel than an inn, but while the Count is here, they behave as well as they are able because the Count insists on it, and he's the most unpleasant one of them all. So from time to time, as insurance, you might say, I do what I can to . . . help him out, and then, when he stays here, the inn and my staff are left in relative peace." He wrings his hands, but whether from genuine distress or mere effect, even he does not know.

"You say that the Count of Murmoor stays here from time to time?" Prince Andre asks, choosing that information to pursue.

"Once, perhaps twice in a year. He is mad for hunting." The landlord reflects sourly that the Count of Murmoor is mad for everything.

"And what do you do for him?" Prince Andre goes on. He may be smiling like a blissful idiot, but he has not forgot everything he learned.

"Oh," the landlord begins, and sees that Leander is still prepared to cosh him if he does not cooperate. "He wants to know who stays here, and what they are doing. He doesn't often do much about it, but he wants to know. He's very jittery about strangers."

Princess Felicia casts a very bored glance at her brother. "Do you mind if I get some rest, Andre? This is nothing more than court intrigue." She does not wait for his permission, but goes to the door, her light, floating walk a joy to behold.

"Princess Felicia," Leander dares to say to her, "you show your superiority in this pose of unconcern while you are exposed to danger, and I admire your fortitude more than words can express. Be assured that I will guard you through the night; in a small way, that will be in compensation for permitting you to be victim of this poltroon's culinary duplicity."

Coming from anyone else but Leander, Princess Felicia would find such sentiments overblown and cloyingly tedious. But spoken with sincerity by a clearly besotted young man who is as beautiful as Adonis, the words take on a vitality and sparkle that piques her interest. "How very kind of you, Leander," she says, and is rewarded with a look of hopeless-but-incendiary passion.

"Fine, fine, get a good sleep," Prince Andre tells her with what seems to Leander to be a total lack of respect and concern. "I'll talk to you in the morning. I'm sorry now we didn't decide to bring a carriage, but it seems so useless to take one hunting dragons. If we had a carriage, we could travel and sleep at the same time."

The landlord nods, not to agree but to attempt to convince Prince Andre that he is on the Prince's side. "You're a very young man, Your Highness," he says, as if this accounted for everything.

"Not so young," Prince Andre counters. "Still, there are things that are a comfort on journeys, and I can't deny that a carriage would be one of them."

"I might be able to provide one," the landlord suggests, thinking of the price such a vehicle would fetch.

"No, no; good of you to offer, but we'll continue as we began." He has finally got to his feet, and as he continues to talk, he kicks bits of the broken chair into the fireplace. "Why would Murmoor want to know what I'm doing? What would it matter to him?"

"That's not for me to say, Your Highness." The landlord is beginning to hope that with luck, Humgudgeon might be left out of it entirely, and the Spy need never be mentioned.

"You might guess. I don't want to find myself held for ransom. My Royal Mother would never let me hear the end of it." He shakes his head thoughtfully. "Who did you send to Murmoor? Does he keep a man here all the time?"

"Your Highness forgets that I was apprehended before I could act," the landlord says, making a serious mistake.

"If that is the case," Leander says in dreadful accents, "then who was the man you sent on his way shortly after Their Highnesses arrived? There was a sinister person lurking here; you spoke with him and sent him on his way. Who was that person and what nefarious purpose did he have?"

The landlord is not sure what *nefarious* means, but he knows that it doesn't matter. "He is one of Humgudgeon's spies." The name of the Protector Extraordinary sticks in his throat like a bit of eggshell. "The place crawls with them when Humgudgeon's displeased."

"Humgudgeon," Prince Andre muses. "What might my dragon hunt mean to him? He's not likely to want to hunt it himself, is he?"

Under other circumstances, the landlord might laugh at such a notion, but he cannot bring himself to do it now. "He likes to hunt other things, Humgudgeon does," the landlord remarks, implying many nasty possibilities.

"I see," Prince Andre says. "Then we'd better be careful, Leander." He winks at his crumpet-baker. "Never know what he might decide to do to us."

"It is like Your Highness to make a jest of peril," Leander says heavily. "Would that I possessed your insouciance, but apprehension deprives me of any capacity for levity."

"Too bad," Prince Andre tells him before looking once more at the landlord. "So you told Humgudgeon's spy that we're here. What good does that do Humgudgeon?"

"Nothing does him *good* at all. His Maleficence isn't interested in doing himself or anyone else good." The landlord sniffs as much from snobbery as from self-pity.

Prince Andre paces around the room, feeling very pleased with himself. "And so we are warned, but neither the Spy nor Humgudgeon knows it. That could be to our advantage, I'd think."

With a marvelous and unusual brevity, Leander confines himself to a one-word response: "How?"

"I don't know yet," Prince Andre admits with a stunning lack of worry. "I'll find out in due time." He pauses, staring at the fire. "I had hoped that there might be bandits on the road. I wanted to get some practice fighting before I hunted the dragon, but it hasn't happened, has it? And we'll reach the

Woebegone Wood by tomorrow, or so I'm told." He points the landlord out the door.

"How could Your Highness say such a thing, when you have your sister in your company? So fine a Princess must be protected and shielded from all the buffets and blasts of misfortune." Leander stands so very straight that it is strange that he can remain upright at all.

"She might think a little misfortune is interesting. Goodness knows that everything else so far has bored her." Prince Andre is not able to sustain this (or any other) thought for very long. He yawns as thoroughly as a cat. "I think I'd better get some sleep. Dinner is catching up with me." He ambles toward the door.

"I will bring a pallet and sleep before Your Highnesses' doors. Rest assured that you will be protected. More shame to me that any mishap has befallen you." He starts after Prince Andre, then looks at the remnants of the chair. "The landlord will want this replaced."

"We'll give him the money," Prince Andre says loudly, confident that the landlord has gone no farther than the hall. "In the morning before we leave."

"He is a wretch!" Leander says with great feeling.

"If you had the Count of Murmoor staying at your establishment, you'd be a wretch, too," Prince Andre says, refusing to go along with Leander's denouncement. "Men of Murmoor's cut are more trouble than they're worth." In the doorway, he waves to an unseen person. "I thought you'd still be here," Prince Andre calls out, addressing the landlord. "Add that chair to the bill in the morning."

The landlord bows double, looking a little like a clothes hanger. "Your Highness is too kind."

Prince Andre beams at him and saunters toward the stairs, very well pleased with himself, and for the moment not caring why.

A Digression

WHILE PRINCE ANDRE tugs off his boots and falls, still half-dressed into bed, and Princess Felicia dawdles over her bath in the deep tub of rose-scented water, the Spy is hurrying through the night, exhausted, uncomfortable, terrified and determined. If anyone told him that Prince Andre at this instant believes that the Spy is having more adventures than he himself, the Spy would assume that the Prince and anyone telling him are crazy. To keep himself moving, he sings an anxious little song:

> *"I am really in a pickle,*
> *In a pickle, in a pickle;*
> *My one last furtive trickle*
> *Of hope has faded now.*
> *If I don't do something quick I'll*
> *Be completely in a pickle:*
> *I'd make my fate less fickle*
> *But I've no idea how.*
> *I am truly in a pickle*
> *In a pickle, in a pickle*
> *And I wouldn't give a nickle*
> *For my chances by tonight*
> *Perhaps an unexpected trick'll*
> *Change my unrelenting pickle*
> *To a chuckle and a tickle*
> *If I just can do it right."*

With any luck, the Spy reckons that the exigencies of the rhyme scheme will keep his mind off his more pressing problems for a while.

In the Woebegone Wood...

ALFREIDA BROOMTAIL IS very pleased with herself. Her initial disappointment at Esmeralda's unpromising size as a dragon has been eclipsed by the news that no less a person than Prince Andre himself is coming to hunt the dragon. That information has had her prancing for joy for the last day and a half, and now she stands near the entrance to her hut, regarding Esmeralda, who is chained to an enormous, drooping tree not far away.

"Liripoop informs me that that insufferable Prince will be here by tomorrow night. Just imagine that, you scaly ninny!" Her laughter has become more cackle-like recently, and she has taken to doing a hopping dance step when she thinks about what is going to happen to the Prince. "They thought that I wasn't accomplished enough to be given a position at some court or other. Well! I'll show some very stupid heads that there's more skill and talent here than a dozen sorcerers and conjurers rolled up and packaged." (cackle, cackle.)

Esmeralda can no longer speak, but she has still retained her sweetness of expression that occasionally drives Alfreida to distraction. Now she gives the witch a long, reproachful stare, her heart-shaped horns glistening like a dented halo over her long, green snout.

"And you can stop looking like that, you great green doddard. You're just as sappy a dragon as you were a person—yech!" She stamps her feet, and little, mote-sized monsters are spawned by the action. Alfreida ignores them, hands on her hips. "See that you give them a proper scare when they arrive to hunt you"—Esmeralda draws up her delicate scaled forefeet in dismay—"or you'll have more to worry about than an energetic Prince with a spear or two."

Esmeralda lowers her adorably hideous head, and a puff of smoke issues from her mouth, which always happens now when she sighs. Miserable, squamous, mute, Esmeralda still would inspire pity in all but the most hardened hearts. She rocks back, balancing herself on her tail, her chain clinking with every movement.

"What a ridiculous creature you are," Alfreida rails at her. "Some people don't know when to take a transformation seriously." With that she turns away smartly, going back into her hut and slamming the door behind her.

Left to herself in the afternoon gloom, Esmeralda would like to give vent to tears, but they do not come easily anymore, and when they do, it leaves her with a headache because of the fire at the back of her sinuses. Instead, she makes a low sort of crooning whimper, which is as close as she can come to speech. She has been telling herself for several days that this is bearable, but has had more difficulty than usual convincing herself of it. She is in the middle of trying to persuade herself that Prince Andre would not really want to hurt her when she sees a movement by her feet and shuffles back.

Liripoop stands there, looking up at her with mad orange eyes. He has been missing for a few days (Alfreida insists that it was because he is jealous of the dragon) and has returned only this morning. He parades back and forth in front of Esmeralda, his tail held aloft in an enormous plume. He is purring loudly and his whiskers are fanned out impressively.

For some reason she cannot explain, Esmeralda is pleased to see the cat. She decides that it's loneliness, for most of the time she has assumed that the cat dislikes her intently. She tries to bend down, to get a closer look at the visitor, but has not yet got the knack of bending forward with all those scales. With a squack of dismay, Esmeralda falls to her side and lies, thrashing helplessly.

Liripoop comes up to her, rubbing his head against her chin, an expression of utmost bliss on his broad feline face.

Very carefully, so as not to scare or startle him, Esmeralda brings up one taloned foreclaw and ever-so-gently begins to scratch him behind the ears.

At the Dragon Hunt

OVER THE TOPS of the trees that hunker in the Woebegone Wood, the sun rides high and shining. Under the trees, the light is anemic and mottled, as if falling through the murk has contaminated it. Ever since Prince Andre and the hunting party entered the Wood, there has been a disturbing silence among them, possibly resulting from a reluctance to make their presence known.

That is not to say that Prince Andre does not continue to ride as splendidly as ever, or that any aspect of his outward demeanor has changed; if anything, he sits straighter in the saddle and keeps his destrier moving at a smart trot, forcing Princess Felicia and Leander to keep up and not ask questions (which he is not able to answer). He has one hand braced against his hip, the other holding the reins with negligent ease, as if he were out for nothing more than a jaunt around the palace grounds. But his destrier's ears are at an unhappy angle, and he minces along as if unsure of his footing, a certain indication that everything is not so perfectly under control as it might appear.

At last there is a widening in the rutted and overgrown road, and Prince Andre reins in and turns to the two behind him. "There; you see? I told you this morning that we'd find a clearing where we can have a camp. This is just what we want. Leander, Felicia, we will camp here, close to the road so that no matter how far afield we chase the dragon, we'll be able to find our way out of the Wood easily." He swings out of the saddle, his movements showing that he is a bit stiff from so much time in the saddle at a trot. "Isn't this pleasant? The trees all around us, casting deep shadows..." (Well, perhaps the shadows aren't pleasant, but they cannot be ignored and

Prince Andre is determined to make the best of circumstances.) "There's a brook nearby, I think. Don't you hear running water?"

Leander dismounts as well. "I believe that there is a river not very distant. I hear the sound, too." By appearances, he is not nearly as stiff as Prince Andre, which is hardly fair, since Leander has been riding a mule of cantankerous temperament.

"But this is exactly like the rest of the Wood," Princess Felicia protests. "It's all nothing but trees."

"That is what Woods are made of, Your Highness," Leander tells her, hoping to console her.

"I know." She sighs, not yet dismounting. "And it's all so boring. Why can't Woods be made of feathers. Or ribbons? Or cake." She gives Leander a long stare. "I require a hand down, Leander," she reminds him, thinking it vastly annoying that she has had to mention something so obvious to him.

At once Leander abandons the mule and hastens to her horse, securing the reins, and then offering her his assistance in getting out of the saddle. "It is a treasured privilege to be able to perform this task for Your Highness."

Princess Felicia nods to him as she goes on, "Woods need not be made of trees, need they? It is unimaginative to limit them to trees. All these trees are very tedious."

Prince Andre is determined not to have his enjoyment dashed by his sister. "Felicia, you knew what it would be like when you asked to come with me. You can't claim to be surprised now."

"No, I can't," she agrees dolefully. "And that's the trouble, don't you see? I *always* know what things will be like. Woods will be made of trees; meadows will be green with grass; snow will turn the world white in the winter; rain will get things wet. Things are so dull."

"But," Leander says, offering Princess Felicia a touch of excitement, "it may be that this calm meadow, so still and grassy, might conceal unrealized dangers, or its very tranquility might lull us into a state of inattention that might bring about terrible risks."

"What sort of risks?" Princess Felicia asks him, regarding him with an attitude approaching interest.

"They're still unknown, Your Highness," Leander says with deference. "That is the danger; that we cannot anticipate what they may be."

"Oh," she says, resigned to disappointment.

Prince Andre is striding around the clearing, inspecting it. "Leander, you set up the camp for us, there's a good fellow. I want to get the lay of the land and see if I can discover something about this dragon."

"Do not, I pray you, put yourself into danger," Leander cautions him.

"But that's what I'm here to do," Prince Andre reminds him in his most reasonable manner. "It is only right that I face some danger while hunting a dragon. That's the whole point." He tries to keep his tone confident and lighthearted, but there is something daunting about the idea of being in danger now that he is actually in the Woebegone Wood and the inadequate light is already beginning to fade for the day.

"One more thing, Your Highness," Leander says to Prince Andre. "What is to become of the Princess Felicia? Surely you do not intend that she should remain here, unprotected? A delicate and cherished Princess cannot be treated as if she were a sergeant of infantry. It is not appropriate to regard her in this cavalier way, for it would mean that she might have to endure ordeals that her refined nature could not sustain." He is holding a sack of provisions, and his attitude is so sincere that in anyone else less noble of attitude and bearing, he might appear silly. Leander is so earnest and so ridiculously handsome that his overblown sentiments seem quite reasonable.

"Felicia's a sensible girl," says Prince Andre in a manner that Leander finds callous. "And you're here, aren't you? You'll look after her."

Leander reaches down for the most imposing utensil in his supplies, and hoists his long-handled skillet (which he uses when he makes crumpets) as if it were a pike or spear. "That's true, and it honors me to think that Your Highness would entrust the care of Her Highness to me. I hope that I may be worthy of the confidence you repose in me."

Princess Felicia gives Leander a long, speculative look. "Leander," she says, as if the word were in some foreign and romantic language. There is something interesting, almost (dare I say it?) exciting about someone preparing to defend another from unknown dangers.

"Rest assured," Leander says to Princess Felicia, "that until the last breath has left my body, I will defend you, dear Princess Felicia. If you believe this declaration to be unseemly, the vow of one forgetful of his station in life, I beseech you to consider the circumstances and recall that were we not here, in the mouth of who-knows-what hideous fate, I would never speak so to you, for I am well aware that you are high above me. Yet I trust that you will not be appalled at what I say to you in this place. You are the treasure of all Alabaster-on-Gelasta, and no one can meet you without succumbing to the charm of your grace and your character."

Prince Andre has not been listening to this effusion, and now he breaks the mood by remarking, "If I am going to be able to start hunting, it would be best if you'd unpack my gear. I want to be ready at first light. A meal, a hot cup of tea, and then it will be time for bed. Before a hunt, it's wisest to get plenty of rest, so that you're ready to face the chase and the beast in the morning." He keeps a strong tone in his words, but little as he likes to admit it, even to himself, his nerve is not quite what it was.

"But it's still light," Princess Felicia protests.

"Well, you're always saying that things ought to be different; then going to sleep while it's still light is a good idea, isn't it? Because it's different. Besides," he goes on more reasonably, "by the time Leander has set up the camp and made a meal, it probably won't be light anymore, and you won't mind getting ready to sleep." He glances toward Leander, hoping that the crumpet baker will add his support to the argument.

For once Leander has almost nothing to say, although he does sigh deeply as he tethers his mule. "I will start with Her Highness's pavilion, so that she may retire from this dismal place, if she wishes. The pavilion is much more attractive than this clearing, if I do not offend Your Highness in taking the liberty of mentioning it."

"Mention it all you like," Prince Andre offers, glad that Leander has not said anything in direct opposition to him. "You're probably right. What do you plan to give us this evening? I warn you, Leander, that I have a hearty appetite with this adventure facing me."

Leander is busy with the bundle of cloth and sticks that, when assembled, make the Princess's pavilion. He pauses to say, in a most respectful tone, "There is little here to aid me, and so I have determined to keep the fare light. I have a soup of turtle and puréed spring peas to begin, then smoked fowl stuffed with currants and raisins, a round of cheese, the fresh herbs I have gathered along the way—although none of them, I feel I must add, have come from this sinister Wood—for seasonings and salad. For dessert, there are candied oranges, and, of course, crumpets." He makes a gesture to show how inadequate he feels this to be, but how helpless he is to change it. "Simple fare, Your Highness."

"Excellent!" Prince Andre enthuses. "Just what's needed when hunting dragons!" He rubs his hands together, determined to keep up morale. "You see there, Felicia, we're to have a simple meal in a forest glade. That isn't your everyday occurrence, is it?"

"No," she admits, looking at Leander and then turning away.

"And tomorrow morning, bright and early, after the dragon I go. Leander, make sure that Hyperion here gets an extra measure of grain." He pats his destrier affectionately, and the horse arches his snowy neck, preening. "He's a fine mount for any man."

"A superb animal," Leander agrees, but convinced that the white horse is better for show than work. "I will see that he is brushed before you ride tomorrow." That, he reflects, is one of the problems of light-colored horses—they are forever in need of cleaning.

"Tell me, Leander," Prince Andre goes on, becoming more voluble, "have you seen any signs of a dragon? Did you notice singed branches or overturned trees as we entered the Wood? Were you aware of any trace of sulphur on the air? Were there clawed footprints in the road?"

"I brought up the rear," Leander reminds him, "and I was not in a position to notice." He has got the pavilion out of its wrapping and is now trying to sort out all the bits and pieces. He has tried to find the least unpleasant patch of grass on which to pitch the Princess's pavilion. This is a frustrating choice, since the entire meadow seems vastly unpleasant to him.

"True, but something might have caught your eye." He takes another turn around the clearing, then decides to address his sister again. "Are you enjoying your adventure so far?"

"I haven't had one yet," she says listlessly. "I have been uncomfortable and I have met some peculiar people I might not otherwise have known, but that is hardly an adventure.

Still, it is less dull than staying at home at the palace, where there's nothing but amusements and Royal Mama fussing, so that makes it more interesting, I suppose." She has found one of three boulders poking up out of the ground, and has seated herself on it, the very picture of beauty in distress. She forgot to bring her lute and the last thing in the world she wants to do is sketch anything, and so she is left to commune with her own thoughts.

"Doesn't that strike you as promising?" Prince Andre asks, puzzled by her (as he has been for the last seven or eight years).

"Nothing strikes me as promising. Promises are as dull as everything else. They have no surprises." She looks around to see that her pavilion is now half up and that Leander is placing a lightly faded white rose over the awning at the front. "It's sweet of him, of course, but so predictable."

"You mean the pavilion?" Prince Andre asks, more perplexed than ever.

"No, silly; the rose." She stares off into the Wood. "Do you suppose that anything hideous is lurking out there? Do you think that there are monsters and other unbearable creatures in the Wood?" Her lips part with anticipation.

"There's a dragon," Prince Andre tells her.

"Yes, but mightn't there be other beasts?" Her eyes glint with hope.

"I . . . imagine there are," Prince Andre says, faltering. It is one thing to hunt something as well-known as a dragon, and quite another thing to be pursuing who-knows-what in a tangled and unfamiliar Wood.

"It would be too much to hope for, wouldn't it?—to see one of them." She notices that her pavilion is standing ready for her. "I think I'll lie down for a little while. When supper is ready, I'll be out." She has a light, floating way of walking, and she trips to her pavilion as if she were crossing a dance floor. As she reaches the doorway of the pavilion, she turns and very nearly smiles at Leander.

The effect of this smile is that Leander spends the next three or four hours in a magical haze, less than half his attention on his work, or his location, or his sworn responsibilities. In his mind he sees himself proving himself worthy of Princess Felicia, accepted by King Rupert as a worthy suitor (his imagination falls short of convincing himself that Queen Hortensia might approve of him), and beloved by Princess Felicia herself. As a result, he puts both coriander and dill in the crumpet batter, but that, he decides, won't be noticed.

Their meal is strangely silent, for now that most of the light has faded, and the flickering of the campfire dispels little of the engulfing dark, conversation seems a chancy thing. No matter what any of them have said before, each is glad to retire to their pavilions (Leander's pavilion is little more than an oversized pup tent) and hope ardently that sleep is not far off, since the cracklings and sounds in the Wood grow louder as the night deepens.

Once the darkness has taken hold, the Trolls (last heard from outside Alfreida Broomtail's hut back in the first chapter) come out to frolick, and, as you might expect from their earlier antics, they do it in song.

"Long leggity beasties are hopping about
And the Wood is a-thrumming with trouble:
You can tell from the ogre's most terrible shout
And the clatter of tum-bl-ing rubble!
Foul monsters are creeping and seeping around
In a slime that's sublime when it's goosh on the ground
With a sob that's a blob of a hideous sound
Like the laugh of an idiot child.

"Soft slithering squeamies all flop through the night
Leaving tracks that are dripping with ichor
That glow full of poison, a wonderful sight
Which we Trolls gather up for our liquor.
And the night is alight with an odious green
Of the kind that you find in a swamp that is seen
Through the murk, and there lurk many monsters so mean
That they better had never be riled.

"Incredible horrors all chortle aloud
Like a chorus that's fresh out of Hades
And the music's enough to make every Troll proud
(Save occasional doubts for the ladies).
Though the place where they race is as grimy as ink
And their cry like a guy who's had poison to drink
Still they swear that their lair is a comfortable sink
That we're never allowed to revile.

"So happily slobber and lollop along
And join in the chorus to jibber.
In the dankest of nights we will burst into song
If you like it, we'll call you a fibber.
And in anguish we'll languish awash on the road
In a way to dismay every frog and each toad.
Then we've raved all depraved when the night never showed
To the world that we're wholly defiled!"

By morning, Prince Andre, Princess Felicia and Leander are all convinced that they never want to hear another minuet in all the rest of their lives.

"I'll need my lance and my spear and my bow, with at least two dozen arrows," Prince Andre tells Leander as the crumpet-baker saddles and bridles Hyperion. "I think that I'd better be prepared for the worst."

"Most perspicacious, Your Highness," Leander declares as he tightens the girth a second time.

"And something to eat, since it may be hours before I return to camp. I rely on you to look after my sister. She's filled with the dismals again this morning. Don't bother yourself guessing why—none of us ever knows what sets her off. Felicia is one of those sorts of girls, or so Royal Mama says."

"I would never claim to have greater knowledge than any member of your esteemed family, Your Highness, however, it appears to me that as fine and sensitive a girl as the Princess is, she is worthy and requiring of the utmost support and tender care. To relegate her sensitivities to caprice—and it appears that you do so, although I trust I misjudge you—is a disservice to her and to all of you in your family, who are known for their acuteness of feeling."

Princess Felicia, who has overheard every syllable of Leander's outburst, smiles to herself.

"You didn't grow up with her, Leander; I did. She's a beautiful girl and she is as well-bred as anyone you might hope to meet, but it doesn't change the fact that she goes into these *states*. She says she's bored, but I ask you: how can that be possible?"

"I don't wish to dispute the matter," Leander says stiffly and mendaciously.

"No time for it, even if you did." Prince Andre slings his bow over his shoulder, takes one last look around the camp, and addresses Leander once more. "Give me a foot up, will you?" He does not wait for an answer, but raises his booted leg, trusting Leander's linked hands to be there to boost him upward.

"A safe hunt, Your Highness," Leander says as he steps back from Hyperion, who is snorting with excitement.

"Thank you," the Prince answers quietly as he turns his mount toward the imposing shadows of the Woebegone Wood.

Princess Felicia pokes her head out of her pavilion and waves a fine embroidered handkerchief after her brother, as if shooing away mosquitos.

Catching sight of her, Leander clasps his hands together and tries to find the nerve to speak to her. "Good morning, Your Highness," he is able to say.

"Good morning, Leander," is Princess Felicia's friendly answer.

It might not be the most promising beginning, but both Princess Felicia and Leander are not displeased.

Prince Andre lets his white destrier canter where the ground appears to be even. He is a fine figure, riding well and dressed so appropriately by his standards that he looks quite out of place in the Woebegone Wood. He makes little attempt to be cautious or quiet in his advance, believing that it is correct to give the dragon full warning of his coming.

Alfreida watches him from her vantage place in the deepest shadows, shaking her head in disgust. "Some people," she mutters, "don't know when to be quiet."

Behind her, Esmeralda shrinks and wishes she could make herself even smaller than she is.

"He might as well send in a herd of cattle, for all the stealth he's showing," Alfreida goes on with her complaints. "He's blundering about, disturbing everything in the Wood. We'll be hearing about this for a long time to come, you mark my word." She cackles suddenly, as if delighted with the notion. "Everyone will remember that it was *my* magic that brought this noisy Prince into the Wood, that *I* was the one who caused all the fuss. Not that I'm boasting, mind you. There are some people who would take advantage and set themselves up as special, but I have more humility than that."

Esmeralda gives a squeak that Alfreida decides to take as a favorable comment. "You've been my servant long enough to appreciate me, and you might try to flatter me because you know how powerful I am. But—" She breaks off as Prince Andre turns toward the place where they are hiding.

"Get back, you great hulking boy!" Alfreida hisses. "I'm not ready to see you yet!"

This is almost more than Esmeralda can stand. She puts her long, pointed snout between her front claws and shivers, little gusts of smoke coming from her nostrils.

Alfreida slaps her. "None of that! I won't have you snivling! You're the one who's supposed to be ferocious, not that overgrown child on the white horse." She folds her scrawny arms over her scrawnier chest. "You're a disappointment! Some people can't do anything the way they ought to!"

Since she cannot answer, Esmeralda only shivers, which pleases Alfreida.

"You little useless wimp!" Alfreida castigates her with rare glee. "You think that you can escape me by degrading my spells, don't you? You assume that you are excused from doing your work for me. Well, that's not the way of it, my little ninny. You'll do as you're told or you'll get turned into a soft-shelled crab in the middle of a group of turtles. Then you'll know you ought to respect me. How can you think you're permitted to behave in this irresponsible way? You're worse than a fool!" Venting her spleen has always been one of Alfreida's favorite diversions. "You get ready, and I'll tell you when to start."

Esmeralda comes as close to swooning as a dragon can.

"Get ready, you horrid creature. I want you to frighten him out of the few wits he has. As soon as he's close enough, I want you to roar and blow flames at him—lots of flames, do you hear? What an ungainly dragon you are, to tell the truth." She braces her hands on her hips and rocks back on her heels. Since she is wearing an ancient and evil-smelling pair of dancing pumps, this is a hazardous maneuver, and she almost loses her balance. "You're going to surprise him, do you understand that?"

"Ho! Dragon!" Prince Andre calls out, hoping that his bravado will keep up his faltering courage. It really is a very dark Wood.

"You're enough to infuriate a bladder-bat, and that's the truth of it!" Alfreida rails. "Why aren't you doing your breathing exercises so you can flame at him."

"Dragon!" Prince Andre shouts, more firmly. "I have come

to do combat. I will fight you, dragon!"

"Listen to him!" Alfreida gasps, cackling once again, her confidence at its height. "Listen to that fool!"

To Esmeralda, Prince Andre does not seem the least bit foolish—rather, he is frightening and gargantuan, an image, if not out of a nightmare, at least one out of a dream. She whimpers again, wishing now that she had not been quite so cooperative with Alfreida when the witch ordered her into the pentagram.

"Beware, dragon!" Prince Andre yells, drawing his sword and swinging it with a satisfying swoosh through the air. "I will triumph over you, dragon, as any Prince worth his salt should! Prepare to do battle! No quarter asked or given, dragon!"

Worse and worse, thinks Esmeralda as she is consumed by misery. Either Alfreida will turn her into something more ghastly than she already is, or the Prince will find her and lop off her head for a trophy. With a squeal of dismay, she bolts from the thicket where Alfreida has been hiding, and makes for the Wailing Gorge as fast as her scaled bandy legs can carry her.

An undersized dragon hasn't a hope in the world of escaping a highbred destrier, and Hyperion, responding to the clap of his master's spurs, is off after her with an alacrity that pleases Prince Andre and makes Esmeralda even more miserable than she already is.

"You!" shrieks Alfreida, watching the dragon scuttle away, "show some spunk! Flame at him!"

Esmeralda is searching desperately for a place to hide. Anything with thorns (which glance off her scales but rip at Hyperion) or tangles is her haven, and she bolts from bush to shrub to berry patch to brambles as quickly as she can.

"Ho! Dragon! I see you!" Prince Andre shouts energetically, shifting his weight in the saddle so that Hyperion can stretch even farther with each galloping stride.

Alfreida bustles after Esmeralda, as well, screeching at her. "You dimwit! *You're* the dragon! *He's* the Prince! I'll turn you into a tadpole if you don't fight! I'll give you to that lout Humgudgeon!" Her laces, always in tatters, are getting more abuse than usual during her pursuit of the dragon (and, by association, the Prince), and in no time at all, she is more disheveled than the most pathetic rag picker.

"Dragon!" Prince Andre calls as he circles a particularly large patch of hawthorn. "Where are you?" He is on the far side of the patch when he sees Esmeralda scoot out of the hawthorn, heading for a stand of nettles. "Dragon!" His sword slices the air as he takes off in chase.

"Get back there and flame at him, you prissy thing!" Alfreida rails, waving her arms in the air. (Above her, three unsuspecting horned owls sprout pigs' snouts and an extra pair of wings, like the wings of huge tropical beetles.) "Get in there and fight! Some people forget what can happen when they defy their betters."

Although all three participants in the hunt are unaware of it, they have been making a huge loop and are now coming up on Prince Andre's camp from the opposite direction to the one he took when he left.

Hearing the approaching commotion, Leander looks about for the means to defend his adored Princess Felicia from whatever danger might be coming.

"Is it the dragon?" Princess Felicia asks as she comes out of her pavilion, breathtaking in a riding habit of the rosiest peach color.

As if in response, Esmeralda's long scaled head pops out of a thornbush.

"It *is* a dragon," Princess Felicia says with satisfaction. "It looks just as I thought it would. My goodness, how boring."

"Come back, coward!" Prince Andre bellows, now losing all patience with the dragon. This is not going the way he had assumed it would.

In a flurry of twigs and leaves, Esmeralda bursts from cover and dives into a clump of poison sumac.

Leander comes to stand at Princess Felicia's side. "Do not let the terrible sight frighten you, dear Princess. Repose your trust in me, for I am sworn to protect you with my life."

"I have you, dragon," Prince Andre shouts as he guides Hyperion round and round the poison sumac. "You can't get out without getting caught. I will catch you, dragon."

Esmeralda is panting, so that little spurts of flame singe the poison sumac; the vegetation starts to smolder. She is almost in flat despair, for there seems to be no place she can hide now where the Prince will not find her, and then . . . She sighs deeply and half the poison sumac leaps into flame.

"That bush will burn down around you, dragon, and I'll

have you." Prince Andre can be excused for the bit of gloating he is doing, since he hardly expected to succeed so easily.

Alfreida, who has finally almost caught up with Prince Andre, takes a stance and begins to make powerful and mystical passes through the air, her spell coming out in gasps and starts as she tries to catch her breath.

Taking advantage of the conflagration, Prince Andre moves around the poison sumac to the one way the dragon can escape. He is eager to see the dragon up close, and to be able to show his valor in the capture. It is hardly properly modest for a Prince to admit it, but Prince Andre is delighted that Princess Felicia and Leander are going to be able to see his triumph.

"Some people are being complete dunderheads!" Alfreida cackles, prepared to do something positively reprehensible to the dragon. She draws back her hands, elbows up, a naughty glint in her small, sunken eyes.

This is too much for Esmeralda, who leaps out of the burning clump of poison sumac, dashing toward the safety of the camp, her head down, her tail dragging behind her with fatigue. With every exhausted step, she imagines she can feel the cut of Prince Andre's sword.

Horrified at the sight of the monster charging the camp, Leander takes up his skillet, holding it at the ready, prepared to bash the dragon with all his might in order to protect Princess Felicia. He is certain that the dragon intends to ravage the Princess, and is equally convinced that he is going to die defending her.

Prince Andre is right on the dragon's heels. He spurs Hyperion on, his sword in one hand, the reins in the other.

"Prepare to be transmogrified!" Alfreida announces, paying little attention to anything but the fleeing dragon.

As Esmeralda flees through the camp, Leander blocks her way, his skillet already descending as he cries, "Save the Princess!"

Metal clangs on metal as Prince Andre's sword deflects the murdurous skillet. "Spare the dragon!" he shouts.

Too worn out to move, Esmeralda sinks to the ground, her long neck stretched out straight, her legs splayed out to the side.

This sudden change causes Alfreida's spell to go awry. Beyond the edge of the camp, a tree convulses and ties its trunk into a knot, shedding leaves and limbs in the process. Alfreida stamps her foot with annoyance. "Not *you*" she tells the tree with contempt. "Some *people!*"

"Look there!" Princess Felicia tells Prince Andre and Leander. The two young men are staring at each other, both baffled.

"What do you suppose that is?" Prince Andre asks when he has swung around in the saddle sufficiently to see what his sister is pointing at.

"It looks just like a witch," Princess Felicia tells them, and then, very picturesquely, she faints, falling into the lavish spread of her skirts like the stamen of an especially perfect flower.

"Aha!" Alfreida bursts out, revving up for another go at the little party. Her elbows flap ominously and her eyebrows are waggling like dancing caterpillars. "Warbul! Warbul! Muydop! Dementia! Ratisrati—" Whatever she has planned is never known, for at her first utterance, Prince Andre springs from the saddle calling to Leander to join him. "You get the left arm," he orders as he strides forward. Having dealt with a dragon with such facility, he is now convinced that he can handle almost anything he might encounter in the Woebegone Wood.

Alfreida lets out a high, keening wail of outrage. She kicks, but there is little she can do with her feet but cause bruises. Once her hands and arms are confined (and they are) she is not capable of magic, which is so galling that she can hardly bear it.

As they drag Alfreida back to the camp, Prince Andre pauses to take a good look at what they've captured. "You know, I believe it *is* a witch, Leander. Felicia was right. A witch and a dragon, all in one morning. Not bad for a first-time try." He glances around. "Is there any rope handy? It might be best to secure her hands."

But Leander, catching sight of Princess Felicia, abandons Prince Andre and, seizing his skillet, hastens to her side, fanning her as he kneels beside her. "You have fainted, dear Princess." He continues the skillet-fanning with one hand, and with the other, dares to take her nearest hand in his. "Princess, o dear Princess Felicia, forgive me, though I shall never be able to forgive myself. I failed to assist you in your hour of peril. I shall count myself the most despicable of mortals if the least harm has come to you because of my inability to protect you as you deserve to be protected."

This outpouring of emotion pierces Princess Felicia's stupor. She opens her eyes and blinks in pretty confusion.

"You have recovered. You are safe. My joy is complete." At last he sets his skillet aside.

Prince Andre has finally succeeded in typing up Alfreida's hands so that she can do nothing more than mutter and hop in fury. He grins at his sister. "Get up, Felicia; there's a good girl." He feels more affectionate toward her now than he has at any time since they set out from Alabaster-on-Gelasta.

"But I was so frightened, Andre. There was a figure, I saw her, so very appalling, that I . . ." She falters as she catches sight of Alfreida. Her hand lifts to her forehead and she wavers. "Oh! The witch!"

As Leander rushes to support her, Prince Andre shakes his head indulgently. "Don't you dare, Felicia."

"Don't ruin everything," Princess Felicia pouts.

"Oh, dear Princess Felicia," Leander entreats her, "do not be too condemning of your valiant brother. He has faced a dreadful creature this day." To emphasize this, he points out the dragon, lying prone not far from the Prince's pavilion.

Princess Felicia is too annoyed at Prince Andre to agree. Instead, she turns a melting look on Leander. "And you faced it, too. It was so brave of you. I haven't seen anyone be so brave before. You didn't even have a horse. I will never, in all my life, forget the sight of you standing there, your skillet upraised, fending off the monster. Oh, why are you a mere crumpet-baker and not a handsome Prince?"

"Dear Princess," Leander says, his voice muffled with feeling; his manly heart is broken. "If only it were true."

Princess Felicia is not used to being thwarted in her desires, and she is not about to accept the idea now. "If you try hard, perhaps you will better yourself in time. Royal Papa will certainly show you some favor for your valor here. In time, who knows what you might attain. I myself will devote much time to bettering you."

"It is so much more than I deserve," Leander says humbly, gazing at her in rapture.

Prince Andre watches them for a bit, and then gives his attention to his dragon (he has already started to think of it as "his"). He walks over to where the dragon is lying, now tucked tidily into a more comfortable and modest position. "Why, what a little thing you are," he says, and is surprised that this does not dishearten him as much as he supposes it ought to do. "No wonder you ran away from me. You, chased by a great hulking Prince like me." He laughs, making it clear that he does not want to alarm the (his) dragon. "Just look at you—you're no bigger than a child's pony. Not even that big." He wants to pat her, the way he would a pony, but he hesitates. "It's hard to believe you're really a dragon, being so little and . . . sort of delicate. Poor thing." He drops down on one knee so that he will not loom over her. "Don't hang back; I won't hurt you—Word of a Prince."

Esmeralda is hopelessly enchanted by her splendid captor, although she is very painfully aware that he cannot know that she is not really a dragon, and will probably never know it. She will have to go through life being, at best, his pet. She makes a strange, squeaky sound, and two perfect smoke rings come from her nostrils.

"You're safe," Prince Andre says at his most soothing. "You don't have to worry anymore."

Worry at this stage is the furthest thing from Esmeralda's mind: lovestruck misery is much closer to the truth. If she could speak (which she can't), she would cry out to him, telling him how much she admires him, how grateful she is for his rescue, how she never, in her most romantic dreams, pictured a finer Prince than he is. She can only make a series of hisses, squeals and grunts, and none of them seem appropriate, so she forces herself to be silent.

"I'll see if Leander has something you can eat. I suppose dragons *do* eat, don't they? And not just Princesses." He laughs again, to indicate this was nothing but a joke.

"Some people think they can fool you," Alfreida shouts from where Leander and Prince Andre have tied her. "And you're silly enough to believe them, you wretched thing. Not harm you. You're safe. Do you hear him? What nonsense he talks. Next he'll be trying to convince you that he wants you for a pet. You know what Princes do to dragons, don't you? *Don't* you? You insufferable, overgrown worm."

"If you come with me, dragon, I'll have Leander make crumpets, and you may have one, if you wish," Prince Andre cajoles her.

"And what will Leander put into his precious crumpets,

eh? Some people think they can get away with murder. And who would care what happens to a scrawny dragon?" Alfreida begins her most awful cackle yet.

"The witch is trying to frighten you," Prince Andre says to his dragon, keeping his tone low and even. "She is jealous that you're going to have crumpets and she's not." He starts toward the rekindled campfire, looking back over his shoulder from time to time to see if the dragon is following him. "Leander, let's have tea now. It's a little early, but after a day like today, a cup of tea and some crumpets would be very welcome."

Leander, who has been sitting with Princess Felicia and therefore has paid no attention to anything else, shakes himself. "What? Did Your Highness call? Is there something I will be honored to do? I am ready, as always, to serve Your Highnesses." His gaze turns back to Princess Felicia.

"Yes, very fine. Well, if it will honor you to make tea, we'd appreciate it," says Prince Andre, with a touch of asperity.

Leander continues to regard Princess Felicia with adoration. "Will it please you, dear Princess, to have a cup of tea? It will be brewed as perfectly as I know how to brew. And a crumpet as well? Oh, my hopes will be fulfilled if you will but allow me to do this humble thing for you."

"Would you really do that for me?" Princess Felicia asks, perilously close to simpering.

"That, and as much more as it pleases you to allow. Perhaps you will be willing to let me tie the laces of your boots, or hold your cloak." He says this with audacity, amazed at how bold he has become.

Princess Felicia positively dimples at him. "I don't know why, but I find you very refreshing, Leander. By all means, let us have tea and crumpets. I know that yours will be the finest crumpets made, since that is like you. It is getting on toward evening, as Andre has said, and it must be tea time. We will have to eat to sustain ourselves through this dark night."

From somewhere far in the distance, there comes the first lugubrious sounds of the Trolls, preparing for another evening of revels and song.

> *Softly in the fading day*
> *Engulfing darkness snatches*

> *Shape and form and sense away*
> *To our glees and songs and catches! . . ."*

"Oh, dear Princess Felicia," Leander implores her, "you must not be afraid. The dangers are all around us, but they will not prevail. I will protect you; I will defend you to my last breath."

"How original of you, Leander. How interesting. How charming." Princess Felicia is all but cooing.

> *"As the final, dimming light*
> *Quails over monstrous trees*
> *Before the great invading night*
> *And our catches, songs, and noisy glees!"*

"Do you hear that, Esmeralda?" Alfreida demands in a rising scream. "The Trolls are coming. They'll be near very soon. Do you know what that means, you little snirt? Some people are all alone in the Wood without protection. There's no one to look after you—"

> *"Now the darkness covers all*
> *As rightness turns to greater wrongs—"*

"—in the way that sickening idiot looks after that insufferable Princess." Alfreida is undaunted by the Trolls' singing; after all, she has had plenty of experience with them. "Before, when you were all pretty and golden, even that lunatic widgeon with the frying pan would have leaped to defend you, never mind the Princess. But there he is, mooning—"

> *"To celebrate, we caterwaul*
> *Our glees and catches and our songs!"*

"—over that dreadful girl. Who of all these will help a dragon? A puny, ugly dragon at that. Some people are stupid, incurable optimists."

Prince Andre has listened to this with some confusion. He is aware that Alfreida would like nothing better than to confuse them so that she might turn this to her advantage. At the same time, he is puzzled by what the witch has revealed in castigating the dragon. *Esmeralda?* What sort of name is that for a dragon? He goes to his pavilion deep in thought, and emerges a little later with a large jar in his hands. "Sigmund gave me this before I left. He said that we might need it."

Leander glances at Prince Andre. "What is it?"

"He said that it's a magic powder. I gather I'm supposed to put it all around our camp to protect us. That seemed to be the jist of it, but you know how Sigmund is." He says this last philosophically. As he opens the jar, he calls out to his *(Esmeralda?)* dragon. "Come inside the circle. You'll be safe here, little dragon."

Esmeralda hesitates, her mind divided. There is always the chance that Alfreida is right (galling thought!) and that she is placing her neck on the chopping block. But there is no one she would rather have chop off her head than Prince Andre, and so, with a little fiery snort, she runs into the camp.

"And what can happen inside that circle, eh? He's a Prince, you're a dragon, remember, you barmy thing? You're at his mercy, you niggling fool!" Alfreida is working herself into a state, quivering with such intensity that the tree to which she is tied threatens to come down around her.

"My dragon is a lot safer here with me than she is out there with you," Prince Andre declares, tired of having his motives impugned. He notices that Hyperion is pawing the ground and snorting, shaking his well-shaped head with obvious irritation and disapproval. "Stop that," he orders his horse. And then, in a milder tone, he says, "You already helped catch my dragon. It shouldn't bother you now."

The horse clearly reserves judgment on that, but he does become calmer.

"Some people are very deceptive, Esmeralda. They lead you right into the trap and then there's nothing you can do." Alfreida is making much more noise than the Trolls are, infuriated that her hands are confined and that she is therefore as helpless as most people in the Woebegone Wood.

"And some people," Prince Andre snaps back, "are trying to frighten my dragon into exposing itself to danger."

Alfreida gives a shower of cackles in a range that any coloratura would blink to hear. "You know there's danger! You admit it! Then what about me, eh? What about me?"

"You're a witch," Prince Andre reminds her tactfully. "Fend for yourself."

A Sidetrip to Addlepate

THINGS HAVE GONE from bad to worse in Addlepate, which delights Humgudgeon no end. There have been three thwarted rebellions in the last two weeks, and he is still wreaking vengeance on everyone who has the least association with any of the conspirators. Vengeance is one of Humgudgeon's favorite sports. He has spent the better part of the day (and he certainly thinks of it as the better part) in the dungeons with his engines of torture and the latest batch of unfortunates. Now he is back in his Throne Room, reclining on the great mound of pillows, and reviewing his progress with his raven.

"It is amazing how determined they are," he says with insouciance, the diversions of the torture chamber having restored what passes for good humor in him. "Nothing but denials, denials, denials, my dear, until the very last. It's a shame they can't be used more than once. I could be so much more inventive that way, and you know how I like to invent."

The raven is silent, which encourages Humgudgeon to continue.

"Yes, there are so many ways I might express my genius, if I had a greater range for my abilities. Destroying parts of Addlepate is all very well, but after a while, there's a repetitive quality, don't you agree? Fire, flood, plague, famine, ruin, war, it's all so much the same. Think of what I could accomplish if I had the scope of my imaginings to draw upon!" This vision is clearly the most captivating he can come up with, and he dwells on it in silence while he nibbles minced dates. "It is time for my wine!" he says suddenly, and reaches out to sound the gong near his hand.

At once, three serving lads hurry into the Throne Room. One of them is in tatters, for he has already tasted Humgud-

137

geon's wrath that day. They all bow so deeply that if their legs were shorter, their foreheads would hit the floor. "Your Maleficence," they say in chorus.

"Wine, my minions. Wine," Humgudgeon orders with a wave of his hand.

They hurry away at once, not only because they know it is best to respond with alacrity, but because they are glad to be out of Humgudgeon's presence—it is much safer out of his presence.

"Yes, the wine will inspire me. I fear, my dear, that I grow stale. I know you doubt that," he says sweetly to his raven, "and I don't question your good sense, gracious no! but you will allow that it has not been as exciting here the last few days as it was earlier in the week, when there were more rebels to be dealt with."

The serving lads rush back into the Throne Room carrying a gigantic tray on which are laid out a vast array of bottles, cups, chalices, urns, jars, glasses and crocks. They set this down beside the welter of pillows, bow double again, and wait to be dismissed, each of them dreading the next few moments.

"That is all," Humgudgeon says in his most languid tone, enjoying their distress. "You may all go. At once."

In obedience they rush from the room, feeling lightheaded.

"Isn't fright wonderful?" Humgudgeon asks his raven as he reaches for the most elaborate chalice on the tray. "They've probably coated the inside with something nasty. Shall we try it?" Without waiting for an answer, Humgudgeon fills the chalice with half the contents of a very old, cobweb-encrusted bottle. "The bouquet is marvelous, isn't it?"

The raven makes a single loud croak and falls silent.

"Yes, my dear, there is much to be said for being a despot. One gets the very best of everything, and as long as my magic holds up, they can do nothing to me." He drinks deeply, letting the potent liquid slide down his throat. He smiles, mouth closed, as he recognizes yet another poison in the wine.

From the door there comes a series of soft but insistent raps.

"I'm not receiving," Humgudgeon calls out mellifluously. "Go away."

"I must speak to you, Your Maleficence," comes the quiet voice beyond the door, filled with urgency. The voice is a familiar one: the Spy has returned.

"You must not," Humgudgeon disagrees. "In fact, I order you not to."

"But I have information, Your Maleficence," the Spy protests, knowing that he is taking his life in his hands by disagreeing with Humgudgeon.

"Hasn't everyone," Humgudgeon says reflectively, thinking of the happy hours in the dungeon.

"About Alabaster-on-Gelasta," the Spy persists, wishing that he could find nerve enough to run away.

Humgudgeon turns to his raven. "Alabaster-on-Gelasta, my dear. What do you think? Shall we admit him, or shall we give him to . . . Chumley? Of course," he continues, "we can do both. Do you favor that, or have you another notion of how to deal with the Spy?" Since the raven makes no response, Humgudgeon sighs. "We might as well hear him out, although why he should choose this of all times to bother me, I cannot think." Taking another, longer swallow of the wine, he closes his eyes for a moment, and then calls out, "Come in, then, Spy."

Reluctantly the Spy does as he is bid. He stands near the door, his back not quite touching the knobbed and studded wooden planks, and taking great care about it, he bows. "Your Maleficence, I walked all night and most of the day to reach you betimes."

"Really," says Humgudgeon, plainly unimpressed with this devotion. "Why did you do that?"

"I have information," the Spy says, trying to keep the whine out of his voice. He knows this mood of Humgudgeon, and he does not trust it (or any other of Humgudgeon's various moods).

"So you say. About what, Spy, that is the question." He savors the expression of apprehension that the Spy is attempting vainly to conceal. "What can you have learned in Alabaster-on-Gelasta that would be the least interest to me?"

"Why, many things," the Spy says, hoping that this is true. "Many things."

"Then you may select one and I will tell you if you are correct." Humgudgeon yawns, as much for effect as anything. He drinks the last of the wine in the chalice, and decides to select another vessel and another vintage. "Continue, or begin, as the case may be."

This is a most unpromising opening and the Spy knows it. He braces himself where he stands and clears his throat.

"There are sinister doings in Alabaster-on-Gelasta. You have been deceived and lulled by King Rupert and the rest of them."

Humgudgeon pours more wine. "Is that so?" He leans back on the cushions. "I'm waiting, Spy."

The Spy drops onto one knee. "They are not what they seem, Your Maleficence. I realize how unassuming and carefree they appear, but that is deception—deception. Why, the whole of Alabaster-on-Gelasta is a rabbit warren of intrigue and plottings."

"Drat," murmurs Humgudgeon, savoring the new wine.

"I know what we . . . I assumed, Your Maleficence. They seem so peaceful and happy, but beneath that surface, much is lurking; there is a sinister power in Alabaster-on-Gelasta, and you ignore it at your peril, Your Maleficence." Just for good measure, the Spy bows again.

"Oh, fudge," says Humgudgeon, his piggy little eyes brightening.

"You cannot imagine what I saw there, and how they toyed with me, Your Maleficence."

"Of course I can imagine," Humgudgeon says, insulted. "You forget whom you are speaking to." He draws himself more erect on the cushions and stares hard at the Spy. "My imagination exceeds that of all others in Addlepate."

"I am aware of that, Your Maleficence," the Spy says at once, taking the most conciliatory attitude possible. "And were it anyone else, I would not attempt to describe what I encountered there, for they would not have the understanding Your Maleficence posseses."

"See that you remember that, Spy," Humgudgeon warns him in dulcet tones.

"I will, I will, I will, Your Maleficence." He draws a deep breath, then plunges back into his report. "Right before my eyes, as if it were the most usual thing in the world, the Torturer produced the most fiendish instruments for King Rupert's examination. He wanted me to try out his rack!" As the recollection stirs, the Spy's voice goes up most of an octave.

"He did?" At last the Spy has Humgudgeon's attention.

"Oh, he was subtle about it, nothing so obvious as arrest, but it was plain to everyone that he would stop at nothing to have me in his clutches." The Spy waits for a moment, hoping that Humgudgeon will say something. When the Protector Extraordinary merely sips his wine, the Spy goes on. "I saw that the Torturer has the ear of King Rupert."

"He does?" Humgudgeon inquires, his interest piqued.

"Metaphorically speaking," the Spy amends swiftly.

"Oh," says Humgudgeon in obvious disappointment.

"They were having a conference, and King Rupert was availing himself of the advice of his . . . advisors." He does not want to give too much away all at once. "The Torturer had a model of a new instrument of torture, one of a long series of instruments that the Torturer has designed for King Rupert. This one might not have been up to his standard, because King Rupert did not immediately approve its use."

"How did Rupert behave during this time? What did he say to the Torturer?" Humgudgeon cannot resist asking.

"He encouraged his Torturer. He commended him for his zeal. King Rupert is not the fool we . . . Your Maleficence thought, Your Maleficence. He's subtle, smooth, fiendish . . . fiendish."

In spite of himself, Humgudgeon feels himself warming to King Rupert. "Yes? Is he? Tell me more."

This is the opportunity the Spy has waited for. "He was there with his magicians and his Torturer having lunch—*lunch* if you'll believe it—and talking about the most terrible things, in the most heartless manner. To hear them, you'd think they'd never hurt a gnat."

Humgudgeon leans forward, grasping his goblet at the base in the event he wants to throw it at the Spy. "What things? What things?"

"They spoke of torture devices, Your Maleficence. They made threats, very definite threats. King Rupert as much as vowed he'd turn loose the power of Sigmund Snafflebrain and Professor Ambicopernicus on Addlepate if any attempt was made to disrupt their way of life in Alabaster-on-Gelasta. It was the most frightening thing I have ever encountered—outside of Your Maleficence." This last is said quickly and with as much sincerity as the Spy can muster. He knows to his grief how proud Humgudgeon is of the terror he inspires.

"Very good, Spy," Humgudgeon whispers. "Did anyone give any indication he knew who you were or who had sent you?"

"That is the worst part," the Spy admits, shame filling him.

"King Rupert saw through all my disguises."

"Un*can*ny!" exclaims Humgudgeon, impressed by this revelation.

"And he . . . he . . ." the Spy falters, afraid to go on.

"Yes?" says Humgudgeon dangerously. "What is it, Spy?"

The Spy swallows very hard, as if he had a pebble in his throat. "He told me to send Your Maleficence . . . his greetings."

"Did he?" Humgudgeon muses. "How do you account for that?" He is being very quiet now, and the Spy is aware that this is a very bad sign.

"He knew all along, Your Maleficence. He sensed everything from the start. King Rupert is more clever than anyone could anticipate, and he was prepared for my visits." He hates to admit this, for it is a bitter pill for a man as experienced as he.

"But how could he have known? How could he have been ready for you?" Humgudgeon's tone becomes very soft, almost caressing. "We've taken every precaution, haven't we? If Rupert was aware of your identity and your mission, Spy, it can only be because . . . you did something *wrong*."

The Spy turns greenish-pale. "No, no . . . no, Your Maleficence," he stammers. "I didn't . . . never. I did everything properly, just in the way you've told me to proceed. I did. I did. I disguised myself very cleverly. I had good disguises. Creditable disguises, Your Maleficence. I was able to have interviews with King Rupert . . ." He can think of little to say in his own defense that Humgudgeon might accept.

Humgudgeon turns to his raven; this is an ominous sign. "Do you believe him, my dear? I realize that your sentiments are harsh, not as gentle as mine, not as subject to tender feelings. You have a more stringent view of the world, do you not? And you find his story . . . his *excuses* implausible, as, I must confess, do I." He clears his throat. "But you have not considered the natural element of his nacient stu-pid-i-ty." Each syllable of the last is as sharp as the snap of a whip. "It makes a difference, doesn't it, my dear?"

The Spy turns a shade even more pale and greenish. "Your Maleficence—"

"Yes," Humgudgeon goes on, blissfully unaware of the Spy's objections, "I thought that might make a difference with you. You are always showing greater vision than I am, which is saying quite a lot, when you come to think of it."

"Your Maleficence—" the Spy interjects.

"Do not interrupt," Humgudgeon tells him. "It is not appropriate for you to interrupt." He gives his attention to both his wine goblet and his raven. "I know the way *you* would deal with him, my dear, and there is no denying that your way has a certain piquancy, a—shall I say—simple forthrightness . . . but you must let me be the judge of what will be the most effective methods at this time. Your way is so shocking. I think that my idea, all things considered, is far better." Having said this, he calls so very sweetly, "Chumley!"

"No, Your Maleficence," the Spy protests, his hackles rising at the horrid thought.

"It has been so very dreadfully long, you know, since Chumley has had a play toy, as he so quaintly puts it. The others are quite worn out, yes indeed, and he's become morose, waiting for another one, my dear." Humgudgeon smiles at the Spy with a sweetness that is as cloying as too much sugar on breakfast waffles.

"But I brought you the information you said you wanted, Your Maleficence," the Spy tries to remind him.

"Ah yes. You told me that King Rupert is subtle, but I knew that—I sent you there because I knew that. You tell me that Sigmund Snafflebrain is crafty and powerful, but that is no surprise to me, either. In fact, now that I come to think of it, all your efforts have been *wasted*, my dear."

The Spy falls to his knees. "You didn't know about the Torturer and his inventions, did you, Your Maleficence?"

"You're clutching at straws, my dear," Humgudgeon says with a wide, insincere smile. "Mere wisps."

Babbling with dread, the Spy goes on, hoping that he might have the right phrase, the right word to keep him out of Chumley's clutches. "The Professor. Professor Ambicopernicus. You didn't know about him, did you? You have to admit that learning about the Professor means something."

"Grovel, my dear," Humgudgeon purrs.

"I can explain," the Spy pleads. "Give me a chance to explain. You'll see that I've done your bidding. You will." He is panting now and he has to force himself not to jig from knee to knee, as if running or needful of a chamber pot.

"You promised me—promised me, Spy—that you would bring chaos to Alabaster-on-Gelasta, didn't you? *Didn't you?*"

Humgudgeon is enjoying himself at last; this is almost as much fun as the dungeon.

"Well, yes, I suppose I did, but—"

Humgudgeon does not give the Spy the chance to finish. Relishing the panic the Spy so clearly feels, he goes on. "And you said that you would deliver the secrets of Sigmund Snafflebrain into my hands so that he could no longer protect Alabaster-on-Gelasta. Didn't you?"

"I guess it seems that—"

Since Humgudgeon likes to draw out the coup de grâce as long as possible, he leans back on his cushions again and drawls, "It's most awfully sad to inform you that you've *failed*"—he says the word magnificently, savoring its sound and effect—"yes, my dear, failed utterly. You are in total disgrace." He takes a deep sip of wine, watching the Spy over the rim of the goblet. "Really, you've not given this the thought you should have. You knew what I wanted, gracious me, how could you not? You know what you vowed to deliver." He addresses his next remarks to the raven which causes the Spy to come close to fainting. "I realize, my dear, that you would use persuasive methods on him, methods of the most *lingering* kind. But I'm not sure that I agree, not yet, in any case. He must find out the *consequences* of shirking his duty, don't you agree? I do feel that my way is better, and you will allow that I am always right."

"Your Maleficence—" the Spy croaks.

There is a pounding on the wall, heavy and persistent, and an ominous, demanding voice calling, "Chumley want play toy!"

Humgudgeon grins at the Spy. "I am going to order you to open that door," he says, indicating the one nearest the pounding. "If you are as devoted to me as you insist, you will not hesitate to do this for me, will you?" If he were a cat, there would be feathers as well as whiskers on either side of his smile.

"That door?" the Spy whispers, pointing.

"That door," Humgudgeon confirms at his most saccharin.

With ever-slowing steps, the Spy makes his way to the door as to the edge of an abyss. Even more reluctantly he draws back the iron bolt and pulls the heavy portal half-open. He can see Chumley hulking in the torchlight, holding something in his hand that looks alarmingly like a shinbone.

"Got no play toy," Chumley bellows. "Chumley want new play toy."

"Yes, yes," Humgudgeon condoles from his resting place on the pillows, "Shortly, Chumley. There is a new play toy for you. Right there. But I want to have him a little longer before you take him over."

"Hurm! Hurm!" Chumley slaps his thigh with his free hand. "That lousy play toy." He lurches back from the door and waits, just beyond the torchlight.

"Your Maleficence . . . you can't . . ." the Spy begs. "You wouldn't."

"Not quite yet, my dear. I was thinking that perhaps the sight of Chumley might, shall we say, jar your memory, help you to recall those little, fascinating details that you might have forgotten and that would mitigate your current unenviable position?" He pauses to smile. "Can you think of any little thing I might want to know about Alabaster-on-Gelasta, something that might convince me to reconsider my decision about Chumley and his play toy?"

The Spy knits his brow with the intensity of his feeling, but thought does not come easily to him with Humgudgeon sitting there, smiling in a way that is more like an ice-cold bath than a warm welcome. "You know about Professor Ambicopernicus, you know about Sigmund Snafflebrain. You know that the Torturer is in the confidence of King Rupert, you know that the Prince is on a dragon-hunt—"

"What?" Humgudgeon interrupts. "The Prince is on a dragon-hunt? Why did you say nothing of this?" He is so excited by the news that he slops much of the wine over the front of his damasked robes and the silken pillows. "What about the dragon and the Prince?"

"There is a dragon loose in the Woebegone Wood, and Prince Andre and his sister the Princess Felicia have set off to kill it or catch it or some such thing." The Spy offers this cautiously, uncertain what Humgudgeon might do in response with it. He might decide that it is just wonderful, or, there is no telling, he might decide that he is being made mock of, and then there will be *consequences*.

"A dragon in the Woebegone Wood?" muses Humgudgeon in his nastiest tone of voice. "How does that come about, do you suppose?"

"I don't know," the Spy is quick to admit, "but I remember

that Sigmund Snafflebrain hinted that there was more to the dragon than meets the eye. He suggested, in his own way, that there was something very special about the dragon. I don't know what it was." He is trying to keep Humgudgeon from accusing him of deception; he might as well hope for fresh apricots in January.

"Go on. Tell me more, Spy," says Humgudgeon with his most crocodilian smile.

"No one would give themselves away, of course," the Spy says, warming to his topic, "but King Rupert let his daughter and his heir go off to the Woebegone Wood with nothing more than a crumpet-baker for company."

"Hmmmmmmmmmmm," goes Humgudgeon, giving no sign of belief or doubt.

There is a thumping on the door to Chumley's quarters, which is still ajar. "Chumley play now?"

Humgudgeon lurches to his feet and goes to lean on the door, pressing it closed. "Not now," he says with a show of patience that is clearly deceptive. "In a bit, perhaps. Be patient."

"They're in the Wood now, Your Maleficence," the Spy continues, hoping that he might be making some headway with Humgudgeon.

"And with nothing but a crumpet-baker, you say?" The gleam is back in his beady eyes. He pours himself another libation, this time from a stoneware crock which emits a strong herbal odor.

"Yes." The Spy is determined now to turn this debacle to his advantage. "They are completely unprotected, and there are no soldiers to come to their rescue. We could kidnap them and then you—"

"*We* could do nothing of the sort," Humgudgeon corrects the Spy in his most emphatic manner. "My dear, you are quite cavalier about my safety, and your own, for that matter. Surely you can see that this is the work of Sigmund Snafflebrain? He told you this so that you would expose yourself— and *me*—to Rupert and his schemes. Why, if you were to go into the Woebegone Wood now, you'd be captured, revealed, tortured, and made an example of." Now that he's said it, he finds the idea rather appealing. "And, my dear, you would deserve it. Yes, believe me, you would."

"I never considered that," the Spy admits in self-condemnation. "I suppose you're right."

"I am *always* right," Humgudgeon reminds him in his thunderous best.

"Yes," the Spy concurs at once.

"And, my dear, it is painfully apparent to all but the very blindest fools that Sigmund was setting a trap for you." He drinks deeply. "He wanted you to follow the Prince into the Wood, and then he would be able to pounce upon you. Well, *I* am not so much a fool to let that happen to me. And you, Spy, ought not to be such a fool, either." His good will has evaporated more swiftly than wine fumes.

"Very, very wise, Your Maleficence. I am horrified that it required your wit to make it clear to me." He is prepared to lay on the compliments with the proverbial trowel if it will gain him any ground with the Protector Extraordinary.

Humgudgeon favors the Spy with a grisly smile. "Which leaves . . . *you!* And you have *failed*. There must be some way, some new and delicious way, that I can use to prolong your agony in order to pay for your bungling."

"Your Maleficence—"

"Before I turn you over to Chumley, I really must try out a few new tricks on you." He beams at his raven, his face a study in maniacal glee. "Not the grotesque sort, my dear, although I am aware that you prefer them. No, this will be refined, exquisite." His face is wreathed in the joys of contemplation. "Done with true delicacy and taste. It will be so very drawn out." He regards the Spy with something approaching appreciation. "You'll be astonished, I know you will. You will be a great many other things, also, but astonishment will be high in your thoughts—you have no *notion* what you can endure. It might take *weeks*."

"Help," squeaks the Spy.

Humgudgeon is filled with his own kind of rapture. "And then, when it is understood that this is how it must be ended, Chumley!" He lifts his glass in a toast, sharing this triumph with his raven. "Doesn't that sound delightful? A true refinement of craft and art, a demonstration of skill that will never be equaled. A loving display of all that might be possible."

"No," mutters the Spy as he fades back into the shadows, deciding that he might as well try to escape since nothing worse can possibly happen to him.

"First, my dear," Humgudgeon proposes to his raven, "to bathe his senses in every attention at our disposal, taking time to linger over everything that can be lingered over. Rack, garrote, thong, strappado, boot, pincers, all of them in sequence, each a virtu*o*so performance. And then, the finale—Chumley!"

An abrupt knocking at the barred door brings Humgudgeon back to himself. "Chumley want—"

"Play toy," Humgudgeon finishes for him. "In a little while, Chumley. Not quite yet."

"Chumley want play toy!" This time there is no mistaking the insistence.

"After I've had my turn, Chumley. You mustn't be hasty." Humgudgeon drinks more of his current wine and licks his mouth. "An interesting savor, that one."

The Spy has almost reached the outer door of the Throne Room, and he is still debating whether or not he should make a dash for it. The renewal of thuds on Chumley's door removes all doubt: he bolts from the room without any trace of hesitation. If the guards catch him, so much the better, for they will only spit him on their halberds. Far better that, thinks the Spy devoutly, than facing the *consequences*.

"Chumley want PLAY!" This last is accompanied by tremendous blows on the door; one of the hinges doesn't seem to be up to this abuse.

"And so you shall, Chumley. I promise you that you will have your play toy when it's convenient for both of us." He is really becoming annoyed with his monster and decides that he might keep the Spy entirely to himself. "I will let you know when you can play."

This is the wrong tack to take with Chumley, who does not like being thwarted. Three shattering impacts from fists as massive as full saddlebags batter the door to kindling. Chumley nearly falls into the Throne Room, his rage apparent in every fiber of his being. He looks around, then shambles toward Humgudgeon, not quite slavering. He reaches out in determination. In a voice that makes it plain that the time for diplomacy has fled, Chumley announces, "Chumley play now!"

Had Humgudgeon taken a little less wine, or spent a longer time in exercise, there might have been a chance for him, but since his habits preclude an heroic battle or even ignominious flight, he is victim to a fate he has meted out to others, coming as close as possible to gaining some sort of poetic justice.

The Morning After

MORNINGS IN THE Woebegone Wood are often strangely beautiful, with sunlight dappling through the heavy leaves and the calls of exotic birds making the place seem far less sinister than the caroling Trolls. At least it appears that way to the dragon-hunting party (and the dragon, as well) when the first golden rays touch the clearing where they are camped.

Princess Felicia expresses it for everyone: "My, what an unusual day."

Leander, who has emerged from his so-called pavilion, is so neat and fresh-looking that it is quite unfair. "It is not so beautiful as the vision of you, Your Highness. No dawn, be it ever so glorious and rosy, is the smallest part as beautiful as you." For Leander, this is a restrained speech, but it is early yet, and he is one of those who takes time to get going in the morning.

Alfreida, still tied to the tree and in a vile humor (even for her), her stringy muscles in knots, has more than she can bear already, and hearing this sentimental outpouring so early brings a caustic rejoinder. "Did you hear what he said?" she asks the air. "Some people don't know what sickening is."

Prince Andre is also up and about, striding through the little camp in his waistcoat and shirtsleeves, his humor as good as Leander's, although his style is somewhat different. "Good morning, good morning. A good day to us all." He looks around the perimeters of the camp. "We have been safe enough. It must be Sigmund's magic powder—he insisted it would work, but it's hard to tell with Sigmund."

Leander looks at Princess Felicia while he apparently addresses Prince Andre. "I shall have to thank him most sincerely upon our return for this thoughtfulness in providing us with this wonderful sovereign." He is warming up. "There are no words to describe, to express with sufficient eloquence, the joy I knew when I awoke and discovered that the Princess Felicia had slept without harm or danger. Did you have sweet dreams, dear, dear Princess? You should have only sweet dreams."

Princess Felicia is enough herself to answer, "I had dreams. The same old dreams." Yet there is a sudden flush to her cheeks that might cause someone to doubt this.

Leander is not as familiar with her habits as he is convinced he is, and so he protests. "But your dreams must be the most beautiful, the most elegant, the most utterly perfect." He turns to her brother for agreement. "Don't you agree, Your Highness?"

Prince Andre has not been paying much attention, and responds in an absent way, "Yes, I suppose so; I don't see why not. Are there any crumpets left?"

"Yes. There are several." He is contrite as he recalls his duties to the Prince and the Princess in their more mundane form. He hastens to make amends for neglecting them, producing crumpets from one of the various tins, pouches and boxes of foodstuffs they have along with them. "Yes, here are two to start. I will build up the fire and bake more in a moment." He cannot stand to ignore Princess Felicia one instant longer. "One should do for His Highness, but you, dear Princess Felicia, I hope that you will deign to eat the other while I prepare a more suitable repast."

"How thoughtful of you," says Princess Felicia as she takes the proffered crumpet. "How original of you, Leander. No one has ever given me crumpets before. I have always received jewels and precious gifts, but none so rare as this crumpet."

Prince Andre disposes of his crumpet in three hungry chomps, and because he is roughing it away from the court, he speaks next with his mouth still full (it makes him feel very assertive and adult). "Very tasty, Leander. And welcome. Now, I propose that after we have eaten that we set out at once for home. We have captured both a dragon and a witch, and I think that we ought to be satisfied with that. We hadn't planned on the witch, after all. We'll go through Addlepate directly—we'll make better time that way." Prince Andre is very brave this morning, and is eager to make the most of it.

"I shall do what I can to discharge Your Highness's orders

with dispatch. Rest assured that we will be under way as soon as I have tended to making a proper breakfast and can pack away the pavilions." It is more of a task than he will admit; he smiles a very manly smile and goes to ready the fire for cooking.

"You are attentive to our every need," Princess Felicia says, watching him prepare the skillet for frying eggs.

"It is the least service I can offer to you, dear Princess; were it for me to decide, there are other offices I would gladly fill for Your Highness." He has become more bold in the last half hour, for he is convinced that his sentiments are returned.

"Oh, Leander, it is going to be very difficult. It would be so simple if you were worthy by birth, because then you would not have to prove your merit by deed—which I am convinced you have, but you don't know Royal Mama—but then, you'd be just like the other young men Royal Mama insists are appropriate for me, and I'd probably be bored with you."

This casual remark strikes Leander to the core. "Princess Felicia, I would prefer to slit my throat with the edge of a stirring spoon than cause you an instant of boredom." This declaration is so impassioned that Leander almost oversets the eggs that are sizzling in the skillet.

"Oh, I don't think you could bore me," Princess Felicia says airily. "But you've never had the opportunity to do that, and so I have to guess. You are very good to listen to me. Almost no one," she goes on darkly, "ever listens to me."

If this is intended for Prince Andre, he is completely unaware of it. He is more concerned with his dragon.

"How's my dragon?" he asks, speaking in a calming tone to give her a chance to respond without fright (if only he knew that fright is furthest from her mind—that reticence comes from emotions very different from fear). "Ready to have something to eat? Leander is making breakfast. I'm sure there is something you'd enjoy, other than a haunch of my sister." He laughs to let her know he could not possibly mean it.

"There's more than one idiot in this Wood," Alfreida declaims to the heavens. "And it's not easy to decide who is the most disgusting. Some people are as perceptive as turnips!"

"Don't let the witch frighten you," Prince Andre says, doing all that he can to make his dragon feel better. He reaches out his hand and pats her shoulder in a kindly way, and is surprised to feel her press against his hand, almost like a cat. "So you're friendlier this morning. That's going to be a help." He pats her again, just to make sure that he was right about the response. "Good dragon," he says, starting away from her, unaware of the bedraggled wisp of smoke that comes from her snout, which is as close as she can come to a sigh.

"Eggs, Your Highnesses," Leander announces, staring at Princess Felicia as he speaks. "And there are kippers and some pomegranates in honey, which are yours alone, dear Princess. They are not as red as your lips."

"Pomegranates are all seeds, and all the seeds are the same," Princess Felicia reminds him, but in a tone of voice that makes it apparent that she is considering the possibilities. She wipes her fingers with a lace handkerchief. "The eggs smell delicious, Leander. I have never seen them cooked that way before. We always have them coddled or shirred. But you have just cooked them on a skillet. How original!" She actually claps her hands once, to show the depth of her enthusiasm for his eggs.

"Your Highness is far kinder than I deserve. If this simple repast pleases you, I cannot tell you how great my satisfaction is in your approval. If I were one day permitted to prepare a banquet instead of this very basic cuisine, then my inspiration would be boundless." Leander reverently slides two of the sunny-side-up eggs onto a porcelain plate with a border of pink flowers. "It should be gold and silver for you, Your Highness."

"Are you going to force me to travel with that incredible looby?" Alfreida demands of Prince Andre. "Why don't you run me through instead? It would be a quicker way to die."

"I'm not going to run you through, unless you force me to," Prince Andre tells her in a robust way. "I'm going to take you back to Alabaster-on-Gelasta with me, and my Royal Papa will decide what to do with you next. He'll probably ask Sigmund and the Professor what to do. He usually does." He stops and looks critically at Alfreida. "It's a pity you haven't something decent to wear."

Now Alfreida is deeply insulted. "I'll have you know that this gown was worn at the annual Necromancers' Ball, and was awarded first prize." She wants to draw herself up straight, but since she is tied to a tree, it isn't so easily done.

"Is that because it appeared to be one of the dead?" Prince Andre challenges her, pleased that he has been able to say something witty.

"Some people," Alfreida mutters, "give themselves airs for no good reason at all."

Esmeralda has got to her feet, and now she begins to follow Prince Andre around the camp, keeping a good five paces back from him, in case she should inadvertently hurt him with a spurt of flame. She has not been very good at breathing fire, but she is certain that if ever she is likely to develop the ability, it is going to be now.

Prince Andre is proud for the way his dragon responds to his training. "I've always thought I had a way with animals," he says to Princess Felicia (who is not paying the least attention) as he deliberately walks all around his pavilion to be sure that his dragon really is right behind him. "Even Royal Mama should be impressed with this."

"There will be kippers shortly, Your Highness," Leander tells Prince Andre before he begins to prepare more batter for crumpets. He has to resist the urge to use up all his supplies right now. He would like to shower Princess Felicia with a cascade of crumpets, anything to demonstrate his ardor.

"Fine, and make sure there's something for my dragon." He goes to where he had left Hyperion hobbled. Until this moment, he has not appreciated the problems of having a horse and a dragon close together. The dragon keeps at a distance, but Hyperion is not impressed. He paws and snorts and tosses his magnificent head with every show of displeasure, a great deal more fierce than the dragon has ever been. "Steady, old boy," Prince Andre says, attempting to jolly his mount into cooperating, his self-avowed ability with animals momentarily an embarrassment.

Esmeralda, realizing that the fuss is because of her, moves back, staying at a respectful distance from the horse. She watches, her snout turned to one side, while Prince Andre grooms his splendid horse. She can feel tears form in her eyes, and she knows irritation with herself for indulging in the kinds of fantasies that might make her feel this way. "After all," she reminds herself sternly for the third time this morning, "he is a Prince and you are a dragon, and there is no way he can understand otherwise."

"Having a little problem, are we?" Alfreida gloats as she watches Prince Andre. "Not going as well as expected? And what do you think is going to happen when you are gone from here, out on the road with that horse and that dragon, trying to ride one and watch the other? What do you think will be the result of a parade like that? Eh? Not that I'm saying you can't manage it, no, of course not; but some people are more audacious than sensible." She starts to cackle, then thinks better of it.

By the time Hyperion is saddled and bridled, Leander has a thrown-together breakfast ready for Prince Andre, and some odds and ends for the dragon. He has even set aside a few misshapen crumpets for Alfreida. That done, he is attempting to find a way to pack and to stay at Princess Felicia's side at the same time.

"I've never packed anything," Princess Felicia admits as she watches Leander take down his tiny pavilion. "Could you teach me, do you think?"

Leander's eyes positively glow. "It would fill me with the greatest pleasure to be able to do this for you, dear Princess. I cannot tell you what rapture would be mine if you were to allow me to show you how these things are packed."

"And you'll let me help you?" Princess Felicia asks, remembering all the flowers she has not been permitted to cut.

"If you do not believe that it is beneath you to undertake such lowly tasks, then I am entirely at your disposal, dear, dear Princess Felicia. It is more than I have dared to hope for, and more than any man can aspire to." He has managed to say this, with hardly a pause for air, as he finishes wrapping up his pavilion, which is impressive in its way. He also has hardly changed color at all, and in one with red-blond hair and fair skin, this is remarkable.

"Wonderful! Andre, Leander is going to teach me how to pack. Isn't that exciting?" She very nearly does a skip in celebration, but that would be going a bit too far.

"Glad to hear it. Anything to hurry us along," Prince Andre says, a bit dubiously, since he is not at all sure that having Princess Felicia to assist him will make Leander work more swiftly.

"Do you see that, Esmeralda?" Alfreida says in an insinuating tone. "That Prince is trying to pull the wool over your eyes." She crows with laughter at the thought of dragons with woolen eyes, then returns to her purpose. "He is hoping to make you think that he will take care of you, and you are just the sort of ninny who thinks that he means it. You hear him say 'Nice dragon' and you think that he intends that to your good. Well, some of us are not so easily misled. Some of keep our wits about us, instead of making moony eyes at a well-turned calf in high leather boots. He has you flummoxed, and there's no other way to put it. What a remarkably doltish thing you are." Her scorn is every bit as cutting as she intends it to be.

Prince Andre overhears the last of this and, for once, hesitates before attempting to convince his dragon that he means her no harm. The witch would only jeer at him, and that stings his pride more than he likes to acknowledge, even to himself. So instead of being persuasive, he pats the dragon on the shoulder. "You'll like Alabaster-on-Gelasta," he says to her. "You'll be able to run and play. It's nothing like this dark, oppressive Wood. There are fields and hills and brooks, and the trees we have are nicer than these."

Esmeralda knows that she would like wherever Prince Andre lives, even if it were a pigsty.

Princess Felicia finds that packing is much more interesting than she thought it would be, as long as Leander is showing her how to do it. She is delighted to find that the pavilions can be folded up into neat mounds of cloth, and that the poles holding them up come apart into sections that can be wrapped up with the cloth.

"You are most adept at this, dear Princess," Leander compliments her as she shoves the last of the poles into the sack that holds the gear. "Would that I had displayed such aptitude when first I learned this task."

Princess Felicia actually giggles.

It is not quite noon when the dragon-hunting party sets out again, with Prince Andre in the lead and Princess Felicia behind him. He would prefer to have his dragon follow him, but neither Hyperion nor Princess Felicia's Rosebud are inclined to permit it, and so Esmeralda follows after Leander on his mule, watching Alfreida, who is tied to the pack saddle, facing backward.

"Just look at you," Alfreida mocks, "coming along meekly, letting that overgrown child take you away from everything you know, and you go right on believing that nothing is wrong, and he'll be fawning over you like that crumpet-baker drools over the Princess. Won't you be surprised when you find out that he doesn't care about dragons, not after everyone's congratulated him on catching one. Where will you be then, with all the hills and fields and trees? You'll be all alone, and no one will care what becomes of you."

Little as she wants to believe this, Esmeralda has the sinking fear that Alfreida may be right. She begins to lag behind, wondering if it might be better for everyone if she simply ran away. The Prince might chase her again (which would be wonderful), or he might be content with keeping a witch and let her go off by herself (a very lowering thought). When they are passing through one of the densest parts of the Woebegone Wood, Esmeralda very reluctantly puts this to the test. She walks more and more slowly, watching the little party dwindle and fade in the gloom as they continue on their way. With dragging steps, she moves away from the narrow pathway, into the tangle of brush that marks the way. She has no notion of where she is or where she is going, and is far too miserable to care. The ground is treacherous—here a mass of roots and vines, there squishy—and she wanders in no direction in particular.

It is some little time before Prince Andre realizes that his dragon is missing, and it comes to his attention because he is aware that Alfreida has fallen silent. Feeling that this is not a good indication, he orders everyone to rein in while he checks on his dragon, a sense of distress lingering in his mind, like a bad taste on the back of the tongue.

"What are you looking for, you great overgrown brat?" Alfreida asks sweetly as Prince Andre reaches her side. "Some people are amazingly careless."

"Where is my dragon?" Prince Andre demands, not in the mood to listen to her version of banter.

"Out there," Alfreida says with a blithe jut of her chin since her hands are tied. "Somewhere."

"When did that happen?" Prince Andre asks, very emphatic.

"A while ago." Alfreida chortles. "She just walked away. No dragon, Prince. Isn't it a pity?"

Prince Andre wheels Hyperion and gives terse orders to Leander and Princess Felicia. "My dragon has got lost. You're to go on to the edge of the Wood and wait for me there. I will be along before sunset, I hope, but tomorrow morning for certain. I want you to make camp and wait. It may take a little time, but I will join you. Don't let that witch convince you of anything else. She's nothing but trouble."

"You could always let me go!" Alfreida carols.

"Don't do that," he tells Leander and Princess Felicia. "No matter what she says, don't listen, and don't let her go. She can't be trusted. I leave it to you, Leander, to see that everything goes well."

"Your Highness, as far as I am capable, and for as long as there is sufficient breath in my body, I vow that I will do everything in my power to discharge your—"

Before he can finish, Prince Andre has spurred back along the narrow path, calling out, "Dragon! Here dragon!"

"Oh, my dear Princess," Leander says to Princess Felicia as Prince Andre is lost to sight, "it is not to be supposed that you are not filled with dread and terror, but I wish to assure you that there is nothing you can ask of me that I will not perform, but to leave you in any sort of danger, whatever."

Alfreida decides that it might have been a mistake to encourage Esmeralda to run away—now she will have to listen to the two lovebirds longer than she had thought she would. She gives a disgusted laugh, and then says, "Some people will do anything for attention," and while she is convinced it is true, she is not sure to whom she is speaking.

As much as Prince Andre would like to rush back along the path in reckless pursuit of his dragon, he knows that the way is too dangerous and narrow to try it—all he would get at best would be a spill from Hyperion. At worst, he might break his neck. So he holds his horse to a trot and tries to make up for the slowness of the pace with greater worry. He cannot imagine what has become of his dragon, and it troubles him to think of that little, doe-eyed creature out in the Woebegone Wood with no one to protect her. "If it were a bigger dragon, then there might be a chance, but a little one like it . . . her, well, there's no telling what might become of her. Dragon!" This shout startles Hyperion, who is not at all pleased to be in the Wood for so long, let alone chasing something as repulsive as that oversized lizard that Prince Andre has taken such an inexplicable liking to. "Dragon!"

From her resting (hiding) place, Esmeralda hears the sound of Prince Andre's voice in the distance, and she is strangely cheered by it. She had been so convinced that she had been abandoned, and yet, he must have come after her. Even if she is only a trophy, she is inwardly pleased that the Prince has come after her. At least, she tells herself, he noticed I'm gone. She has to decide what to do next, for if she remains where she is, Prince Andre might not miss her. At the same time, she does not know how to reach him, or where he is going, and for the first time the enormity of her predicament nearly overwhelms her. She drags herself from her resting (hiding) place and starts to search out some way to get back to the path through the Wood.

That is more easily decided than done. Now that she wants to move with purpose, she finds no way that is not blocked by huge fallen trees and odoriferous bogs that would suck her down as soon as bubble. She wallows through one stagnant pond, and emerges from it with a terrible slime clinging to her scales. It is so disheartening that she almost gives in to defeat. Only the sound of Prince Andre's voice fading from her gives her the impetus to take one more try at scrambling through a vast network of vines and rubble, hoping that she is not too late. Her talons scrabble for purchase on the crumbling stones, and she almost falls more than once, and by the time she drags herself and her tail out of the last of it, she is too tired to do more than hunker down on her haunches and puff smoke rings. She is convinced that Prince Andre will never find her, and that she will be left here in the Woebegone Wood until the vines grow up around her, or the Trolls find her and drag her back to the Wailing Gorge. That dismal thought drives her on, and she is plodding ahead, watching only where she is putting her sore clawed feet, when she sees, not far ahead of her, a snowy white destrier mincing toward her.

"Dragon!" shouts Prince Andre, vaulting out of the saddle and rushing toward her. "You're safe."

This is more than Esmeralda can bear. She lowers her snout and gives way to emotions so complex that she hasn't the vaguest idea if they are positive or negative, only that she is pathetically glad to see Prince Andre. And if, she says to herself, he wants to turn me out to pasture as a pet, then that will be fine with me. She can't dismiss the sinking sensation that this acceptance brings, but she does her best to put on a brave smile (not the easiest expression for a dragon) and lets him drop a lasso around her neck.

"I'm not going to let you get away again, dragon," he warns her, but with more concern than anger. "What made you run off like that? It was probably that witch, making you think that you're going to be treated badly. Wasn't that it, little dragon?" Prince Andre is the sort of person who talks to animals as if they are slightly deaf children, and so he tends to speak more loudly than usual when addressing Esmeralda, which makes her flinch. Prince Andre assumes this is more fear and he tries to convince her that he means no harm. "Come closer, little dragon. I won't hurt you. You see—nothing in my hands, not even a riding crop."

Esmeralda longs to tell him that she understands every word, that she knows that she is in no danger from him, and all she can do is make a low grunting noise, which produces bursts of smoke from her nostrils.

"Come on, little dragon. You come back with me and I can promise you that nothing bad will happen to you." He smiles his most winning smile, the kind he usually reserves for unfriendly ambassadors, wondering all the while if dragons know what smiles are.

Esmeralda does as she is bid, and hopes that Prince Andre sees that she is trusting. It is very frustrating to be not only mute but a dragon as well.

Knowing that Hyperion does not want to be too near the dragon, Prince Andre puts the horse on a long lead, then walks beside Esmeralda as they make their way out of the Woebegone Wood. And as they walk, he sings to her:

> *"Oh, tho' the Wood is dark,*
> *It is lit by the day above*
> *And the sun beams fall*
> *Thru' the gloom and the pall*
> *Like the music of a lark*
> *Or the mourning of a dove.*
>
> *"And tho' the dark is vast,*
> *It's alive with a million lights*
> *And they cast their shine*
> *In rays long and fine*
> *From the first of time to last,*
> *Like a jewel with facet brights.*

"All around you shadows gather
Anyone would be afraid.
Leave the darkness if you'd rather
Turn from Wood and night and shade.

"Poor dragon all alone
Walk from this place and see
That you needn't fear
All the darkness here,
That your nightmare dreams have flown.
Walk in the light with me.
Walk in the light with me."

A Matter of Consequences

WITH THE LONG OVERDUE fall of Humgudgeon IX, Protector Extraordinary of Addlepate, the people of the capital are so hysterical with joy that they have decided to award the Protectorship to their deliverer—Chumley—perhaps on the assumption that he cannot be any worse than his predecessor. These long beleaguered unfortunates have taken to the streets for a day and a night, throwing off all restraints in a manner that is in its way as alarming as the oppression of Humgudgeon was.

Prince Andre, who has been anticipating his arrival in the capital of Addlepate with trepidation, is puzzled to discover that instead of grim foreboding and silence, he and his little party are met at the gates of the city by a drunken, rollicking crowd, many of its members singing (though not all of them are singing the same song) and dashing through the streets in their continuing celebration. Periodic shouts for "Chumley" and others of "Huzzah!" ring through the narrow streets, and flags of all sorts stream from windows, clotheslines, doorways, and even more inconvenient places.

"What is going on?" Prince Andre asks of one passerby who appears less intoxicated than the rest.

"Celebration," answers the lugubrious fellow.

"Of what?" Prince Andre continues.

"Chumley," is the response (if you can call it that).

"Who's Chumley?" Prince Andre shouts after the man who is being carried away by the crowd.

"New Protector," is the answer, and the first bit of useful information Prince Andre has received since he and his party have entered the city.

Shouting in order to be heard, Prince Andre addresses the others with him, "Let's find some place quiet."

Leander nods in an exaggerated way to make it plain that he hears and understands what Prince Andre has said, and then points toward a side street and performs a complicated pantomime that suggests that there are very few people in that direction. Even in silence, he is overblown.

"That way, then!" bellows Prince Andre.

Alfreida says something sarcastic, but cannot make herself heard over the din.

Slowly, and with much shoving and jostling, they force their way to the side street Leander has indicated, and there, a bit breathlessly, they gather to compare notes.

"They say that there's a new Protector," Prince Andre tells them, still puzzled by the information.

"Not Humgudgeon?" Alfreida asks in accents that imply she is not wholly disappointed.

"Apparently not. There's a new one, someone called Chumley, I think," says Prince Andre, not wanting to be too certain of anything yet. "It must have taken place recently."

"What took place?" Princess Felicia asks, not the least put off by the chaos she has seen.

"A change of Protector," Leander says, doing his best to break it to her gently. "It is as well that we are not required to learn the sordid details. One so gently reared would doubtless be greatly distressed to learn of this."

In fact, Princess Felicia would relish a few sordid details, but she is too well-mannered to say so; she only sighs. "No Humgudgeon, then. I was hoping to see him. I was wondering if all the stories are true."

"Depends on the stories," says Alfreida, smacking her thin lips. "In Humgudgeon's case, they probably were." She rocks back on her heels, humming to herself and taking no more interest in what is going on around her.

"The question is, how are we to proceed?" Prince Andre ventures, and provides his own answer. "We came this way for speed, not convenience, and if we are to be delayed by all this commotion, then it might be better if we took another route." He glances at his dragon. "It isn't fair to ask so much of you, walking all the way to Alabaster-on-Gelasta. It's the only way we can get there, unless that witch is prepared to transport us magically."

"Do not even consider that, I implore Your Highness," says Leander with great emotion. "Your Highness cannot trust a witch, and she is clearly avowed your enemy. Take no chance, I urge you, to play into her hands, for her wiles are great and she would not stop at anything to harm you."

Alfreida snaps out of her reverie. "Some people are not nearly the dolts they appear," she announces, then adds in her best cryptic style, "and others are more."

"Be quiet, you," Prince Andre orders her. "You've caused us more than enough trouble already."

"Untie my hands, you twerp, and you'll learn a thing or two about trouble." Alfreida's cackle is so loud and unnerving that it attracts the attention of some of the mob in the cross-street, and a number of flushed faces peer toward them.

"Be quiet," Prince Andre hisses. "Who knows what may happen if we're discovered."

Esmeralda, who has been watching the street with a sense of dread, now reaches out to grab Prince Andre's sleeve.

"Dragon?" Prince Andre inquires, very proud at the way his dragon is coming along as a pet.

Before she can impress him with their danger, half a dozen large, drunken men reel toward them, singing loudly and diversely, clearly determined to have Prince Andre and the rest join them, or else. Since this is Addlepate, there are still *consequences*.

"Jhoin 'nah c'bra'shun," one of them breathes at Prince Andre, seizing his arm in an aggressive manner.

Firmly but diplomatically, Prince Andre does his best to disengage the grip. "You'll have to excuse us," he says, speaking slowly and distinctly. "We're strangers here, and we have a long way to travel."

"Tha's no way t' b'have," the man informs Prince Andre, becoming offended at once. "Polozhize!"

"What?" Prince Andre asks, more confused than affronted.

"So yu' shink y'r too hi'n'mithy f'r ush," the fellow goes on more belligerently than before, weaving as he tries to take a punch at Prince Andre. His comrades are quick to enter into his cause, and it takes very few minutes for everyone in the dragon-hunting party to be drawn into a melee.

In vain, Leander tries to reach his mule where the skillet is packed, so that he can lay about with it. He is knocked on the head and sent sprawling to the ground, dazed and disoriented, and aghast that he should fail Princess Felicia so utterly when her need of him was at its greatest. He condemns himself for a fool as he tries to get his eyes to focus properly.

Two of the men make a grab for Princess Felicia, but she, having seen them start to fight, is ready for them. She kicks out at the nearest in a most un-Princess-like way, her foot connecting solidly with a spot that gently reared Princesses are not supposed to know about, let alone kick. As the poor fellow doubles over, his face the color of whey, Princess Felicia uses the sharp, dainty high heel on her shoes to scrape the shin of the other man, and then she spins, her arms up and akimbo, and her elbow bashes the other man's nose.

Disheartened and demoralized, the others retreat, dragging Prince Andre with them.

Alfreida gives Princess Felicia a long, appraising stare. "Some people might think that this was an unusual thing for a Princess to do," she says in her shrewdest tone.

Princess Felicia, her eyes shining, laughs. "I've always wanted to find out if that works. It does."

"That it does," agrees Alfreida. "You show more nerve than some ninnies I could mention." Here she shoots Esmeralda a vitriolic glance. "Dragons are supposed to be fearsome creatures, you insufferable worm!"

Esmeralda hangs her head, but more from worry about Prince Andre than from shame at her lack of action.

By now, the two who attacked Princess Felicia have hobbled off, one of them swearing comprehensively. Both are more sober than they were three minutes ago.

Leander, still on the ground, has managed almost to sit up. He has a large bruise over his brow and cheek, and he moves as if each and every bone in his body aches its entire breadth and length. He cannot face the eyes of his adored one. "I did not come to your aid when you were in need."

Princess Felicia grins at him. "Yes, you did; now I've come to yours." She starts to kneel down to help him, but he raises his hand to protest.

"You will soil your clothes and sully your hands touching such a despicable knave as I have proven myself to be." He has never felt more wretched in his life, and the knock on the head is the least of his infamy. "I am a complete blackguard."

Princess Felicia pays him no mind. She half kneels beside him and takes out her handkerchief to wipe his face. "You're talking nonsense," she chides him gently.

"It's about time you noticed that," says Alfreida with asperity. "Did anyone bother to remember which way they've taken the Prince?"

With a whiffling noise (since Lewis Carroll, it has been imperative that dragons, like Jabberwocks, whiffle from time to time), pointing down the alley and hopping on one foot, her tail launching her into the air, Esmeralda tries to make it clear that she knows where they have taken the Prince.

"I think the dragon is trying to tell us something," says Princess Felicia, watching these antics with a good deal of curiosity. "The dragon hasn't done that before."

"Small wonder," sniffs Alfreida, impressed in an odd way, with how determined Esmeralda has suddenly become. "There are those who might think that this is a trap," she cannot help but to suggest, out of her habitual malice as much as anything.

"But if the dragon"—Princess Felicia is still uncertain if this is a he or a she dragon—"saw, then we must try to learn from . . . the dragon." She has been holding her hand to Leander's forehead, doing her best to lessen his pain.

"We must persevere if we are to aid the Prince," Leander announces as he starts to recover. His chagrin is increasing by the moment. "I do not know if I am able, but it may be that I still have sufficient strength to combat any opposition we may encounter." He knows that it would be wise for him to get up and show that he is prepared to do his utmost on behalf of Prince Andre (for Princess Felicia), but it is not easy to tear himself away from his present position. He rebukes himself sternly for his loss of self-discipline, but it lacks the usual power to goad him.

"Don't try to get up yet, Leander," Princess Felicia says sweetly. "You're not yet recovered. I am thrilled to hear you say you are ready to aid my brother, but for now, you must let me be the judge of that."

Leander is overjoyed to be overruled. "I . . . confess that I am dizzy yet," he says, offering it as a sop to his conscience.

"Well, while we stand here blathering, that mob is getting the Prince farther and farther away from us. Some people might think that this is a disadvantage. Some people might wonder how much you truly wish to find the Prince." This evil dart finds its target.

Princess Felicia gets to her feet so suddenly that Leander almost falls back to the cobbles. "How dare you speak to me like that!" Her face is flushed, and the animation of her anger gives her more beauty than her characteristic ennui. "Andre is quite right not to trust you, vile old witch that you are." She turns to Leander. "If she speaks to me like that again, bash her with your skillet!" In some ways, Princess Felicia is very much her mother's daughter.

Leander, more stunned by this swift turn of events than by the knock on his head, is able to nod once or twice, each time fighting a wooziness that horrifies him. "I will do my best to carry out any orders and instructions Your Highness is kind enough to give me," he promises her while hoping that he will not be sick.

"Something must be done," Princess Felicia tells the others, her hands on her hips. "If we wait here, some more of those disgusting ruffians may find us, and then who knows what might happen. We will have to find a parlor or . . . taproom, I suppose, where we can talk and plan."

"There are some of us who might think that a taproom is likely to be filled with more ruffians," Alfreida says with a smug smile. "After seeing what the streets are like, taverns could be worse. Not that such things matter to a creature like me, being vile and all."

"Do you suppose that our mounts are still back at the guard station?" Princess Felicia wonders. "We might need to move quickly once we have secured Prince Andre."

"That is very nearly a sensible observation," Alfreida tells her briskly. "There are inns near the guard station, and they might not be so hectic as here. Not that you should pay any attention to the likes of me, of course." She stands as if she has folded her arms, although her hands are still tied behind her. "Some people are very dense."

At last Leander is back on his feet, and while it is true that he is not yet capable of walking without weaving from side to side, he is determined to behave properly. "Permit me to precede you, dear, dear Princess, for it may be that there will be others wishing to evince their debased passions, and it is not seemly that you should be forced to endure such improbity again."

"It might be better if the witch or the dragon goes first," Princess Felicia says when she has given the matter a little thought. "Not even those rascals are going to want to grab either of them. If they're so drunk that they want to try, they'll be too drunk to be much danger." She touches Leander's forehead again, pushing back his bright hair from his injured face. "You will need to take care of yourself, Leander. We're all depending on you."

Leander feels his heart swell within his breast, and he has to steady himself against the nearest wall. "Oh, there are not sufficient words to reveal to you what your affirmation of confidence instills within me. Courage is an inadequate word, and one that merely hints at the obligation I feel at this unexpected and undeserved approbation."

"The mule is at the mouth of the alley," Princess Felicia says prosaically. "It's probably best if we catch it, and then return to the inns near the guard station."

"About time that something was done," Alfreida says loudly. "Some people would spend the whole night gabbling about their sentiments instead of tending to what has to be done." She glares first at Leander and then at Esmeralda. "You make sure you keep with us, you contemptible dunderpate! Some people are enough to make an astute witch doubt her capacities. Not that I mean to be immodest." She finds herself walking beside Princess Felicia, who has set off at a brisk pace.

"Say what you want, you're still tied up, and you'll remain that way." She points to the mule. "He's not running away. Can you reach him, Leander?"

"It would be worse than folly if I failed to do so," Leander vows, stumbling after the mule which regards him in the obdurate way of mules. Leander succeeds in catching the reins on the first try, which is just as well, since it is doubtful if he is up to a chase.

"Very good, Leander," Princess Felicia commends him with emotion. "I don't know why it is, but since I've known you, I've only been bored about half the time."

"Your gracious perspicuity quite unmans me, Your Highness," Leander says as he brings the mule closer.

Now that they are back near the main street, the noise envelops them like a suffocating blanket. Princess Felicia can only make herself understood with quick signs and a few determined shoves. In no time, they are making their way through the press of the crowd, Esmeralda in the lead with Alfreida, Princess Felicia in the middle, and Leander in the rear with the mule, his skillet now firmly clutched in his white-knuckled hand.

The third inn they come to is called the Broken Window, and it appears to be the least busy of any of them. Princess Felicia orders the others into the main room of the inn, then she goes in search of the landlord. "He's bound to be here somewhere, even if he's passed out behind his own taps."

"It is not vainglory which prompts me to say that this apparent tergiversation displayed by our dear Princess must be perceived as the revelation of depths hitherto unacknowledged in her already superior character," Leander says to Alfreida, possibly in an attempt to make his version of smalltalk.

"Twaddle!" counters Alfreida, keeping her eye on Esmeralda, who is wandering about the room in a listless way.

"Doubtless she will not be dissuaded from her determination to secure a release for Prince Andre, no matter what has become of him," Leander goes on, unfazed by Alfreida's uncordial attitude. "It cannot surprise any who have had the opportunity to observe her that she would persevere in this, as in all other matters. Her resolution must inspire us all with similiar determination and purpose." He has found a stool to sit on, but is too well-behaved to use it until Alfreida has found a place for herself.

"Fie!" Alfreida snaps, her patience with Leander almost exhausted. "You overblown quopper, I'd turn you into almost anything that doesn't talk if I had my hands free."

Leander nods. "I have been aware since we caught you that you have nothing but disdain for those who receive warranted adulation from others."

Alfreida gives a long, disgruntled hiss. "Some people would do better to consider what they say before they say it."

"On this, witch, we can agree," Leander says, and is puzzled when Alfreida starts to stamp her feet and mutter.

Fortunately, Princess Felicia returns just then with the landlord in tow. This worthy is much the worse for wear, having spent the greater part of the last two days in downing libations to the new Protector Extraordinary. He regards these intruders with bleary eyes, and decides that he must not indulge anymore, because one of the party gathered in his front parlor looks decidedly green and tailed. He remembers to bow, which he does badly, and then to wait for more instruction.

"First, some food. No drink, sir. Then we will want to be left alone. There are two horses at the guard station, and you will be rewarded if they are cared for and safely here when we return tomorrow." Now that she is getting the hang of being in charge, Princess Felicia is enjoying herself tremendously.

"As you say, Your..." He isn't sure of her title and has decided to say nothing rather than use the wrong one.

"And we will need rooms for this evening. One for Leander there, and one for the rest of us." She speaks briskly, one toe tapping in cadence with her words.

Alfreida shakes her head. "Won't do any good to remain here, you goose," she points out. "That dolt of a brother of yours could be anywhere by now, and you won't find him by waiting for him to come sauntering through the door."

"As reluctant as I am to endorse anything this frenzied creature says," Leander says, still wishing that that woman would sit down so that he could get off his feet, "I must agree that in this instance she displays remarkable lucidity."

"You lack-witted joltskull," Alfreida scoffs, apparently unaware that he has just given her a compliment.

"I hope that we are all ready to take action," Princess Felicia says with pluck. "And that includes the dragon."

At the mention of the word *dragon*, Esmeralda turns toward Princess Felicia, excitement beginning to replace the numbness of despair that has consumed her since she saw Prince Andre dragged away from them.

"Landlord, get us some food," Princess Felicia orders, then lowers her voice as the door closes. "While he's away, I'll tell you my plan."

Meanwhile, In the Protector Extraordinary's Castle...

FOR THE FIRST day or so of celebration and festivities, Chumley had a marvelous time. He had more than enough to eat and drink, and it pleased his simple soul to be surrounded by those who were eager to serve him. But now, he is not as gratified as he was, for he has not been permitted to have any play toys and everyone around him keeps asking him to tell them what to do. This not only baffles him, it is starting to irritate him, which is a risky business with Chumley.

He has taken over the Throne Room, cushions and all, and has yet to find a really comfortable position on them. All the drink he has consumed has left him with a gonging head and a terrible taste in his mouth. Every time he is offered a new beverage, he becomes more surly. There are a few members of the court who are beginning to suspect that the new Protector Extraordinary is not temperamentally suited to the job.

Thus it is with trepidation that the Captain of the Guard enters the Throne Room and abases himself in front of the cushions. "Your..." He mumbles something that ends in "icence," since a title has not yet been found for Chumley.

"Hurm," says Chumley.

"Ah... there is a... prisoner, I think, for you to question, or whatever you want to do with prisoners." The Captain of the Guard fumbles with his weapons, then gets to his knees. "Some of the townspeople found him in the streets. He's a stranger, Your (mumble)icence. Looks to be important."

It takes Chumley a little while to digest what he is being told, and when he is pretty sure he has it right, he says with great deliberation, "Chumley want see."

"Yes. Here? Now?" He has not yet learned how Chumley wants his court conducted, and has learned over the years not to make assumptions.

169

Again Chumley gives himself to laborious thought. It makes his headache worse. "Here," he orders at last, and in a tone of voice that indicates to the Captain of the Guard that it would not be wise to keep the Protector waiting.

The Captain of the Guard scurries from the room and goes to get the prisoner, pondering the change of Protectors as he goes. As soon as he has Prince Andre in his custody, he warns him, "You better not make any trouble, that's all I can say."

Prince Andre favors the Captain of the Guard with a disdainful look. "Why? Are you afraid?" He is able to laugh, which is as amazing to him as it is to the Captain. He shakes himself free of the Captain of the Guard's grasp. "I will come quietly. You needn't maul me."

"If you think this is mauling, sir, you're very much mistaken, I can tell you that." The Captain of the Guard is clearly insulted by the inference, and his tone is huffy. "Mauling's what we do *after* the Protector gives the order, if you take my meaning, sir."

Prince Andre, in fact, takes it all too well, as he remembers every unpleasant tale (and there have been so *many* of them) he has ever heard of Humgudgeon. If this new Protector is half the creature Humgudgeon was, Prince Andre fears he is in very serious trouble. He tries not to think about that as he enters the Throne Room and bows gracefully and deeply. "Your Majesty." He has no idea that the ruler of Addlepate might have another title. Prince Andre calls all rulers Your Majesty out of habit and good manners.

Chumley beetles his brow at this new arrival and shakes his lumpish head. "Not play toy," he says sadly. He had great hopes for the new arrival, but even he knows that it would be going too far to use this young man as a play toy.

"Just so, Your (mumble)icence," says the Captain of the Guard, who remembers the very recent days with Humgudgeon when almost anyone might be made a play toy at his whim.

"Want play toy," Chumley says in a surly tone.

"One will be found," the Captain of the Guard declares, a bit sharply since he has been the one to hear most of the complaints recently.

"It is an honor to greet you, Your Majesty," Prince Andre goes on in his best court behavior. "I understand I am the first foreign Royal to call upon you, which is my great good fortune."

"Hurm," says Chumley, who has understood about one word in three and who is trying to sort out what it all means.

Perceiving that whatever Chumley may be, he is not the capricious sort that Humgudgeon was, Prince Andre continues with caution. "Your Majesty will doubtless be planning a gala to celebrate your rise to the Throne of Addlepate. If there is any way I might be of service during this time, you have only to ask me and I will place myself at your disposal."

"I wouldn't put it that way, sir, if I was you," the Captain of the Guard warns Prince Andre, too late. "He gets notions about things, you know."

Prince Andre does not know, but he does his best to appear calm. "Certainly there is no danger in offering to serve another ruler."

"As to that, sir, I couldn't say," says the Captain of the Guard, watching Chumley out of the corner of his eye. "But I will say this, and it is that we never had such a ruler as this one in Addlepate, not in all the history."

"Really," responds Prince Andre, hoping to bring out more information before he has to speak to Chumley again.

Chumley, who has been cleaning his nails with his teeth, looks up and says, "What is celebration?"

Prince Andre blinks. "It is . . . a party, Your Majesty. There are feasts and dances and state processions and other similar happenings." He pauses, uncertain as to how to go on. "They can be quite pleasant, Your Majesty, but they take a lot of planning, and some persons find them tiring." He recalls Queen Hortensia's method of party preparation, which is to give a great many (often contradictory) orders, and then retire to her apartment to lie on her chaise so that she might be fresh for the occasion when it finally arrives.

"Play toys?" asks Chumley wistfully.

Prince Andre is aware that this phrase has been the most prominent one on Chumley's lips, and so he gives a hearty laugh. "If that is what Your Majesty desires, then doubtless you shall have them." Only after he has said this does he notice that the Captain of the Guard is desperately trying to catch his eye. "Doubtless," he goes on, hardly missing a beat, "special arrangements will need to be made."

"Bad idea, sir," the Captain of the Guard whispers.

"Want play toys," Chumley tells them with determination.

"Of course, Your (mumble)icence," the Captain of the Guard promises him mendaciously.

"Want play toys now," Chumley says, with an alarming display of animation. "Play toys!"

"Just so," the Captain of the Guard says, as if speaking to a fractious five-year-old (which, in a sense, he is). "You have only to issue your instructions and it will be tended to." He feels fairly safe there, because he is reasonably certain that Chumley is incapable of doing it.

"Your Majesty," Prince Andre interjects, having a better sense of the way things are. "It would be my privilege to help the Captain of the Guard, and whomever else you wish, to prepare a celebration for you. If you authorize us to do this, we will try to arrange a party that would be everything you might like."

"Play toy?" Chumley has had trouble following Prince Andre, but he has the jist of it, and it suits his current frame of mind. "Lots of play toys."

"If it is possible, naturally we'll give it highest priority." He is not quite sure how this is to be done, but he knows that if he is to get out of this place, it will not be by might or courtesy, but by guile. "If the Captain of the Guard might be allowed to advise me? I fear that I haven't much knowledge of how things are done here in Addlepate."

"Get play toys." This has more the sound of a mandate, and Chumley, to make himself clear, throws a goblet across the room, watching with satisfaction as it smashes against the wall.

"I will do everything I can, Sire," Prince Andre says with a bow in perfect form. "May we withdraw?"

The Captain of the Guard plucks at Prince Andre's sleeve. "Better not to wait for that, sir. The new Protector don't stand much on form, if you see what I mean." He pulls Prince Andre toward the door, giving more consideration to haste than form. Once they are in the hallway and out of range, the Captain of the Guard takes Prince Andre to task. "What was you up to, filling his head with notions about play toys? We've been trying to get him off that for over a day, and we were doing pretty well until you reminded him about them. Now we shall have our hands full, and no doubt about it. He's the Protector, but there's no denying that he's a simpleton. What he has in mind, sir, you wouldn't want to know about. The old Protector," the Captain of the Guard goes on, hardly pausing for breath before launching into a recitation of some of the horrors Prince Andre would not want to hear. "Humgudgeon used to give things to Chumley, if you know what I mean by that."

"The play toys he wants now?" Prince Andre asks, hoping to follow all that the Captain of the Guard is saying.

"That's what he calls them, yes, sir, but that's not what they are, you see. Whenever someone displeased Humgudgeon, why, he'd call in Chumley to take care of the situation. Chumley would carry off the offender, and that was all there was to it." He folds his arms and gives a very unlovely smile. "That's what the Protector wants when he says he wants play toys."

Prince Andre's brows raise. "He wants to . . . ?"

"Precisely," says the Captain of the Guard with a swift, graphic gesture at his throat.

"And he finds that amusing?" Prince Andre asks, needing no answer.

"It was Humgudgeon's fault, really. He set him on to it, if you understand, sir. He gave him the taste for it, and now there's nothing we've been able to do that fills the gap. It will probably come down to letting him have a criminal or two every week or so." He sighs. "He's not as difficult as Humgudgeon, of course, I'll say that for him, but I can tell that this is not going to be as simple as it seemed at first."

Prince Andre starts to pace in the confined space. "Are the people aware of his . . . proclivities?"

"Oh, I shouldn't think so, not yet. They're glad to be rid of Humgudgeon, don't you know, and so Chumley seems to be their deliverer, and an inoffensive one, at that. Have a look around the nobility if you want to have your hackles raised, young fellow. Not much to choose between 'em, and they're all snapping at one another like a pack of rabid dogs. They'll all be waiting for a chance to do away with the poor looney in the Throne Room and take his place so that Addlepate can be run proper again."

"Run proper?" Prince Andre repeats, both hoping and fearing clarification.

"You know, the way Humgudgeon was doing it. We're used to it here in Addlepate, and we don't like to have our Protectors turn out to be too mild. We don't like soft rulers, the way the rest of you lot seem to. We like rulers who can rule, you understand me? and no bones about it. Whenever I hear about other kingdoms where there aren't the sorts of rulers we have here, my heart fairly stops in my breast, so it does, because I don't know how they go on with such a state of affairs." He breathes deeply, lifting his chest with what he believes is justifiable pride. "In Addlepate, the ruler is always the one who makes the rest obey, and obey they do, none of this shilly-shallying around as the rest of you seem to like. I'll take the Protector any day, no matter how tricksy he may be, against any soft-tempered ruler. Mark my words, young fellow, it's the Humgudgeons who hold the world together, you'll see for yourself before you're much older."

Prince Andre does his best not to appear aghast at what the Captain of the Guard has told him. "In the meantime, there is the question of a celebration."

"Oh, I should think we can put that off, sir, if you follow me. It would merely give the others a chance to do away with Chumley, and they'll do that soon and soon in any case. We'll have the cooks make him some pies and we'll find a few clowns from the carnival to come and balance plates on their noses for him, and that should keep him happy for a while." The Captain of the Guard gives an indulgent smile.

"And the . . . play toys?" Prince Andre inquires.

"Oh, I fancy we'll think of something, young sir, and that ought to satisfy the Protector." He chuckles suddenly. "It's a simple enough request to fill, compared to some of the things that Humgudgeon was always asking for. Still, finding what he wants will take a little time, I should think." He beams at Prince Andre. "You won't have much to do but read until the ransom arrives."

"Ransom?" Prince Andre asks, not as surprised as he would like to be.

"Of course. You didn't suppose we wouldn't hold you for ransom, did you? It was that or offer you as some sort of sacrifice, but that almost always leads to war, and with Chumley on the Throne, well, young sir, anyone can see that war would not be his strong point, not at all." He finds this amusing and permits himself to laugh at his own humor. "We'll get a messenger off one of these days, and then they'll pay, and you'll be able to go home. It shouldn't be too unpleasant, not if you mind your manners and stay where you're put. If you try to escape, that would be another matter, if you get my intention, and you would have to be put in a

dungeon cell, where who-knows-what might happen to you."
He raises a finger in warning. "Be careful, lad, and don't
waste your time getting yourself into more trouble than you're
already in. We're not patient folk here in Addlepate. You'd
regret being impetuous."

"Held for ransom," Prince Andre says to himself. "After
all this, to be held for ransom."

"Don't get yourself downhearted, sir," the Captain of the
Guard says at his jovial best. "We'll see that you're entertained properly, and you won't starve here."

"How good of you," says Prince Andre with a sarcasm that
is entirely wasted on the Captain of the Guard.

"We try to please, sir," he remarks to Prince Andre before
he strolls away.

Left to himself, Prince Andre frowns at the wall, as if
trying to decipher a message in the stone. He is irritated with
himself for being in this ridiculous position, and he is equally
concerned that his companions might be in a worse predicament than he is. He tries to think of a way to find out about
them, but nothing suggests itself to him, and finally he abandons the problem entirely, before he gives way to despair.

The Question of Rescue

"THAT'S THE MOST shatterpated notion anyone has come up
with yet." Alfreida sneers at Princess Felicia and the author of
the idea she has such a low opinion of, Leander. "What's to
stop the soldiers from arresting you as you sneak into the
palace, tell me that."

"If I go in through the kitchen they should pay no notice of
me," Leander says. "The perspicacity of the kitchen staff is
not an issue in this instance."

"And who's to say they won't mention this to the Guard, and the next thing you know, you'll be in the next dungeon, and they'll be snipping bits and pieces off you." Alfreida does one of her very best cackles.

"I am so indebted to His Highness that there is no sacrifice I would not make on his behalf. If it falls to me that I should suffer with him, then I will submit to—"

"Oh, no you won't," Princess Felicia says with determination. "If there's any sacrificing to be done, you're not going to be the one to do it. If anyone goes to that castle for a spy, it will not be you." Her elbows are on the table and her lace cuffs are pushed up. Her rosebud mouth is set in a very firm line.

"What!" protests Alfreida, who is the only other candidate.

"We will have to arrange a way for us to remain together, at least for the time being," Princess Felicia goes on, paying no attention to Alfreida's outburst. "If we let ourselves be separated now, there's no telling what will become of us. If we remain together, we have some chance of success."

"You could send a message to your father, you berserk mooncalf," Alfreida suggests, stamping her feet under the table.

"What good would that do?" Princess Felicia asks mildly. "He would have to find someone to act for him, and that would take time, and we haven't time to spare. It is up to us to find the way to rescue him."

"Let me reiterate my first notion," Leander puts in. "We can disguise ourselves as entertainers—it is appropriate for a new ruler to be entertained upon his ascending the Throne. Doubtless this Chumley is not unlike all other new rulers, and would be pleased to receive us."

"And what then?" Princess Felicia asks. It has become quite dark in the tavern, and there is little light from the dying fire. For the most part, they speak in whispers, as if wanting to share the stillness of the hour. "Once we are in, we dare not reveal our identities, and how are we to find Andre if we don't?"

"There must be ways." Leander says, shocked into simple declarative statement.

"There must." Princess Felicia's gaze wanders around the darkened room once more, and this time lights on the dim figure of Esmeralda, where she huddles near the fire (dragons, like all the lizard clan, love heat). "Entertainers," she says speculatively, her eyes still on the dragon.

"Oh, dear Princess Felicia, what has occurred to you? I acknowledge your right to determine the means of rescue, and it is apparent that you have gained new inspiration. Indulge in speculation, for our benefit, I urge you."

"It appears to me," Princess Felicia says in careful tones, "that there is a problem both in getting in and in getting out. We therefore have to find a way to do both, and without risk, or as little risk as possible. If we become entertainers, to have the chance to be admitted to the castle, then we ought to offer something unusual." Again, her eyes wander to the dragon. "Since we aren't real jugglers or performers—"

"Some people are not; others are," mutters Alfreida. "And if I had my hands free, I could show you a thing or two. I'm not boasting when I say that there are many witches out there who would give half their herb gardens to do what I can do. It may not have occurred to you, but I am a witch of importance and reputation, not that I mean to make much of myself."

"—or have other talents that we can use," Princess Felicia goes on pointedly, "we must take advantage of what we can do. And we do have a dragon."

"Imprecations!" Alfreida expostulates. "Aren't you listening to me, you jabbernoll? Is talking all you're good for? Some people would try the patience of a tree!"

Very deliberately Princess Felicia folds her hands and gives Alfreida a long, enduring stare. "Very well; say what's on your mind."

"Why, you could let me go. I could have us out of here in no time at all. Everything they say about the new Protector indicates that he hasn't the least magic about him, and therefore there's no one around who could stop me. Give me the chance, and I could whisk us all away from here in the batting of an eyelid." She flaps her elbows, as if to prove a point.

"And you would whisk us back to your hovel, no doubt, and into cages or worse." Princess Felicia shakes her head briskly. "I don't think so."

"But I could give you my word." Alfreida's smile is so crafty, so wholly untrustworthy that even Chumley would be skeptical about her propositions.

"What good would that be?" Princess Felicia counters even as the dragon moves forward, one small talon lifted in warning. "A witch isn't bound by her word, or so Sigmund told me once, and Sigmund really *does* know everything, when he can remember it."

"Drat!" rasps Alfreida.

"I will keep your suggestion in mind, however. I might yet find a use for it. And there's no denying that you're very picturesque. We ought to be able to use you to some effect." Princess Felicia looks thoughtfully at the dragon again. "I wonder if it knows any tricks?"

Hearing this, Esmeralda moves forward, her small front limbs lifted up. She does a shambling sort of leap, and then cavorts around the room in an ungainly but endearing fashion. She is prepared to do almost anything to rescue Prince Andre.

"What an egregious display," says Leander, much impressed (and not positively) with the dragon's performance. "Surely you cannot wish to employ that creature? It is a dragon, and that must create many doubts in your mind, dear Princess. It is a dangerous, unpredictable monster, and it is most implausible that the beast would cooperate with you in your venture. Let me be the one to enter the castle, so that you need not expose yourself to anything but the most minimal danger." He very nearly takes her hand in his, but that would be going too far.

"It is like you, sweet Leander, to offer this, but I think that my idea might have the better chance of success. Besides, someone must guard this witch, and it's apt to be a more difficult task than getting into the castle." Princess Felicia rises. "What's needed, I think, is some sort of costume. I believe I will go and cut up my rose riding habit." This is said with the sweetest of smiles. "Come along, witch. You can advise me."

"Piffle!" scoffs Alfreida. Then, with a very angular shrug, she gets up and goes to the door with Princess Felicia.

"Have a care, dear Princess. That witch is, as you have remarked, an unpredictable and capricious being who might attempt blandishments that would lead to your releasing her from her bonds. You must permit me to guard you."

"I won't listen to anything she says," Princess Felicia tells him. "I'm merely going to study her clothes." If she sees the look of utter outrage that Alfreida gives her, she does not acknowledge it.

As the door closes behind them, Leander stares at the fire,

ignoring the dragon huddled near it, small plumes of pale smoke rising from her nostrils. He gives vent to his feeling in song:

> *"Ensorceled by a double charm, I stand*
> *Between despair and my highest aspiration;*
> *Fatality has gripped me by the hand*
> *To confound me or to grant me exaltation.*
>
> *"Were it possible, I would at once reveal*
> *To that epitome of every delectation*
> *What evil charm that to woe from weal*
> *Wrought me by malefic transformation.*
>
> *"Fairest Felicia, garden amid the blight*
> *You, the source of all my inspiration*
> *You, the dawn that vanquishes my night*
> *And lends my heart vast revivification:*
>
> *"I vow that what I tell you now is true*
> *And simply stated—oh, do I love you."*

Esmeralda, being Esmeralda, is very touched by Leander's song (though, naturally, she liked Prince Andre's better), and she wishes there were a way she might be able to tell Princess Felicia about it. On the other hand, she would hate to embarrass Leander, so perhaps it is just as well that she can say nothing of what she has overheard.

Upstairs, Princess Felicia has set to work with a pair of shears, taking the elaborate lacing and braid off her rose-colored riding habit, and then cutting back the sleeves until they are only little shredded caps at the shoulder. Next, she hacks away at the neckline until it is low enough to make Queen Hortensia, should she ever see it, swoon.

"Fashions are silly these days," Alfreida growls at Princess Felicia as she watches the destruction of the garment with relish. "In my day, let me tell you, there was real grace and elegance, not like these overdone and ridiculous things you rig yourself out in today."

"This is hardly going to be fashionable," Princess Felicia says with alarming reasonableness.

"It doesn't matter," Alfreida sniffs. "The thing was silly to start with. Look at it: no dash, no élan, no style." She shakes her head. "When I was a girl, you should have seen how beautiful we were, in the laces and silks, with the standing ruffs and ribbons everywhere. Osgood used to tell me that no one had a way with spider-web lace that I had." A reflective light comes into her eyes. "You can't imagine."

"Very likely not," Princess Felicia says abstractedly as she does untold damage with the shears. Most of the skirt has been snipped to an uneven hem, varying in length from knee to lower calf, and will reveal far more of her leg than it is seemly for a Princess to reveal to anyone but her nurse and her eventual Prince. "It's a pity I haven't a pair of sandals, but I suppose my slippers can be cut up, too."

"It isn't going to work, you dunce. You want to show off to that brass-haired lout in the parlor, that's all you want to do." Alfreida delights in her scorn.

There is just enough truth in this accusation to bring a flush to Princess Felicia's cheeks. "That," she says primly, "has nothing to do with it."

"Nothing to do with it, nothing to do with it," Alfreida mocks. "I'm not some zany witling, you giddy-skull. You've got your little heart set on entrancing that daft crumpeter, not that you need to bother. He's already dizzy from you, and this is nothing but wasted energy."

"We have to get my brother out of that castle," Princess Felicia insists with a good deal of sense. "And I believe that I and the dragon have the best chance of doing it. The other is . . . beside the point." She makes a particularly vigorous slash with the shears and the last of the petticoat is reduced to tatters. "There. This looks more the thing."

"For what?" demands Alfreida.

"For what a dragon-tamer might wear, of course," Princess Felicia says curtly.

"Dragon-tamer?" Alfreida echos. "Do you really suppose that that deranged undersized clodhopper is going to be any use to you? Why, she'd faint at her own shadow if she had an ounce more sense than she does." Alfreida squirms in her bonds. "Let me go, and I'll help you. Left to you and Esmeralda, everything will go wrong."

"You call the dragon Esmeralda?" Princess Felicia asks with genuine amusement. "How quaint. Esmeralda."

"Fat lot you know about anything," Alfreida says, sulking.

"You with your scissors and your plans, you're as crack-brained as any of them. Not that you ever had me fooled."

"And you don't have me fooled, either," Princess Felicia says. She has to pause to choke back a giggle. "You would love to get out of the bonds and work a spell or two, to teach us all a lesson, I suppose. Then you'd be back into the Woebegone Wood, leaving us in goodness-knows-what condition. It's a pity you can't be trusted, because we could use your help, but it would be far too costly." She makes a few random slashes on the riding habit and then stares at it critically. "I think this will have to do it. I suppose I could tie it in knots and roll it around the floor a few times, to make it a bit grimy."

"Humph!" says Alfreida to indicate her idea of the whole plan.

"Yes, you would say that," Princess Felicia agrees most cordially, which only serves to infuriate Alfreida the more.

While Princess Felicia ties her ruined habit into several lumpish knots, she goes on, explaining her idea as much to herself as to the witch. "We'll arrive, and being only a simple maiden and her pet performing dragon, no one will suspect that we are up to anything. We'll ask if we can perform for the new Protector and any visiting dignitaries, and then, when we are admitted to the Throne Room or the Great Hall, we will hope that Andre will be there. If he's not, we'll have to find out where he is. Perhaps I will say that we wish to travel to other countries and wonder if there are any visiting nobles who might give us an introduction or a safe conduct. That would be reasonable, wouldn't it?"

"I don't know. It has nothing to do with me. It's not my plan, and if it were, I'd know better than to use it." Alfreida is determined to be contrary, and she does it very well.

"If you haven't a better one in mind—and one that is practical—then this is the one I'll have to use. I do hope that your dragon will be able to do some tricks. If not, perhaps the sight of her will be enough." She gets down on her knees and begins to scrub the knotted habit over the dusty boards. "I must say," she adds reflectively, "I think it's very unfair that espionage and spying and all the rest should be left to hirelings. It's quite a lot of fun, really. You never know what's going to happen next."

"You might not like what happens next. Some people are

very blind to reality," Alfreida says darkly, but with a note of satisfaction.

"You mean that we might be discovered and captured and all the rest of it. Yes, I can see that it could happen, but that's what makes it interesting, don't you realize? That element of uncertainty, what a delightful thing it is." Satisfied with the state of the habit, she rises and begins to untie the knots. "We had all better sleep well tonight. Tomorrow is likely to be a hectic day."

Into (And Out Of) The Jaws Of Danger

THE GUARDS OF the Protector's castle in Addlepate have seen just about everything over the years, what with the whims of all the Humgudgeons, but most of them are surprised when a pretty Gypsy-like girl comes to the castle gate, leading a small but genuine dragon.

"What's a sweet maid like you doing here?" leers the Sergeant of the Guard (it is expected of him).

"To perform for the new Protector, and perhaps get a decent meal and a few coppers for my pains," answers Princess Felicia in what she hopes is a saucy tone. She has never actually seen a Gypsy, nor is she certain what a saucy tone is, but she has an excellent imagination and it stands her in good stead.

"You think the Protector would want to see the likes of you?" jokes the Sergeant of the Guard.

One of the men standing near him plucks at his sleeve. "You never know," he says timorously. "This new Protector might like—"

"Yes!" barks the Sergeant of the Guard. "Very true." He is still more used to Humgudgeon than Chumley, but the point, he realizes, is well-taken, and this new Protector has simpler tastes than the former had. He looks at Princess Felicia with a bold eye. "Will you give us a kiss for an open door?"

"My dragon will," Princess Felicia declares fearlessly. "I'm not for the likes of you, Officer." Since she isn't certain of his rank, she decides to choose a safe title. "I have a lover who would break your skull with one blow should you take liberties with me." Which is true enough.

The Sergeant of the Guard takes this in good part, laughing loudly. "Fierce, aren't we. Does your dragon eat more fire than you, wench?" He shakes his head and goes to lift the enormous exterior bolt that closes the gate on this side. (There is an even more enormous bolt on the other side, to hold the gate against the occasional insurrectionists.)

The castle of the Protector of Addlepate is nothing like the palace of Alabaster-on-Gelasta, except that both are very large. The courtyard of the castle is gloomy, a small, dark patch of cobbles surrounded by towering, imposing dark granite walls, with only occasional windows (and very small ones at that) to relieve the starkness of their fronts. Armed men are everywhere, and none of them seems friendly.

A skinny page runs up to Princess Felicia and Esmeralda and makes a sloppy bow. "I'm supposed to take you to the Protector, so the Sergeant of the Guard orders." He has a pinched, ratty face, and it is not unlikely that this boy will grow up to be very much like the Spy.

"Good of you," says Princess Felicia in her most flirtatious manner. "We're anxious to see him and his court."

"Court?" the page asks, nonplused.

"Or whomever the Protector keeps with him," she adds with a shrug.

The page says nothing, but he scampers off into one of the gulletlike tunnels, not quite cringing, but close enough to make Princess Felicia almost feel sorry for him. If only he had some character, she thinks, some strength to give him worth, but she can perceive none in him.

"Come along, dragon," Princess Felicia orders when Esmeralda hesitates at the entrance to the passage. "There are torches to light the way." Then, as if this behavior required some explanation, she says, "They don't like the dark, you know, in strange places. It's their tails."

"Oh, yes," mumbles the page as he leads them to a narrow, curving staircase.

"Do we have to go up there?" Princess Felicia inquires, suspicious now.

"It leads to the Throne Room," the page tells her with an ingratiating grin.

"Why not take us by the main staircase?" Princess Felicia wonders pointedly.

"This *is* the main staircase," the page informs her, trying to smile and making a mull of it.

"Oh. Well, it might be difficult for the dragon," Princess Felicia declares, thinking that if getting up is hard going, coming down is sure to be worse. She realizes with chagrin that she had not anticipated such a problem when she worked out her plan. Sternly she banishes her apprehension, and signals to Esmeralda to follow her.

"Watch out for the trip stairs," the page warns. "There are two of them."

"How clever," Princess Felicia says, trying not to become too irritated with the situation.

Outside the Throne Room, the Captain of the Guard is waiting with four soldiers, all standing at attention with weapons in hand. This is hardly encouraging, but Princess Felicia tosses her head and swaggers past them, making sure that they all can see she is unafraid and wholly able to handle herself. She is a bit miffed that they do not see through her disguise enough to bow to her, as is only proper, but she does her best to reconcile herself to lowly position.

"An entertainer, Protector," the page announces as the Captain of the Guard lets him and Princess Felicia and Esmeralda through the door.

Chumley is lying back on the cushions trying to play cup-and-ball, with very little success. No matter how he tosses the ball on the string, it never seems to land in the cup. He is glad to abandon the pursuit and to let someone else do the work for the time being. "Hurm!" he declares as he catches sight of the dragon.

"Your Majesty," Princess Felicia says as she sinks into a perfect curtsy (she is as well-mannered as her brother). "My dragon and I are here to entertain you." Nothing in her face reveals the shock she feels at the sight of the new Protector Extraordinary. Extraordinary indeed! she tells herself. Humgudgeon she was prepared for, but Chumley . . . She conceals her bafflement and starts into the little speech she concocted the night before. "Your Majesty, my pet and I are here to astound you with our skills. You and your court, your guests, are invited to watch and wonder as we perform for your entertainment."

"Play toy?" Chumley asks hopefully.

"I beg your pardon?" says Princess Felicia, thinking she has misunderstood.

"Want play toy," Chumley tells her, sighing deeply.

"We will...uh...try our best," Princess Felicia says, looking toward the page and the Captain of the Guard for some hint as to what is going on.

"These aren't play toys, Your (mumble)icence," says the Captain of the Guard firmly. "They are to watch. They will amuse you. You'll like it."

Chumley shakes his head with disappointment, then lowers his eyes, the better to stare at the dragon's feet. "Funny," he tells Princess Felicia.

"Apparently," Princess Felicia agrees. "If there are any others?" She had assumed that it would simply be a matter of finding the Protector to find Prince Andre, and now she is becoming confused. She forces herself to think clearly. She turns to the page and the Captain of the Guard. "It might be best if we had a larger audience. It is easier to perform when there are a few more people, and it might make it...more enjoyable for the Protector?" If they refuse her, she does not know what she will do next.

"I take your meaning, Miss," says the Captain of the Guard with a knowing wink. "Not very attentive, our Protector."

"So it seems," Princess Felicia says, trying not to sound too much like herself.

"Well, you get started and I'll see what I can do about bringing a few more people in. There are one or two nobles hanging about who might like to watch a dragon, though, if you'll pardon my mentioning it, that isn't much of a beast, is it?"

"She's young yet, Captain," Princess Felicia informs him crisply. "It's best to train them young."

"I should think so," says the Captain of the Guard as he goes to the door. "Back in a bit. Start with the easy things, as you might say. No sense wasting the best on him."

Ordinarily, Princess Felicia would retire to her apartments and stare dreamily out the window when events frustrate her,

but she is not at home in Alabaster-on-Gelasta, and she has no
apartments to retire to. For the first time, she begins to think
that excitement might not be all that it is supposed to be.
While Princess Felicia would never use a word like *afraid*, she
will admit to a few qualms, which in her case is much the
same thing. She forces herself to stand straight and to smile,
and she pulls on the lead to bring Esmeralda closer. "Bow to
the Protector, dragon," she orders.

Esmeralda slashes her tail to the side and does the best she
can to bow. Her thoughts are awash with dismay, but she is
determined to do all that she can to help save Prince Andre,
and if dancing for this ungainly lump of a Protector will be
useful, she is determined to do it.

"Very good," Princess Felicia says, patting the dragon's
shoulder (she does not like the way the scales feel under her
hand, but that is a small price to pay), and wishes that she had
some sort of treat to give the dragon for doing well, though
she hasn't any idea what dragons like as treats. She knows
that it is carrots and apples for horses and bones and old socks
for dogs, but dragons?

"Hurm, hurm," goes Chumley in appreciation.

"Now the dragon and I will dance for you, Sire," says
Princess Felicia, sorry that there are no musicians to play for
them. "The dragon will begin." She tugs the lead. "Now,
dragon, dance."

As a girl, Esmeralda dances with a lithe grace that is truly
breathtaking. As a dragon, the reaction is not so favorable.
She shuffles forward three steps, then hops sideways, trying to
keep to some steady rhythm but without much success. Spin-
ning is even harder, since her tail drags behind her, and when
she tries to stop, it pulls her around farther. Staggering and a
bit dizzy, she lurches to the side again, almost loses her footing, and then rocks back on her tail, kangaroo-style, to keep
from falling.

For any other audience, this performance might be greeted
with derision, but Chumley is absolutely enchanted. He bun-
dles his cushions all around him and braces his elbows on his
knees and his chin on his knuckles as he gives the dragon his
rapt attention.

Noticing that she is getting more success than she anticipated, Princess Felicia is happy to take advantage of it.
"Dance, dragon," she urges Esmeralda. "The Protector is
pleased with you."

This does not please Esmeralda as much as it pleases Princess Felicia; she has had more experience with those of uncertain temper and intellect than the Princess has, and it has taught her several worrisome lessons. She hops back onto her feet and begins to do a slow sort of skip, hoping that she will keep her balance as she careens around the room.

Chumley whoops his delight.

This is not at all what Princess Felicia had in mind when she came up with her plan, and now that it is going so strangely, she is becoming flustered. She pulls hard on the lead and clears her throat. "Dragon, stop."

"Want more!" Chumley protests, not at all graciously. He glowers at Princess Felicia and waits for her to obey him.

"In a moment, Your Majesty," Princess Felicia says, bowing to him. "Dragons tire easily when indoors, and then they cannot control their flames. You don't want the room to catch fire, do you?"

Chumley does not understand all this, but he knows what fire is, and he is dimly aware that dragons can do it. He leans back, not wanting to push the little luck he has. "Dance," he tells her, but more as a request than an order.

"Shortly, Sire," Princess Felicia promises him. "In the mean time, the dragon will balance on one foot." From what she has seen of Chumley, Princess Felicia is fairly certain that will satisfy him for the time being.

Esmeralda quivers, not sure she can perform this feat, but willing to try. She finds a spot in the center of the room and carefully shifts all her weight onto her left rear foot, gradually raising the right, and finally, her tail. The support is precarious, but she is able to do it for more than a minute.

Chumley's delight is almost boundless. He slams his huge palms together in applause and rolls on the cushions like an enormous kitten waiting for a new mouse. "Good. That good!" he hollers.

Princess Felicia keeps her opinion to herself and hopes fervently that they bring her brother quickly, for she is certain that the longer this goes on, the more reluctant Chumley will be to part with the dragon, which would hardly be fair to the beast, and which Prince Andre would not permit, in any case. "Now, dragon, roll over."

Esmeralda is offended by this suggestion, and she wants to scream out that she is not a puppy, but all that she can do is hiss, and then try to think of how to manage the thing. Her tail makes so many actions difficult.

Before this command can be executed, the door opens and the Captain of the Guard returns with half a dozen men in tow. "This is where the dragon is, and you're to watch it with the Protector," he is telling them in a brusque fashion. "Find places to stand, and mind you don't upset the Protector. He's had a difficult day, if you follow my meaning."

One of the men, a grizzled veteran more than half gone in drink, gives Princess Felicia a bleary greeting, then, when he reaches the wall, he falls back against it, sliding down it slowly until he ends up in a snoring heap.

"Wait a little longer, Miss. There'll be a few more coming." The Captain of the Guard gives her a gesture of encouragement. "He seems to take to the dragon, by the looks of it."

Annoyed at this interruption, Chumley pounds his cushions with his fists. "Want see play! Want see trick! *Now!*" This last order is in stentorian tones.

"Shortly, Your Majesty," Princess Felicia says, attempting to be charming to him. "The dragon has to do things slowly."

"NOW!" bellows Chumley.

This is more frightening than what has come before (little as Princess Felicia would like to admit it), and she seeks to find a way to please the Protector without making the dragon completely miserable. "Dragon, I don't need you to roll over yet, but for the time being, I want you to hop and skip again. These gentlemen have not seen you hop and skip." It pleases Princess Felicia that the dragon understands her so well, and she begins to think that she has underestimated the intelligence of the beast.

Obediently Esmeralda begins to hop and skip, doing her best not to get too near any of the men who have come into the room. Most of them remain silent, but Chumley makes up for them all, hooting and clapping in the most persistent way.

"Not much of a trick, if you ask me," says one of the newcomers. "Hop on one foot, hop on the other. I ask you, what's so remarkable about that?"

"A dragon's doing it," one of the others reminded him.

"There is that," the first says philosophically. "Still, not much of a trick, if you ask me. If it juggled at the same time, that might be better."

"Dragons have talons," the second points out. "Probably can't juggle."

"Oh," says the first, losing interest entirely.

Little as she wants to admit it, Esmeralda is beginning to tire. Her feet are sore and her tail is so heavy that her muscles are starting to ache as she pulls it around. It's one thing to manage walking, she thinks as she continues her ungainly jig, but this dancing and performing are more than she's ready to do. Only the hope of getting Prince Andre out of this place keeps her going. Under any other circumstance, she would want to faint from embarrassment, since she knows she is doing her dancing badly. It's all right, she tries to console herself. They don't expect as much of dragons.

"Rear back on your tail, dragon," commands Princess Felicia, who is, in a strange way, enjoying herself. "Talons *up!*"

With less alacrity than she had shown at first, Esmeralda does as she is commanded.

"Want more! Hurm, hurm, hurm! Want more!" crows Chumley. The men of his court try very hard to act as if they are here by accident.

As Esmeralda rocks down off her tail, the door opens again, and another eight men are rudely shoved into the room. Prince Andre is one of them. Esmeralda nearly falls over as she catches sight of him.

If Esmeralda is shocked, it is nothing compared to Prince Andre's reaction. He recognizes his sister at once, and gasps at the ridiculous clothes she is wearing. At the same time, he sees his dragon, and he is horrified that it should be brought into a place like this. He flushes with indignation.

"Now, turn, dragon," Princess Felicia orders sharply. "Quickly!"

Chumley's delight at this is boundless. He guffaws and pounds the pillows, feeling happier than he has since he made Humgudgeon his play toy. His noisy outbursts cover Prince Andre's reaction.

"Felicia! What do you think you're doing, bringing my dragon here?"

"Hush, Andre; we're rescuing you," Princess Felicia responds merrily. "We're almost ready."

"What are you—" He is not able to finish because Chumley gets up from his cushions and lumbers forward, his massive arms out, preparing to embrace the dragon.

"Want dragon. Want play with dragon. Want play. Chumley want dragon to play." For Chumley, this is a long and complex speech, and some of the courtiers are impressed in spite of themselves.

This is too much for Esmeralda, who has been pushed to the limit. It is one thing to dance for that hideous creature, but to have to play with him is more than she is willing to bear. She swings her tail around, catching Chumley across the legs and sending him caroming into the wall, knocking over two courtiers in the process.

"Now, now," warns the Captain of the Guard from the door, his weapon swinging forward.

Esmeralda flings her long-snouted head back, opens her mouth and breathes out four feet of flame, and watches with unacknowledged satisfaction as the Captain of the Guard retreats, leaving the way clear for escape.

"Now!" Princess Felicia cries, seizing the moment and her brother's arm as she bolts for the door, shouting to the dragon to clear the way.

In the doorway, Esmeralda turns and spews out another fiery breath. She gives herself only a few seconds to watch the hangings and the cushions start to smolder before she rushes for the twisting staircase where Princess Felicia and Prince Andre are waiting for her.

They tumble down the stairs, and at the foot, Esmeralda once again shows her pyrotechnic talents, bringing several little fires and a great deal of chaos to the halls and courtyard that front the castle. They rush across the courtyard as the portcullis is being lowered, its long spikes descending on the avenue to their freedom.

"Roll!" shouts Prince Andre, following his own order and dropping to his side. He drags Princess Felicia after him and reaches out for the dragon (he is more worried about the dragon than his sister, since the dragon is so specially his) as he passes under the lethal spikes. He hears his sleeve rip as he slides free.

Esmeralda gives a hiss and an involuntary belch of flame as the portcullis snags a few scales of her tail. She scrambles to her feet and turns on the soldiers on the other side of the iron barrier. She gives them one last dose of her fire, then lurches after Princess Felicia and Prince Andre, who are shouting to her to follow.

The three fugitives dart down the nearest side street (most of the streets in Addlepate are side streets), hoping to elude any possible pursuit. They shove passersby and vendors out of their way, and when a donkey stubbornly blocks their path, it is Esmeralda who rushes forward to shove it out of the way. They continue until all three of them are out of breath and they are thoroughly lost.

"What . . ." pants Prince Andre "ever possess . . . ed you to . . . try an . . . idiot stunt like . . . that?"

"We got . . . you out, didn't we?" answers Princess Felicia, breathless as he is.

"I would have . . . managed it somehow," he tells her, clearly offended at the implication that he would require rescue.

"But when?" Princess Felicia asks, still gulping air.

"Soon," is his evasive answer.

"But why wait? We . . . didn't know what was . . . happening to you, and for all . . . we knew, you were being tortured, or worse." She pauses, one hand to her throat.

"I would have managed," Prince Andre insists, sulking a little.

"No doubt, but we wanted to help," Princess Felicia says, and there is no arguing with this.

"Thank you," Prince Andre says, more surly than polite. "But why did you have to . . . bring my dragon? She might have been hurt."

"*I* might have been hurt," Princess Felicia reminds him, a bit offended herself.

"Yes," Prince Andre says hastily. "I didn't mean that the . . . way it sounded. But Felicia, the dragon . . . how could she know what might happen? You exposed both yourself and her to real trouble when you brought her along." He reaches out and pats his dragon's shoulder. "And look—she's got a cut in her tail."

"And you've got a rip in your coat," Princess Felicia points out. "And it seems to me having the dragon along was very lucky. Without the dragon, we wouldn't have got out of there so easily." She is determined not to have her adventure blighted by her brother. "I think that we did very well, getting you out the way we did."

Prince Andre sets his jaw. "Of course," he grates. "But only because of my dragon."

"Of course," Princess Felicia says, willing to let him have that much.

Hearing this, Esmeralda is both thrilled and oppressed. She

would have done anything to save Prince Andre, and she is glad that they are all out of that terrible castle, but it pains her to think that all she is to Prince Andre is a clever pet, while to her, he is the sun and the moon and the stars (and unlike Peter Pan, he is not a child). She is also worn out. All that dancing and running and flaming has left her exhausted. She tries to persuade herself that some of her misery comes from that exhaustion rather than her disappointment, and to some degree, she succeeds.

When, an hour or so later, Prince Andre, Princess Felicia and the dragon arrive at the western gate to the city, they find Leander (in a perfect frenzy of apprehension), Alfreida (her hands still tied), and their mounts all waiting for them and their last stage of the journey back to Alabaster-on-Gelasta.

"Oh, my dear Princess," exclaims Leander as he catches sight of the bedraggled company dragging out of the gate. "What dreadful thing has befallen you? Do not hesitate to tell me, for there is no burden, no matter how onerous, that would not be a privilege for me to bear for you."

Affection is a strange thing. If Prince Andre had said anything half so sloppy as that, Princess Felicia would have been outraged and been so angry that she might not have spoken to him for days, but since it is Leander who has said it, she gives a tremulous smile and very nearly bursts into tears for this expression of concern. "Oh, Leander, you're so good," she sighs.

"Altercations!" Alfreida expostulates in disgust. "That goose of a Princess hasn't learned a thing!"

"You need not fear that anything you relate to me would decrease by an iota the fondness and respect that fills me. You are so far above any mishap, dear Princess, that your qualities would shine from the depths of a tarn." Leander does not forget himself as he would like, but goes so far as to take her hand in his. "What other woman is as intrepid as you, as courageous as you? What other woman would risk so much for a beloved brother?"

Deep inside herself, Esmeralda wants to shout, "I would! I did!" but being a dragon, she only lets out two exasperated plumes of smoke and hangs her head unhappily.

Prince Andre reaches over and gives her a gentle pat. "You're a good, brave dragon. You did as much as my sister, didn't you?"

"Pets are hardly the same thing," Leander says, determined to keep Princess Felicia cast in the role of absolute heroine.

"Some people can't blink for blinders," declares Alfreida at her most cryptic.

Prince Andre goes slowly to Hyperion, who has been regarding all this with a jaundiced eye. "We'd better get under way," he tells the others. "We won't be home until tomorrow afternoon, as things are going now, and that's not a moment too soon for me."

Obediently the others fall into their positions, and then they start off toward Alabaster-on-Gelasta, content to go at a slow and steady pace as they make their way home.

A Very Grand Finale

WHEN THE DRAGON-HUNTING party wakes on their last day of adventure, Leander at once proposes that as soon as he has finished making their breakfast, he should hurry on ahead to inform all of Alabaster-on-Gelasta of the coming triumphant return. "For, as Your Highnesses are no doubt aware, Their Majesties are greatly concerned for your welfare and must be eager to learn that you have escaped all danger unscathed."

"That's not a bad idea," Prince Andre says reflectively. "I'll tell you want, Leander; when we're through with breakfast, saddle Hyperion. I don't mind riding one of the other animals. In fact, it is easier for the dragon to travel with the donkey than with Hyperion."

"Your Highness!" Leander cries. "I am overcome with so great an honor. To be permitted to ride that superb animal, to be allowed to carry the news on so fine a horse, it is too much distinction for me."

"Well, I do insist," Prince Andre says with a smile. "It would be faster, and you'd like the ride better."

"Your Highness," Leander begins, aware that he should offer further protest, but unable to summon up the courage to turn down Hyperion.

"Leander," Princess Felicia says, her huge eyes turned toward him. "I think you should do as Andre suggests. It is fitting that you should carry such good news on Hyperion. It is more appropriate than for you to arrive on a mule."

"That is very right," Leander says, deciding to accept the offer. "For an occasion of this nature, I do realize that it behooves me to present such tidings in the most worthy manner possible, and for that reason, and that reason alone, I humbly accept that magnificent horse as my mount. Do not fear that in so doing I will have notions that are above my lot in life, for that is not the case."

"Goodness, gracious, no," Prince Andre says, a twinkle in his eyes.

Princess Felicia glares at her brother before she once again gazes at Leander. "Hasten to Royal Mama and Royal Papa on my . . . our behalf, and tell them that they can prepare for rejoicing. They'll know what to do; they've done it many times before." A touch of her old boredom comes back into her voice. "It will be much the same as always."

"I trust not, Your Highness," Leander tells her with strong emotion, "for nothing in their reign has come close to this event for remarkableness and accomplishment. Do not fear that your feats will go unnoticed and unsung; you have my word that Their Majesties will know all of what has transpired on this momentous journey."

Alfreida, who has listened to Leander's rhapsodizing with increasing disdain, now says, "Does that dolt talk in his sleep, do you think? Some people are beyond all patience."

No one pays any attention to the witch, except Esmeralda, who gives her a worried look before tagging after Prince Andre.

"You're getting very tame, dragon," Prince Andre says as he suits his pace to Esmeralda's. "That's wonderful. I never knew it would be such fun to have a dragon."

Fun is not the word that Esmeralda would choose, but she ducks her head, hoping that he will understand the nod for what it is.

"I'm going to think of something nice to do for you after I present you to Royal Mama and Royal Papa. They'll be impressed, I know they will. Perhaps Sigmund will have a suggestion or two." He frowns a bit at the thought. "It might not be possible to find out what they are, just at first, but in time he's bound to come up with something."

Leander has almost finished making the breakfast crumpets, and he can now devote more of his attention to Princess Felicia again. "While I ride, dear Princess, you have my every assurance that my thoughts will be with you. Were it possible to be in two places at once, I would not leave you to complete this errand, but I am constrained to perform this task, and so great is the honor of the commission that I beseech you to forgive me for leaving your side."

"How sweet you are, Leander," Princess Felicia says, looking at him through her lashes. "Perhaps in time, Royal Papa will favor you with advancement for all the service you have performed for us."

So great is Leander's emotion that for once all he can do is offer Princess Felicia a crumpet and stare at her with hopeless longing.

The meal is soon over, and Leander once again has Princess Felicia's help for packing the pavilions and loading the animals before he has to saddle Hyperion.

It is true that Hyperion is a magnificent horse, with a fine, arched neck, small, alert ears, a beautiful head and the conformation of the best of his line. Almost any rider would look good on him, and Prince Andre certainly makes a fine figure on his back. But Leander, even in his simple garments, is so impressive that even Alfreida has to admit that he is a remarkable vision: Leander's staggering good looks and his superior horsemanship make the sight of him on the destrier enough to take the breath away.

"He rides well," Prince Andre says to Princess Felicia as they watch him head off.

"Yes," she breathes, with a world of comment in that single word.

"For a total noddy, he's convincing on a horse, I'll say that much," Alfreida growls. "Pity he hasn't got any common sense from his curls to his big toes."

Prince Andre chuckles. "Careful there, witch; you're getting soft." He indicates their other mounts. "Time to be going."

Princess Felicia lets her brother give her a leg up into the saddle, and she adjusts her leg over the horn (being a proper Princess, she rides sidesaddle—and hates it), and fixes the drape of her skirt so that its pleats and folds fan out along the side of her horse. "I'm ready," she says, and giggles at the sight of Prince Andre riding a donkey.

"It doesn't bother the dragon and the dragon doesn't bother it," Prince Andre says with a touch of huff in his tone as he gives the signal for them to start.

Traveling at a good clip on Hyperion, Leander reaches the gates of Alabaster-on-Gelasta not long after midday. He passes through the gates (which, naturally, are not guarded) and goes up the wide, tree-lined avenues toward the palace. Everywhere people turn to look at him, to point and smile and whisper as he continues on his way.

A groom takes charge of Hyperion once Leander has reached the palace and dismounted, and Leander hurries at once to the Throne Room, rehearsing in his mind all that he has to tell King Rupert and Queen Hortensia.

At the door to the Throne Room, he is stopped by not one, but two pages. Leander recognizes Francis (or Frances), but the other is a new and unfamiliar face—in fact, the face is so ordinary that Leander forgets it almost at once. (The new page is none other than the Spy, who has come to his senses at last and knows a good deal when he sees one.)

The new page throws open the door to the Throne Room and calls out: "The crumpet-baker has returned, Your Majesties," then stands aside so that Leander can enter and bow with exquisite grace to the King and Queen.

King Rupert sets aside his knitting, an expression of interest on his kindly features. Beside him, Queen Hortensia moves her lace handkerchief from under one brimming eye to the other. "Oh, don't tell me the dreadful news. I cannot bear to learn that my blossoms have been blighted."

"Knit two . . . aha!" King Rupert has heard all of Queen Hortensia's predictions of disaster since the dragon-hunting party left, and so he pays them little heed. However, the announcement that Leander is back gets his attention.

Leander drops to his knee, the very image of the knights of old, and so indescribably magnificent that it is difficult to imagine him a mere crumpet-baker. "I am come, at the behest of Their Highnesses, to impart to you the details of a great and remarkable victory."

"A victory?" King Rupert repeats with growing excitement. "Francis! And you other one! Bring Sigmund and the Professor to the Throne Room at once. Leander has brought us news."

"At once, Your Majesty," say two voices from beyond the door, followed at once by the sharp sound of retreating footsteps.

"Imagine that, my dearest," King Rupert says to Queen Hortensia. "A victory, and so soon. Isn't that delightful."

"If only it proves not to be Pyrrhic," Queen Hortensia says in hollow accents. She has been caught up in a welter of noble suffering and she is not about to stop it without very good reason.

"Oh, I doubt that it is anything so questionable as that," King Rupert soothes her, doing his best not to be put out at her attitude. "Leander would not have left them to come to us, if that were the case. Would you, Leander?"

"To do so reprehensible a thing, I would have to forsake all honor and abrogate my oath as well. Rest assured, Your Majesties, I bring no word of disaster or unpleasantness. There is cause for rejoicing." Leander lays his hand over his heart, looking with clear-eyed fortitude from King Rupert to Queen Hortensia.

"Rejoicing, did you hear that, my love?" King Rupert says as he puts his knitting aside for the moment. "When the pages return, one of them must go to the kitchen to give orders for a feast."

"The crumpet-baker can do that," Queen Hortensia states.

"Why, so he can," King Rupert tells her, "but then we should have to wait to learn of what has happened to Andre and Felicia, and I hardly think that is what you would wish. I know that I am eager to learn of their adventures. You would say that they had adventures, wouldn't you, Leander?" King Rupert asks, seeking corroboration.

"Definitely that," Leander says, so succinctly that an uneasy quiet descends when he does not elaborate.

"How exciting," King Rupert declares, and looks up as the Throne Room door opens and Professor Ambicopernicus strides in, yet another enormous tome in his hands. "Professor, come join us. Leander is going to tell us all about the dragon hunt once Sigmund arrives."

"Leander has returned?" Professor Ambicopernicus says,

and then covers this gaffe by saying, "Late last night it seemed that the stars promised events of great portent."

"How splendid," King Rupert says as he picks up his knitting again. "It must be very reassuring to be able to see such things in the stars. They're a perfect muddle to me, but there it is. Some are gifted that way, and others are not. You've devoted your life to the study, and there it is: you're able to foresee these events. Knit one, yarn over, knit two . . ."

"That can be the results of study, but few can interpret with accuracy all that is writ there," the Professor says portentously. No one is paying much attention.

"How my heart quivers at the thought of what my adorable babies have endured," Queen Hortensia announces to the room, but does not yet elaborate.

"Professor, you must have some notion of what Leander will tell us. How jolly for you." King Rupert returns to his knitting again, but now he is humming.

"Sigmund Snafflebrain, Your Majesties," says the Spy as he shoves the wizard through the door.

"Excellent, excellent," King Rupert enthuses. "Now, page, whoever you are, go to the kitchens, will you, and tell them to prepare a victory feast. They'll know best what it's to be. Since the weather is so fine, we can plan to have it on the terrace, that's the ticket. Knit two, purl three, knit two. Gracious, this is so exciting that I can hardly keep track of my stitches."

Sigmund blinks benignly at the persons in the Throne Room. "Is there . . . was I . . . What . . . ?"

"Leander is about to tell us of the dragon hunt, Sigmund. I knew you'd want to hear." King Rupert motions his wizard closer to the throne, in what might be a distinction for the wizard, but is more likely a precaution against his straying during the tale that Leander is going to tell.

"Oh, Leander," Sigmund says, as if he believes it is significant or perhaps associated with something he had already said (and it probably is, though who knows when he said it).

Leander, still on his knee, inclines his head to the wizard. "The Princess Felicia and Prince Andre are most grateful to you for the protection you granted them," he says with enviable sincerity.

"Oh?" Sigmund remarks, clearly unaware of what has been said to him.

"Tell us about the dragon hunt, Leander," King Rupert suggests. "We're all here now and we're listening."

Obediently, Leander takes a deep breath and begins his narrative. "May it please Your Majesty to hear: we went, as you know, through neutral territory on our way to the Woebegone Wood. It was not an unpleasant journey, though the Princess stood in peril for much of the time, and her courage in withstanding these hazards was such that the most benighted of savages must admire her and acclaim her quality and character. Prince Andre showed himself determined to pursue the dragon and was most decisive on his course, no matter the risks that were associated with the venture."

"Risks!" moans Queen Hortensia.

"Eventually, the initial and minimal obstacles overcome, it was possible to reach the Woebegone Wood itself, and once we entered its forbidding borders, it was of primary importance to find an appropriate location for our camp so that Princess Felicia need not be exposed to any greater unpleasantness than was absolutely necessary." Here Leander pauses, sighing with the force of his sentiments at this memory. "I cannot begin to express adequately the fortitude that Princess Felicia showed while on the journey and once camped in the Woebegone Wood. Many another would have fled from the place and not be thought craven for the action. Whether dealing with malicious innkeepers or only aiding in the selection of a preferred campsite, the Princess was at all times composed and admirable in her deameanor, and her behavior provided an excellent example to all of us."

"Who would have thought that of Felicia, my dear?" King Rupert asks, plying his needles with energy. "Goodness, how very exciting this is. Do go on, Leander. You say that once you reached the Woebegone Wood, you made camp?"

"In a clearing, Your Majesty," Leander confirms.

"Good place for . . . you know . . ." Sigmund begins, but is distracted by some inner reflection.

"Most enterprising. You should listen to this, my love," King Rupert says, trying to coax Queen Hortensia out of the brown study she has fallen into.

"Oh, Toby." Her mouth quivers, and her handkerchief is brought into play once more.

"Just as you wish," King Rupert says with the ghost of a sigh. He has grown used to Queen Hortensia after all these years, but he has never lost hope entirely. "Pray continue, Leander. This is fascinating."

"We had barely established our camp when night fell. In such a place as the Woebegone Wood, night is a dreadful thing, and it was made more hideous by the moanings and howlings of terrible monsters." (It is not likely that the Trolls would want to have their performance described in this way, but no artist truly likes critics.) He squares his jaw. "It lasted all through the night and made sleep very difficult. Only the noble determination of Their Highnesses sustained us through that night. It was most inspiring to see that in the morning, Princess Felicia was able to bring herself to eat a morsel of food and to make light of the ordeal that had passed."

"Oh!" cries Queen Hortensia. "My dearest child; so like me."

"Felicia isn't so fragile, by the sounds of it, dearest. Your nerves are more sensitive," King Rupert tells her with a display of the diplomacy that has made Alabaster-on-Gelasta the happy place it is. He nods to Leander and gives a forceful thrust with his knitting needles.

"Once the morning was underway, Prince Andre set off in search of the dragon."

"Very proper," Professor Ambicopernicus approves.

"It was a harrowing time for Princess Felicia," Leander goes on, returning to his favorite theme. "She was required to remain in camp, and she listened to the cries and shouts that issued from the unknown depths of the Woebegone Wood as His Highness chased the dragon."

"The Woebegone Wood is that sort of place, as I remember," Professor Ambicopernicus says reflectively.

King Rupert hesitates. "Wait, Leander. You say that Prince Andre chased the dragon?"

Leander would much rather speak about Princess Felicia, but he knows it is best to answer such direct questions. "Oh, yes. With energy and purpose."

"The dragon didn't chase him?" King Rupert goes on, just to be certain.

"Not that I am aware of, Your Majesty," Leander says with utter candor.

"Curious. Do resume the tale, Leander." Contentedly, he resumes his knitting.

"It happened that in the course of the pursuit, the dragon

turned toward the camp itself, and was prepared to assault it. When this dire beast appeared, it greatly menaced the Princess, who endured the horrid sight as long as her gentle eyes would bear the vision, and then she swooned." Leander lowers his head in chagrin, as if the telling brought new shame to him.

Queen Hortensia gives a shriek and claps her hand to her brow. "I don't believe I can bear to hear this."

"Nonsense, my love, you will be the better to learn how they escaped the danger, for they must have done so, mustn't they, Leander?" King Rupert intervenes in his most amiable and reasonable manner. "Goodness, if anything terrible had happened, Leander would not be here like this to tell us about it."

"True; very true," says Sigmund, although it is not certain if he is speaking about this or some other matter entirely.

"As I have said," Leander resumes with some force, "the beauteous Princess swooned at the sight of the monster. I, your humblest of servants, your most devoted subject, stood by the Princess, prepared to defend her to the last drop of my life's blood. The dragon charged upon us, and it was only through the greatest good fortune that Prince Andre fended it off, and then captured it." He pauses to regain his breath and to allow the others a chance to speak.

"I knew I should never have let them go," Queen Hortensia sobs.

"So Prince Andre captured the dragon!" King Rupert exclaims. "Why, this is excellent news. Tell us more, Leander."

He hardly needs such an invitation. "The Princess was saved and—"

"Mercy!" Queen Hortensia bursts out.

"Yarn over, change hands, knit two, and try it again," King Rupert says, trying to salvage his knitting. "Please, do let Leander finish, dearest. Go on, Leander."

"Yes," Leander declares. "The Princess was saved. Her lustrous eyes opened upon the world again. She, as is typical of her, insisted that she was able to aid her brother in his securing of the dragon, and then in capturing a witch who was lurking in the Wood and in some way influencing the dragon. It was more appalling than you can imagine. Our intrepid Prince was able to confine the witch so that she could not work any of her malignant spells upon us, or upon the dragon. By night, the terrible monsters returned and tried to do us mischief, but in this we were fortunate, for Sigmund's protective powder saved the Princess from any harm."

"My powder?" Sigmund asks, not certain which one is being discussed.

"The powder!" Queen Hortensia agrees, her expression changing. "Sigmund's powder. You told me you were going to provide them with magic powder—do you mean that you actually did?"

"If . . . he says so . . . I must have . . . given . . . powder. . . ." He favors Leander with a contemplative stare. "Did I . . . give it to you? . . . that is . . ."

"You gave it to Prince Andre, Sigmund," Queen Hortensia reminds him emphatically.

"Oh!" Sigmund says, delighted.

"Dragons! Witches! Magic powder!" King Rupert enthuses. "How very thrilling. Tell me, Sigmund, what sort of magic powder did you give them?" He beams at his wizard and waits, as one must, for some sort of answer.

"Protective? . . ." Sigmund asks. "Powder . . . the Prince . . . the Princess . . . the Wood . . ." He claps his hands, at last recalling the incident. "Yes! The powder was . . . sugar . . . just sugar . . . thought it might . . . make them feel, you know . . . safe. That's it . . . safe. Sugar. . . . Didn't mention it was sugar. . . . no help if I did. . . . mention . . . sugar. . . ."

"Very clever of you, Sigmund," King Rupert says.

"Clever . . . ? Was it? . . . Oh, yes . . . I suppose . . . suppose it . . . was . . . clever . . . that is . . . ?" His mind once again wanders.

"Can it be?" Leander demands indignantly. "Forgive me, Your Majesty, for it is not my place to rebuke your servants, or to behave in this fashion, which is not proper, as well I know. But I must not remain silent on this occasion, for then I would fail in duty rather than in manners. How can you approve the methods of your wizard, and condone his lack of responsibility? He was obliged to provide an aid, a protection, and yet he admits that all he gave was sugar. This is more than reprehensible!"

"But it worked, didn't it, Leander?" King Rupert reminds him. "No harm came to any of you, so what does it matter what the powder was made of? Perhaps sugar has special properties in the Woebegone Wood."

The Throne Room door is thrown open and both Francis (or Frances) and the Spy tumble in. "Your Majesty," Francis (or Frances) blurts out, "they are sounding the trumpets at the gate. Prince Andre and Princess Felicia have returned."

"This is marvelous!" King Rupert exclaims. "Goodness, yes. By all means, send word that we're expecting them here, at once. Huzzah! My dear, our children are back!" He remains on his throne, but he clicks his heels together several times as if he were dancing. "What wonderful tidings."

Leander cannot bring himself to continue his reprimand. Not only is he aware that he is well outside the bounds of his authority, but he cannot argue with King Rupert's conclusions: whatever the powder is, it worked. He rises and moves back from the dais where the thrones are, so that Prince Andre and Princess Felicia will not have to trip over him to reach the King and Queen. While he is yearning to see Princess Felicia again, he is saddened by the realization that this must mark the end of their adventures together. How bittersweet the moment is, he tells himself, but it doesn't make him feel any better.

A cacophony of trumpets and horns rings through the air, and a roar of genial acclaim. The people of Alabaster-on-Gelasta have turned out to welcome home their Prince and Princess and to see what they have brought with them.

In the Throne Room, everyone waits, listening, since conversation quickly becomes quite impossible without actual shouting. King Rupert uses the time to do another row of knitting, Queen Hortensia has a good cry, Professor Ambico-pernicus finds himself a place by the windows where he can read more of the volume he carries. Sigmund, newly entranced, goes to examine the tall, ornate clock that stands opposite the thrones (he rediscovers this clock about once every three or four months—it always intrigues and delights him).

There is a clatter and banging in the distance, the brasses suddenly burst indoors and the noise is much louder. The servants and staff of the palace all turn out to hail Prince Andre and Princess Felicia and to gawk at the dragon and the witch. On his throne, King Rupert leans over and yells in Queen Hortensia's ear.

"Very soon, my love!"

Queen Hortensia waves him back with her handkerchief. She isn't through with her cry yet.

Finally the Spy rushes into the Throne Room and shouts, "Prince Andre Victor Halli—"

Prince Andre strides through the door, his dragon right behind him. "It isn't necessary," he says to the Spy as he passes. "They know who we are." He has been in a very good humor for the past few hours and now he cannot help but be pleased with himself as he brings his captives into the Throne Room. "Royal Papa, Royal Mama, see what I have caught!" He had intended to be more nonchalant with his announcement, but now finds that he does not want to be.

"Knit three, purl one, knit two, purl four, knit five, purl . . ." King Rupert says, hoping desperately to finish the row without error. "You've made me lose count, Andre." He looks up from the needles. "Gracious me! How amazing. See, Hortensia, my love. A dragon, and—yes, indeed!—a witch. Leander said it and there they are. Very good, Andre. Commendable effort on your part, I'm sure."

With an effort, Queen Hortensia takes her handkerchief from her streaming eyes. "Is it really you, my poor wilted violets? Have you returned to me at last, thinking better of this dangerous and ungracious venture? How could I have thought you'd turn against my heartfelt, my poor wishes, the deep concern of your mother's tender love?" Then she interrupts herself to give a squack that a very large squashed pig might make. "Where did you get *those?*"

Princess Felicia curtsies and grins, showing dimples that no one knew she had. "We got them in the Woebegone Wood, both of them. Now Andre has caught his dragon, and we have a real witch. Everyone rescued everyone else. It was almost exciting."

"Exciting?" echoes the Queen, her face a study in dismay. "Oh, my poor, poor darling children. How very hideous it must have been for you."

"It was, sometimes," Princess Felicia says, considering the matter in as unbiased a way as she can. "Most of the time, it was fun."

At this, Queen Hortensia turns away and gives herself up to another satisfying bout of tears.

King Rupert has been studying the creature who stands beside Prince Andre, and a little behind him, as if seeking protection from all the strangers in the room. "Bring that dragon a little closer to me, will you, Andre? I've never seen a real one before, only read descriptions." His kindly gaze goes over Esmeralda, who still hangs back. "This must have been a real disappointment to you, Andre," King Rupert says at last.

"Not at all," Prince Andre protests.

"It's a shame that you couldn't have found anything larger, but there it is. With dragons, I suppose you must be content with what you get. Nevertheless . . . Dear me, I didn't know they came this small. Perhaps it will grow larger." He is doing his best to be encouraging, but it is clear that he expected a more massive creature than this dragon is.

"Unlikely," announces Professor Ambicopernicus, looking up from his book. "It is not the larger phase of the moon."

Alfreida, who is on the other side of Princess Felicia, snorts. "Some people don't know when to keep their mouths shut." She is not in the mood to have her work criticized.

The Professor's book closes with a snap. "How odd. How strange. It must be all the remembering I've been doing since there was all this talk of the Woebegone Wood, but I thought I heard my long-lost love's voice just then." He comes away from the window, the better to explain himself to this bedraggled stranger. "Permit me, Madam, to say that when you spoke, you reminded me of my life-long sweetheart. I saw her last forty . . . no, fifty-seven years ago, combing the gnats out of her tangled hair in the most filthy rain that has ever fallen. It was a time of confused stars, and the weather was capricious that year. She—my love—was dressed for a great festival, and the picture of her my memory has enshrined, fresh and unsullied through the fading years." He bows, his great turban almost touching the floor.

"Memory!" Alfreida scoffs. "A fine thing memory is. Some people would forget the colors of their . . ." Her voice trails off, and when she speaks again, it is in a very different tone. "Did you say fifty-seven years?"

"He did; that was the figure," King Rupert corroborates, helpful as always.

"Yes, Madam, I did. I abandoned the happy life of a country alchemist, never realizing, alas, that in so doing I would lose the one who was dearer to me than all knowledge." He wipes his brow with the large square end of his sleeve. "But I do not mean to burden you with this. Forgive my impertinence. And you as well, Your Majesties." He bows to the King and the Queen. It is an afterthought, but a wise one.

"Oh, don't mind me; don't mind me," King Rupert says in great humor. He indicates the others in the room. "And you needn't mind them, either."

Alfreida takes a very cautious (for her) step forward. "It was fifty-seven years ago that my only love went away from the Woebegone Wood. I long ago gave up any hope of seeing him again. Is it really you . . . Osgood?"

Professor Ambicopernicus (whose first initial, as you will recall, is *O*) blinks and stares, then a disbelieving smile dawns on his face. "Alfreida?" Then, with more feeling, more happiness he repeats her name. "Alfreida!" He closes the gap between them and beams down at her. "You are every bit as ugly as I remember you. How fine of you not to change over the years."

"Osgood." Her face isn't used to smiling joyously, but she does the best she can. "I thought for sure you ended up with the warlocks in the Marshes on the far side of the Ululating River. They were always doing such experiments, and I know how inquisitive you are. I thought . . ." She has to bite back a sob. "I thought you were lost to me forever, but you're not."

It is time for a duet, and it is Professor Osgood Ambicopernicus who begins it:

> *"It's you, it's you, it's you!"*

And since it is a duet, Alfreida takes up the tune:

> *"It's you, it's you, it's you,"*

And both together:

> *"Oh joy, oh joy, oh rapture!*
> *It's you, it's you, it's you."*

Alfreida:

> *"My dreams have all come true!"*

The Professor:

> *"The sky has turned to blue!"*

Once again, together:

> *"Oh joy, oh joy, oh rapture*
> *It's you, it's you, it's you!*
> *We've caused a great to-do.*
> *A happy ending, too!*
> *For happy ever after—*
> *It's you, it's you, it's you!"*

While the Professor and Alfreida are celebrating their reunion a familiar face pokes through the door: it is Eustace, the Official and Hereditary Torturer. He pauses at the sight, saying to anyone who might be listening (although no one is), "Your Majesty, I thought I heard . . . Oh!" This last exclamation comes when he catches sight of the dragon and the witch, for he can envision all sorts of possibilities with such subjects.

"Come in," says King Rupert, gesturing to his Torturer. "Yes, Eustace, come in."

The Torturer's eyes gleam with anticipation. "Your Majesty, how does this come about?"

"Oh, Prince Andre has caught the dragon and a witch as well. Isn't this splendid?" King Rupert smiles broadly at Eustace.

"Very splendid," Eustace agrees at once, coming closer. "Do you think there might be the slightest chance, Your Majesty, that you could spare me one?"

King Rupert shakes his head. "I don't think so, no. Regrettable, of course. I am sorry," he tells Eustace, doing his best to reconcile his Torturer to more disappointments.

"But they are so perfect," Eustace protests, and refuses to lose all hope.

"I don't think—" King Rupert begins, and is interrupted by Alfreida, who is regarding Professor Ambicopernicus with skeptical adoration.

"Osgood, you always were filled with surprises. Have you kept up your magic, or are you busy with other matters? Some people get remarkably sloppy if they don't practice." By the angle of her head, she does not include herself among the sloppy ones.

"I have kept my hand in a little," Professor Ambicopernicus says modestly. "In general I confine myself to astrology, but every now and then, I will do a little something: a charm here, an enchantment there, a few spells. Nothing worth mentioning, certainly nothing meriting your attention. I've never attained anything like your prowess."

Leander, who has been watching this surprising turn of events, is moved at last to speak (as you might expect). "Oh, what an affecting scene. The tenderness of this meeting cannot but fill my heart with the noblest sentiments. If only Princess Felicia were as kindly inclined on my behalf, then I might bear my feelings in silence for as long as the Professor has, and longer."

"Who would have thought you'd end up here, in Alabaster-on-Gelasta?" Alfreida marvels. "I assumed that you were gone far away years ago. It is ironic that you were so near and I never knew."

Professor Ambicopernicus laughs shakily, not quite in control of his feelings. "And I was certain that you had gone away from the Woebegone Wood long since. A witch of your reputation and talent must certainly have had attractive offers. You always said that you wanted to establish yourself suitably. Doubtless many have sought you out."

"A few; a few," Alfreida says, blushing for the first time in over forty years.

"And yet, today," the Professor goes on, his eyes directed upward, as if his glance would pierce the ceiling, "as I scanned the stars, I knew that events of great portent were to occur. How could I know, even then, that you would be returning to me at last?"

The Official Torturer has come farther into the room and is regarding the dragon with an appreciative smile.

"I was convinced," the Professor continues, "that this would be a great occasion, but I was wholly unaware that it could have direct bearing on my life, let alone so happy an outcome." He takes Alfreida's hands in his and grins wide as a livestock gate.

"How touching," Leander sighs.

"Humm . . ." says the Official Torturer as he walks around Esmeralda. "Excuse me. I need to get a closer look."

Princess Felicia is as enchanted as Leander. "The Professor isn't bored. How astonishing."

"You're more than I remembered, Osgood. I can see that the potential you had when we were young has flowered. Some people might not recognize your abilities, but you can't conceal them from me. Not that I wish to boast, you understand." For Alfreida, this is a very restrained and tender statement.

"Without you, Alfreida, I had only my studies, and I did

what I could to perfect them in order to forget." He touches
his turban, making it a significant act.

"I do not wish to interrupt, Professor," says King Rupert in
a gentle tone, "but when I took you into my service, it was on
the condition that you work no more magic. It was fine for
you to study the stars, but that was all we agreed you would
do. If you have performed any magic, woven any spells since
you came here, will you be kind enough to undo them now?
Knit three, purl three and repeat to the end of the row." He
pauses in his knitting to see what his order might bring about.

"There's only one important spell, and it was done for Your
Majesty's best interests, I assure you," Professor Ambicopernicus says, oozing good will and fellow-feeling now that he
once again has Alfreida with him.

The Official Torturer is more entranced by the dragon than
ever. In spite of Prince Andre's attempts to keep him away
from the dragon, he has continued to speculate the creature's
uses. "I could fasten a pulley here . . ."

"If you will undo the spell, Professor?" King Rupert asks
in his most amiable manner.

"How *can* you, Toby?" demands Queen Hortensia in a
voice of loathing. "With ladies present!"

Leander has been contemplating Professor Ambicopernicus
and Alfreida with the air of one inspired. "To think," he says
to himself (but loudly enough for Princess Felicia to hear
him), "that the Professor was willing to live with his hopeless-
ness and his undying passion. I must take him as my example,
unworthy as I am to seek the hand of the most perfect of
womankind."

Professor Ambicopernicus actually laughs. "As to that,
young man . . ." He raises his hands and begins to mutter in a
strange tongue, making peculiar passes in the air. He sways,
and his silken robes move hypnotically with him.

And what is the result of all this? The Throne Room
darkens, and there are unaccountable bits of light speeding
through the air as a buzzing sound grows louder. Next, a
crackle like beginning lightning shivers in the air, followed
almost at once by a thrumming cloud that is dark and light at
once. It descends over Leander, and then—*poof!*—is
gone. . . .

"My gracious!" gasps Queen Hortensia.

For Leander now stands revealed in satins and laces,
bejeweled and crowned, as it has always seemed he ought to

be. If he were handsome before, he is dazzling now.

"Oh!" sighs Princess Felicia. "Leander." She might swoon, but she cannot bear the thought of losing sight of him.

"Amazing!" says Prince Andre, bemused by this transformation.

Sigmund, startled out of his reverie, wanders over to Leander who is gazing raptly at Princess Felicia. "Strange . . . very strange . . . I wonder how he . . . did that? . . . Ought to have been a frog, though . . . if he was . . . what he was . . ."

"What are you saying, Sigmund?" inquires King Rupert, who should be much more startled than he is.

"A frog," Sigmund explains. "After all . . . a Prince . . . enchanted . . . ought to have been . . . a frog. . . . The Prince . . . not right that he wasn't a frog . . . not right at all. . . ."

"A frog?" repeats Queen Hortensia, repelled. "Did you hear what he said? In this room! Ugh!"

The Official Torturer is still examining the dragon. "And pincers, oh, yes! I could use pincers!"

King Rupert pays no attention to this, but bends his kindly gaze on Leander. "This is an agreeable change, is it not, Felicia? It saves all sorts of difficulties. No midnight elopements, no invented titles. Very, very convenient. I am delighted to see you this way, Leander . . . er? . . . Prince Leander. It is Prince Leander, isn't it?"

"It is, Your Majesty." His bow is more perfect than before, if such a thing is possible.

Now King Rupert hesitates. "Although, in some ways this is most awkward. I suppose I must apologize for what you've endured here, doing the crumpets and all. But, well, I couldn't have known, could I? Knit one, knot two, purl one . . . Could I?"

Impetuously, Prince Leander approaches the throne, taking hold of Princess Felicia's hand on the way. "Oh, Sire, I cannot begrudge one instant that I have spent in your kingdom of Alabaster-on-Gelasta, no matter how lowly my estate or how mean my circumstances, for it was here that I first beheld this true epitome of all that is beautiful and adorable in womanhood—"

"Yarn over, purl one, knit one . . . Go on, Leander; we're all listening." King Rupert smiles his encouragement over his needles.

Leander does as King Rupert commands. "—and been privileged to hear her voice and see her smile."

"Some people," says Alfreida acerbically, "would put syrup and honey on marshmallows!"

"It was a rather nice little spell, wasn't it?" Professor Ambicopernicus asks her, with a smug little smile on his lips.

"Showoff!" Alfreida scoffs. He may be her long-lost love, but she is not now and has never been blind to his faults. "You always were a showoff, Osgood. Well, some of us still do better enchantments than you do. Some of us are true experts." With this remark, Alfreida begins to hop around the Throne Room, waving her hands and hissing through her teeth.

Zing! and the valentine-shaped horns soften and melt into curled, golden locks. Whirrrr! and the scales begin to run and fuse, turning back to soft skin and pretty cloth. POP! and where there had been a dragon (and a small dragon at that) Esmeralda is once again her very sweet self.

Only Eustace is disappointed. He takes off his wig, flings it to the floor and stomps on it. "It's not fair!"

Prince Andre smiles giddily at her. "How extraordinary! Look at you. I thought all along you made a very poor dragon." His expression is almost as silly as Prince Leander's.

King Rupert stares, for once genuinely startled. "This is most amazing. Yes, indeed, most amazing. I must say that I didn't anticipate anything quite like this when I let you go gallivanting off to the Woebegone Wood." He puts his knitting down and motions to Esmeralda. "Come here, child."

"Her name," says Prince Andre shrewdly, "is Esmeralda. Isn't it, Esmeralda?"

She nods to Prince Andre and curtsies to King Rupert. "Your Majesty?"

"You're not frightened of me, are you?" King Rupert asks when it is apparent that Esmeralda is reluctant to approach him. "Why, you're not to be frightened of me. I'm just a man in funny clothes and funnier hat who knits all day. Nothing to be afraid of, dear me, no."

It would take a far more timorous soul than Esmeralda to be put off after this display of affability. "Whatever you wish, Your Majesty."

Both Francis (or Frances) and the Spy appear in the doorway. "The celebratory feast," they say, almost in unison, "is served on the terrace."

"Marvelous," King Rupert says. "You may go and supervise it, both of you," he tells his pages, then gives his attention to Esmeralda. "I gather that you were . . . uh . . . enchanted by that witch into a dragon. A very unpleasant form. It didn't become you at all, not in the least."

"No, Your Majesty," Esmeralda agrees with feeling.

"Not that the ninny," interjects Alfreida, "will do any better with this one."

For once, Alfreida may very well be wrong. Prince Andre takes Esmeralda by the hand. "You must tell me . . . us how you came to be enchanted at all. It wasn't anything like what I expected, hunting you and catching you. And to see you this way, it's very surprising. And wonderful."

Esmeralda blushes, and she is every bit as flowerlike in her loveliness as she was before her transformation. "It is a very long story, Your Highness."

"I'm anxious to hear it, all of it." He draws her away from the throne, toward the terrace where the feast is waiting. "Remember, I caught you. I have a right to know."

"Really?" Esmeralda asks, suddenly breathless.

Without warning, Queen Hortensia surges to her feet, her bosom heaving with her turbulent emotions. "Is nothing to be the way I planned it?"

King Rupert smiles at her. "It seems not, my love."

"Oh, Toby," she says plaintively, "I meant well."

King Rupert puts a comforting arm around her shoulder. "Yes, my love, so you did. I know. We'll go out on the terrace and have our feast, and then we'll decide how to manage it all."

Being good courtiers (and hungry), the rest follow King Rupert and Queen Hortensia, leaving the Throne Room quite empty, except for Sigmund, who makes a few arcane gestures, and then waits.

A Shape (you remember the Shape from the Interludes?) drifts in through the open window, and settles slowly, like a huge, sooty leaf, at Sigmund's feet, where it becomes a large feline form, rubbing Sigmund's leg and purring like a mill-stone.

Sigmund beams and bends down to pick up Liripoop, who at last has returned to his rightful owner. As he scratches the cat behind the ears, he says, "Shall we see if there are any fishes for you?" and grins as his familiar closes his eyes in ecstatic anticipation.

An Epilogue in Slightly Irregular Verse

(courtesy of Sigmund)

I know that once I had a thought, I had it in my head;
And if I ponder long enough I think I will have said
Whatever thing I thought it was that ever I did think,
But every time a thought will rise, another thought will
*   sink.*
This leaves me going round and round until my brain is
*   dizzy,*
And leaves me feeling very odd and looking very busy.
I think I can remember when the Prince was starting
*   out,*
Although I can't seem to recall what it was all about.
There was something about sugar that I gave him in a
*   jar*
To keep him safe from dragons—I'm getting none too
*   far.*
There was some talk of dragons and the mention of a
*   witch;*
Just when I think I've got it right, my mind does a sort
*   of twitch.*
The dragon turned into a girl, at least I think it did,
But thinking on it now, my thoughts begin a kind of skid.
The crumper-baker who was here turned out to be a
*   Prince;*
That alteration's just the thing to make a strong man
*   wince.*
And it was quite the kind of change to leave me all
*   agog,*
For I thought each enchanted Prince was turned into a
*   frog;*

*Then that Professor did a turn and called the witch his
　　love;*
*He and she danced up and down—what were they
　　thinking of?*
The dragon is the sweetest girl I ever hope to see,
*It's good to know that things turn out the way they
　　ought to be;*
For all and sundry now will live in bliss for ever after,
*Free from all dismay and harm, and filled with joy and
　　laughter,*
And loving one another all content, without travail
(As you recall, we said at first, this is a fairy tale).
*With Liripoop returned to me, I know I'll sort things
　　out:*
It seems that I knew all along what it was all about.
*I know that I can think it out if I think with all my
　　might—*
And so, dear reader, fond good-day. . .

*　　　　　　　　　　　　　　or is it fond good-night?*

TROLLS QUASI MAZURKA

Pomposo, andantino

Grue - some - ly churns the wa - ter down Bring - ing us vic - tims, hey - ho!

Hors - es and rid - ers wash - ed down Who sim - ply for - got to say woah!

Murk - y and damp our hous - es are deep in the slime and mud caves

While to the tune of fright - ened screams our mom - my whim - pers and

raves Cho - rus! Lol - lop - ping, slob - ber - ing mon - ster - ous

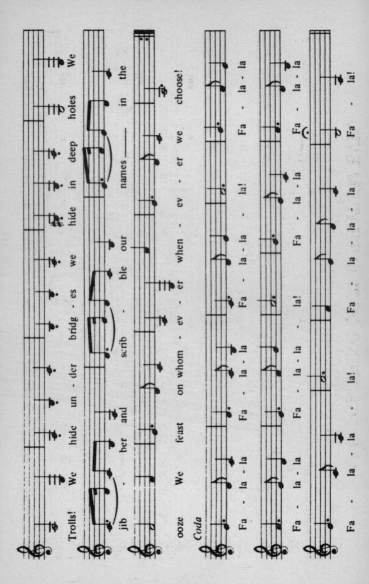

Trolls! We hide un - der bridg - es we hide in deep holes We

jib - ber and scrib - ble our names —— in the

ooze We feast on whom - ev - er when - ev - er we choose!

Coda

Fa - la - la Fa - la - la - la! Fa - la - la - la!

Fa - la - la Fa - la - la - la! Fa - la - la Fa - la - la - la!

Fa - la - la - la! Fa - la - la Fa - la - la Fa - la!

AND THE THING OF IT IS THAT I'M EVIL

A HARMLESS LITTLE HOBBY

WHERE DID I GO WRONG?

Con gran sentimento, troppo dolcissimo

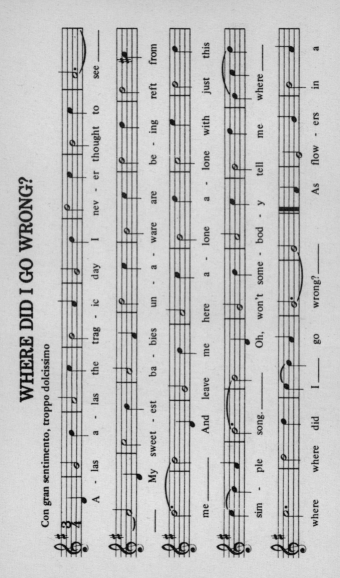

A - las a - las the trag - ic day I nev - er thought to see

My sweet - est ba - bies un - a - ware are be - ing reft from

me ___ And leave me here a - lone a - lone with just this

sim - ple song. ___ Oh, won't some - bod - y tell me where ___

where where did I ___ go wrong? ___ As flow - ers in a

IT CAN NEVER, NEVER, NEVER, NEVER, NEVER, NEVER, NEVER, NEVER, NEVER, NEVER HAPPEN HERE

Energetico

1) Prince Andre

1. Brav - er - y! That's the thing turns a Prince to a

2.
3.

King Teach - es fools to be wise, cuts a brute down to size

It can nev - er, nev - er, nev - er, nev - er, nev - er.

nev - er, nev - er, nev - er, nev - er, nev - er hap - pen here!

Languidoso
2) Princess Felicia

1. If — on - ly the sky were oth - er than blue   Or the trees were oth - er
2.
than — green   Then I would - n't care much   if the weeks ran through

all the months in the or - der they've been.   It can nev - er, nev -

er, nev - er, nev - er, nev - er, nev - er, nev -

er, nev - er, nev - er hap - pen here.

Moderato e staccato

3) King Rupert

1. I sup-pose that if I lis-ten to your sage ad-vice and coun-cil
2. I will rap-id-ly per-ceive that all my king-dom is a mess But if I has-ten to ig-nore you with your words of world-ly wis-dom There's a chance that we'll con-tin-ue in our bliss-ful hap-pi-ness! It can nev-er, nev-er, nev-er, nev-er, nev-er, nev-er hap-pen here.

IT CAN NEVER, NEVER, NEVER, NEVER, NEVER, NEVER, NEVER, NEVER, NEVER, NEVER HAPPEN HERE

– all together, last verse

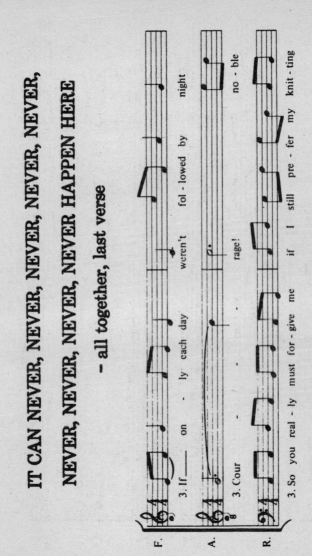

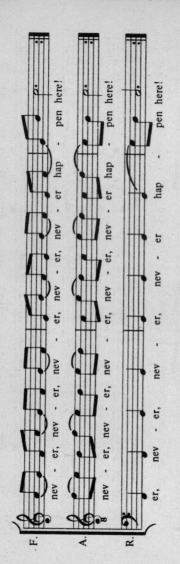

BUT IT'S MUCH TOO PRETTY TO CUT

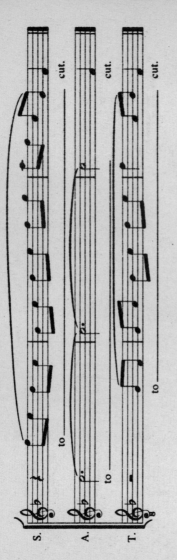

IN A PICKLE

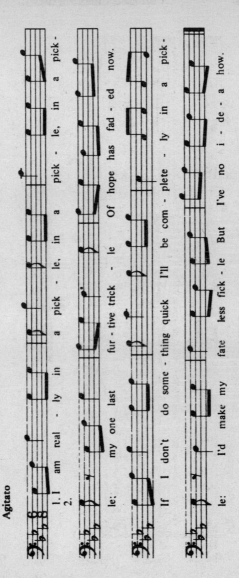

Agitato

1. I am real - ly in a pick - le, in a pick - le, in a pick -
le; my one last fur - tive trick - le Of hope has fad - ed now.
2.
If I don't do some - thing quick I'll be com - plete - ly in a pick -
le; I'd make my fate less fick - le But I've no i - de - a how.

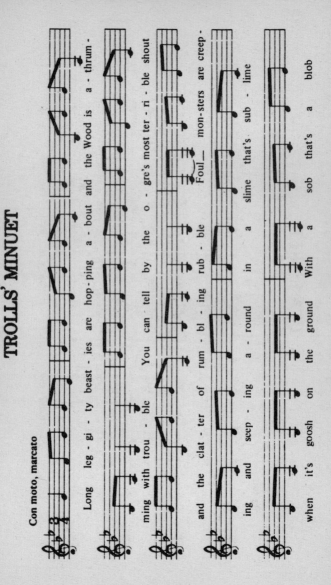

of a hid - e - ous sound like the laugh of an id - i - ot chi - ld.

PRINCE ANDRE'S SERENADE

Dolce e semplice

1. Oh, tho' the Wood is dark, It is lit by the day a - bove And the
2.

sun beams fall ___ Thru' the gloom and the pall ___ Like the

mu - sic of a lark, or the mourn - ing of a dove.

Poco rubato

All a - round you shad - ows gath - er An - y - one would be a - fraid.

Leave the dark - ness if you'd rath - er Turn from Wood and night and shade.

LEANDER'S LOVE SONG

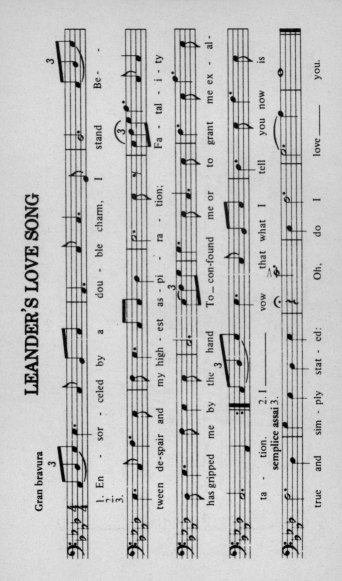

IT'S YOU, IT'S YOU, IT'S YOU

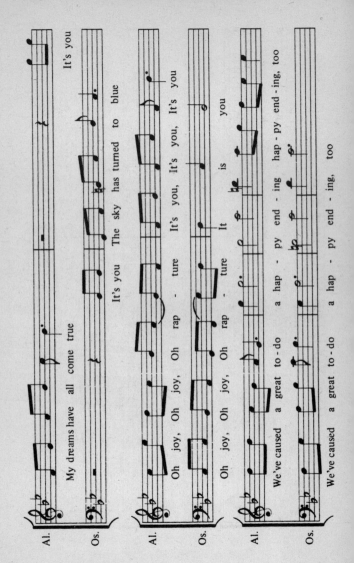

ACE ANNOUNCES A NEW DIMENSION IN SCIENCE FICTION AND FANTASY PUBLISHING

ACE HARDCOVERS

The #1 publisher of paperback science fiction and fantasy proudly announces the launch of a new hardcover line. Featuring the finest quality fiction by top, award-winning authors, and striking cover designs by today's most respected cover artists, ACE HARDCOVERS will make an impressive addition to your science fiction and fantasy collection.

COMING IN SEPTEMBER 1986

THE DRAGON IN THE SWORD by Michael Moorcock. *The first new novel in fifteen years in the classic Eternal Champion epic. This swords-and-sorcery adventure takes the Eternal Champion to an alternate world and a confrontation with the heart of evil itself.*

THE FOREVER MAN by Gordon R. Dickson. *The author of the* Childe Cycle *explores an exciting future where scientists are trying to solve the puzzle of a man who disappeared two centuries before—and has returned with his mind and soul merged with the circuitry of his ship.*

And look for more Ace hardcovers by Steven Brust, Clive Barker, Alan Dean Foster, Patricia A. McKillip, and Jerry Pournelle!

Ace Science Fiction and Fantasy

THE BERKLEY PUBLISHING GROUP
Berkley • Jove • Charter • Ace

Discover New Worlds with books of Fantasy by Berkley

____	**FAITH OF TAROT** Piers Anthony	09553-3/$2.95
____	**THE KING OF THE SWORDS** Michael Moorcock	09201-1/$2.95
____	**DAI-SAN** Eric Van Lustbader	07141-3/$2.95
____	**WATCHTOWER** Elizabeth A. Lynn	06195-7/$2.75
____	**THE NORTHERN GIRL** Elizabeth A. Lynn	09308-9/$2.95
____	**THE BOOK OF MERLYN** T.H. White	07282-7/$2.95
____	**THE ONCE AND FUTURE KING** T.H. White	09116-3/$4.95
____	**THE WANDERING UNICORN** Manuel Mujica Lainez	08386-1/$2.95
____	**THE HERO AND THE CROWN** Robin McKinley	08907-X/$2.95
____	**WHITE MARE, RED STALLION** Diana Paxson	08531-7/$2.95
____	**MOON-FLASH** Patricia A. McKillip	08457-4/$2.75

Available at your local bookstore or return this form to:

 BERKLEY
THE BERKLEY PUBLISHING GROUP, Dept. B
390 Murray Hill Parkway, East Rutherford, NJ 07073

Please send me the titles checked above. I enclose _____. Include $1.00 for postage and handling if one book is ordered; 25¢ per book for two or more not to exceed $1.75. California, Illinois, New Jersey and Tennessee residents please add sales tax. Prices subject to change without notice and may be higher in Canada.

NAME_____

ADDRESS_____

CITY_____ STATE/ZIP_____

(Allow six weeks for delivery.)

76M